DEDICATION

To Olivia Black for giving me invaluable advice about gayrom.

And Kenna Greebo, here is your story about Turk…finally!

A DANGEROUS REALITY

BOOK 1 OF THE BENT ZEALOTS MC

BY
LAYLA WOLFE

Quicksilver
Books

Copyright 2015 © Layla Wolfe
Print Edition
ALL RIGHTS RESERVED

Cover art by Red Poppy Designs
http://poppyartdesigns.com
Edited by Carol Adcock

Bobby Creighton photographed by Island Male Graphics

This book is copyrighted intellectual property. No other individual or group has resale rights, auction rights, membership rights, sharing rights, or any kind of rights to sell or to give away a copy of this book.

This literary work may not be reproduced or transmitted in any form by any means, including electronic or photographic reproduction, in whole or in part, without express written permission.

All characters and events in this book are fictitious. Any resemblance to actual persons living or dead is strictly coincidental.

Keep your lovers close—and your enemies in bed.

TURK

My club sent me to track him down. And when my mission was over, I never wanted another one again. When I found him, I kicked the crap out of Havelock Singer. I issued the mightiest beatdown of all time. Problem is, we're evenly matched. We're equals in every way, and when we finished whaling on each other, exhausted, we fell into each other's arms.

It's been the ride of my life. But loving another man in the MC world is a risky business. As if our business isn't already brutal and ruthless enough, Lock's sergeant-at-arms Stumpy blackmails us into doing some of his dirty work, or be exposed for what we are—a couple of deviants.

This run into the Indian reservation is sleazy and beneath us, but now I'm cornered, and I'll do anything to keep my sweet Master from being lynched by his club.

LOCK

When that kingpin Carmine Rojas got a load of my beautiful stallion Turk Blackburn, he'd stop at nothing to have him. It's my fault we're in this situation. I should've kicked Turk's ass and sent him packing back to The Bare Bones.

I can hear my destiny calling me. Either I'll slink back to my club like a slimy bounty hunter with no morals—and no respect from anyone in my own backyard—or I'll step up to the plate and be the lion of the day.

Either way, we're screwed. Our clubs are going to hound us underground or into another country before we escape this mess—if we don't die trying.

Publisher's warning: This book is not for the faint of heart. It contains scenes of gay sex, consensual BDSM, illegal doings, dubious consent, and man-on-man violence.

Living off the grid and being kind of an outlaw brings a dangerous reality.
—Ron Perlman

CHAPTER ONE

TURK

I was antsy and restless.

The last several runs hadn't ended well. Our club, The Bare Bones, was at war with the Presención cartel, and the tension was wearing on everyone. We weren't in lockdown per se, but we may as well have been. Our clubhouse, The Citadel, was truly becoming one now, a fortress with futons strewn in the War Room like a pack of playing cards, sweetbutts draped from every coat rack like lingerie displays, patch holders camped out in tiled bathrooms where the plumbing hadn't worked since the Vietnam War. Men kept watch at broken windows, cleaning and polishing their weapons, peering out as though at the lunar wasteland scene of a Jewish ghetto, wisps of battlefield smoke rising from the desert spires and mesas.

We were hunkered down like soldiers in our dismal, depressing trenches. The aura of rancid bacon grease permeated everything, as if bacon was the only thing bikers knew how to cook. It was a rainy winter and spring, and everything made of leather started growing mold. I became irritated by the same old, same old sight of my brothers. Even the nearly twin, stunningly handsome faces of the Illuminati brothers, Ford and Lytton, were becoming like nails on a blackboard to me. Standing next to them in the Crowd Pleaser toilet trailer, pissing side by side, brothers in arms and all that, made me want to take them by the neck, throttle them, and toss them into the airplane hangar like grenades.

So I got out on a few runs. But there seemed to be a black cloud hovering over us, some kind of hellhound karma that we couldn't seem to shake. Riding down to Nogales to hit a Presención trap house only wound up in a clusterfuck of epic proportions. I guess we had the wrong intel or the wrong code knock. When no one answered the door, although we could clearly see the flickering glare from at least one TV through the closed blinds, we busted on in there like a SWAT team. Unfucking-fortunately, instead of finding our mortal enemies waiting to engage in fair, competent, hand-to-hand battle, we were suddenly pointing our Russian ladies at a BDSM dungeon full of poor fucks who just wanted to have a little spin on the St. Andrew's cross.

One girl was cuffed there, her blubbery ass being whipped into a froth by some smelly devil in a PVC Y-harness that went up his ass crack. He wasn't messing around, either—his cat was slicing actual bloody welts into her skin. She bit down on her ball gag and tears dripped copiously down her face. Another guy chained to what might pass for a spanking bench wore a total latex hood with a closed zipper for a mouth. I've been to a few bondage clubs in my time but never had I witnessed extreme "play" like this. A urethral sound was jammed up his dick, and another moron was whacking the hell out of his johnson with a wide leather belt. The heavy pewter buckle even smacked his bare thighs. His shrieks were muffled by the latex hood.

I'll tell you. It was enough to shame you out of the entire bondage world. It even struck me that these "submissives" weren't there voluntarily, knowing the human trafficking world the Presenciónos moved in. Engaging in the play of a power exchange always involves the tiniest bit of acting, no matter how gung ho one is about it. And I'm telling you, these victims weren't acting. They were there under duress.

But I was a seasoned patch holder. I had patched into The Bare Bones fourteen years ago and I wasn't about to lose my shit because someone's flogging technique lacked finesse. These idiots were just runners, low-level spitters who probably used more drugs than they sold. It wasn't our position to enlighten them on the finer points of sub-drop or cock-and-ball torture. We were in the thugs-and-drugs game, too, foot soldiers trying to win a war.

"Let's just grab the dope and irons and leave," I suggested to Ford.

He nodded curtly. We'd come up together since the short pants days—we knew each other's shorthand and thoughts. We'd seen some Mossbergs in the front room, and a coffee table where someone had been bagging dope. As we pivoted around to head out, the dungeon lit up with the sudden strobe-like flashing of our Prospect's Kalashnikov.

Mergatroyd shrieked like a woman as he sprayed the backs of the floggers with his rounds. Ford and I looked on, horrified, as Mergatroyd re-enacted some fucking scene from a *Rambo* movie. "Die, you fucking douchebags, die!" he yelled, like some war-torn, PTSD-riddled combat vet. "Take this, you sick fucks! This'll be the last time you chain anyone up against their will!"

"*Mergatroyd!*" Ford barked. He even bashed the stupid Prospect on the skull with his own gun butt, causing a look of glazed stupor to wash over Mergatroyd's pupils.

But the damage was done. The Prospect wielded a Russian lady, and those bullets don't stop for anyone. A human torso isn't as dense as a tree, for instance. The assault rifle rounds had gone right through the disgusting offenders as they flailed in a dance that was half Marquis deSade, half who-the-hell-is-shooting-me.

It would've been funny to see that harnessed fucktard twitching like a disciple at a revival meeting, if only the bullets weren't going right through his body and into that of the poor Mexican victim. Her head lolled against her shoulder, her jaw relaxed so much the ball gag fell from her mouth, hanging like a clownish necklace. The scene was repeated with the poor hooded guy. The fuckwad brandishing the heavy belt twitched like a dreaming dog as rounds carved little channels in his back. He crashed to the floor in a pile. It was probably a blessing he was put out of his misery, but we didn't know what sort of scene they had going on. We tried to never intervene in things that didn't directly involve our business.

"Oh," breathed Mergatroyd. "Jeez." He gazed at the carnage as though waking in the middle of a dream.

"*What the fuck is wrong with you?*" Ford seethed.

"I...I don't know what came over me..." Mergatroyd gulped. He gazed at his rifle in vague horror as though it were a turd.

"Never mind," said Ford, his eye as always on the prize. "Let's grab the stuff and blaze."

It was a given that Mergatroyd's prospecting career with The Bare Bones was over. He was a good man, but we couldn't afford to have a loose cannon like that operating with us. We had a Prospect once who, at the slightest drop of a hat, would rip someone's throat out if they looked sideways at him. It gave us too much exposure having a pit bull like that running around randomly getting tweaked over shit that wasn't important in the long run, like making a catcall at his old lady, or having the bad taste to order a Coors instead of a Bud. Acting out while wearing club colors reflected badly on all of us as a unit, and the collateral damage brought on our heads was never worth it. That guy never did wind up earning his top rocker, and neither did Mergatroyd.

But I'm getting ahead of myself. Scenes like this were repeated all over the state of Arizona that winter and spring. We had lost our golden touch, starting this feud with the Presenciós. For a while, it sure seemed as though our glory years were behind us.

In fourteen years I had never once questioned the righteousness of being a Boner. The man-to-machine relationship was the finest and foremost apex of my life, the crowning glory, the highest high. Riding with my brothers was a holy rebirth, a sacred temple for my fragile identity. It helped that Ford and his pop Cropper Illuminati had taken me in as a kid, so the outlaw life was literally in my bones. They had taken a devastated, terrified, homeless kid under the protective wing of the MC, and I had flourished and blossomed.

Not being an expert at blowing shit up like Ford, I hadn't joined the SEALS, but had managed the Bones' army surplus store first, living in the back or at the Bum Steer bar and grill until they refurbished the old army airplane hangar that would become The Citadel. Not once had the slightest shadow of doubt crossed my mind that the club was anything other than a great, protective bond, a noble and holy shield—the colors of The Bare Bones MC.

My brothers in arms went to the wall for me through thick and thin. All MCs had their brothers' backs, but The Bare Bones was different. We lost our President Cropper during a shootout in the desert near Nogales. The new boss wasn't the same as the old boss. We rallied around Ford, tighter, stronger, more closely knit than ever before. When a half-brother of Ford popped up, threatening to take down the club, we were like the phoenix emerging from the cleansing fire. We'd taken Lytton into our fold, too, his skills and strengths enhancing the club, adding to the depth and breadth of our power in the Pure and Easy area. I wound up running a medical marijuana dispensary downtown, one of the Bones' many legitimate concerns. A Joint System specialized in the long-flowering sativas Lytton grew at his Leaves of Grass farm up on Mormon Mountain. Our initial fussing and fighting over how to manage the dispensary turned Lytton and I into staunch, rock solid allies.

We were an untouchable tribe, a closed society that could not be dented, scratched, or marred in any way. Then all of a sudden things began to go south.

The Presenciónes started to hit back. My budtender August was hit in the bathroom at a Hempcon in Phoenix. The mild-mannered, unarmed biker was brained with a ball peen hammer and nearly depantsed before he'd made his escape, too shaken up to continue manning A Joint System's booth. Our old school brother Duji had shot his way out of a Pottery Barn while backed into a corner by a bunch of *sicarios*—hit men. Another founding member, Faux Pas, was jumped at a U-pick apple farm by some cartel members disguised, appropriately enough, as migrant workers. Luckily Faux Pas had one of those long-handled apple picking implements in his hand at the time, and he wielded it like an Asian stick fighter.

"I was tossing beaners right and left!" Faux Pas cried in his thick French accent. "They were flying like trapeze artists, rolling like hedgehogs, stumbling over the fallen apples! But they could not touch me, because I was a jiu-jitsu fiend! I whacked one in the head with the metal basket and the fingers of the cage actually got stuck in his skull, like some kind of horror movie. That's when another one came at me with one of those things you use to plant flowers—"

"A trowel," I suggested.

"A trowel, stabbing overhead at me with it. Another one climbed the apple tree and jumped me from fifteen feet above. You see this cut on my shoulder? That's from the trowel! The only thing that saved me was, well…"

"Sapphire?" Ford filled in, mentioning Faux Pas's wife.

Faux Pas looked abashed. "Not Sapphire."

Duji frowned. "Sophie?" That was Faux Pas's teenaged daughter.

The Frenchman instantly protested, holding up his hands. "She is an ace softball pitcher! She is already being scouted for the minor leagues!"

I chuckled. "Your daughter hit the *sicarios* with apples?"

Faux Pas scowled. "They can be quite painful when thrown as hard as Sophie can throw."

Things were getting just a bit too hot for our comfort, especially when it became obvious we were being hit while doing everyday, innocuous things, endangering family members, innocent bystanders, even kids. We needed to protect our flank, so we basically went on lockdown. It was easy to protect The Citadel, being in the middle of a flat treeless mesa, built as it was for military aircraft to land and take off. Old runways and revetment areas crisscrossed the mesa like landing strips of the gods, so the only way they could hit us there would be a drone or a remote detonating IED, if anyone could sneak up and set the charge, that is.

But we were all going stir crazy. Everyone was raring to go on runs, no matter how trivial. You should've seen the clamor to be picked for a Farmer's Market run. Great Caesar's Ghost, you should've seen the stampede that ensued when someone needed to go to Home Depot for light bulbs. It was like a Who concert, and poor Kneecap really *did* stumble and fall under the weight of several pairs of engineer boots. We knew something had to give.

Ford called a meeting in the chapel. I happened to be standing next to Knoxie as we waited to toss our cell phones into the bucket, so we made small talk. Pretty much even the small talk had been exhausted by this point, so Knoxie said,

"Where's Carrie been? Haven't seen her for about a week."

Carrie Gunslinger was this cum factory snatch I had been "hitting" for a few months. I wasn't sure how effective of a beard Carrie was, having no real idea to what extent any of my brothers realized I was gay. Over the years, there had been a few cracks about it, especially coming from Ford. The way we referred to it was so subterranean it wouldn't even have been noticeable by an outsider. That was the way it had to be—unacknowledged. Uphill gardeners were so despised in the biker world, we had to find an entirely new row to hoe. If it was going to be done, we had best dig a hole to China and come out on the other side of the planet before even *thinking* about it.

I shrugged. "Ah. You know. It's not the height of excitement around here, and I didn't want to endanger her."

Knoxie nodded. "Plus, she's set to headline that new flick, *Lord of the G-Strings.*"

"Right," I said, eager to highlight Carrie's important career outside of The Citadel. Knoxie should know, being a former performer at the Triple Exposure Studios himself. "She doesn't have time to hang around here. She just wrapped *White Men Can't Hump*. I wonder what's on the agenda here today?"

Tuzigoot, in front of us, turned around. "Someone probably needs to go to 7-11 for a Snickers bar."

We chuckled half-heartedly. The MC lifestyle wasn't always full of shits and giggles, drama and angst. Lately it had been as boring as a factory full of power drills.

Once Ford called the meeting to order, it was his half-brother Lytton who took the pulpit. I didn't know in that second that life as I knew it was about to undergo a game changer.

I had been chomping at the bit for a new mission.

For my sins, I was given one.

Lytton orated, "As you may have heard, some condom breath has been running around the western part of Arizona, we think up and down the Colorado River, selling weed under my trademarked names, Eminence Front and Young Man Blue." These were his two most popular strains from his plantation. They were by far the most asked-for strains at my dispensary, and their fame ranged far and wide. A customer had brought me some of that fake dope to check out. I ruptured the resin glands to inhale the volatile terpenes, but it was harsh and rank, without any of the lovely lavender and skunk overtone of Lytton's signature product.

Lytton went on, "It's utterly and completely bogus, and what's worse, it's dirty schwag weed. It's obvious from the stems and the amount of seeds it's that crap from Chihuahua."

August, my budtender, nodded sagely. "Instead of tiny rockets of THC, it felt more like firecrackers of meth."

I added my two cent's worth. "Instead of the hazy citrus aroma, there was a distinct overtone of moldy leather."

Everyone nodded emphatically, being all too familiar lately with that particular scent. All my senses were pricked up. I was on the edge of my seat to hear what Lytton proposed to do about it. At a time when even a jaunt to the car wash would've been the height of excitement and men were haggling over the *Super Mario* joystick and the new copy of *More* magazine, well, this was right up my alley.

And Lytton delivered.

"As you all know, the annual Laughlin River Run is coming up in a week."

The low mumbles around the table burst into outright huzzahs and whoops. Every year, tens of thousands of bikers rumbled into the gambling village of Laughlin on the Nevada side of the Colorado River. It was the biggest rally west of the Rockies, with vendors and headline music acts, packed with exhibits. I'd only gone once, in '03, the year after that brutal Angels and Mongols clash on the Harrah's gaming floor had left a bad taste in everyone's mouth. So I was told that things were normally not that sedate in Laughlin, and sure could've fooled me. It was the biggest debauch my twenty-year-old brain had ever seen. We just fucked—girls, at the time, mostly—up and down Casino Drive, drinking and smoking our way through one exhibit after the other, test driving rides, getting inked, and I'm pretty sure I even somehow participated in a bikini bike wash.

Now, seeing as we'd been stuck inside playing pool and watching *Wheel of Fortune*, the prospect of attending the Laughlin run was an even bigger prize to dangle than normal. Everyone sat up straight, suddenly silent as the grave when Lytton raised his hand.

"It makes total sense to send a couple of you boys into Laughlin to check on the general lay of the land. See if you can track down the source of this bogus weed."

"Those Assassins of Youth dirtbags are based just over the river in Bullhead City," Ford noted. Every outlaw biker who wasn't a Bare Boner was automatically a dirtbag, and everyone around the table nodded in assent. Some of those clubs we had amiable dealings with, but the Assassins weren't one of them.

Lytton said, "Right. They could easily be the source of this crap weed, knowing their control over that whole Highway 95 river area. It's not our backyard, but I want to start pushing back on this. It's pissing me off on a personal and professional level. I can't go, seeing as how I'm going to Dallas for NORML's Marijuana March in a couple days. And Faux Pas will be in LA working on the newest *Paranormal Activity* movie."

My cock was actually stiffening with anticipation, my hands flat on the table, leaning forward so far my arms actually stung with a sharp ache. I would've torn the tabletop right off the legs if Lytton hadn't spoken my name.

"Makes the most sense to send Turk, of course. That shouldn't come as a surprise to anyone. He knows his weed and—"

Nobody else probably heard the rest of Lytton's yammering, either. Everyone exhaled mightily as one unit. A giant gust of wind swept across the table as twenty pissed-off brothers glared at me with jealousy, sending knives shooting from their eyes like those comic book hypnotists.

Of course, I wouldn't go alone. Maybe I could choose someone to accompany me. August would have to stay to manage A Joint System. And, if I chose a discreet partner, there was a very real possibility of a passionate, bruising, thunderous hookup with Dayton Navarro of our Flagstaff charter.

My lover. My Master.

I was so certain I'd choose Wild Man, a casual, laid back sort of guy who liked to make bongs out of Pringles cans, carrots, and mannequins. I wasn't even terribly let down when I heard Ford say,

"We think the best person to accompany Turk is Twinkletoes."

Everyone mouthed the word *Twinkletoes?* in horror, as though just the word would give them Ebola. Twinkletoes himself wasn't in the chapel at the time. Being a Prospect, he wasn't invited to church. But being a Prospect made it even stranger he'd be chosen for such a plumb assignment.

Not so strange, actually. Ford went on, "Twinkletoes' medical necessity to use pot makes him an excellent candidate for this run. Do you agree, Turk?"

"Sure," I babbled happily. I would've agreed to Tinkerbell as well as Twinkletoes, I was so tickled. "He's pretty knowledgeable. Every time he comes into Joint System we discuss the various strains in depth. I know he's your computer guy, your eyes and ears man, and that might be valuable in Laughlin, too."

Lytton slapped the table with his palm. "It's settled, then. The rally starts the twenty-third of April, but you can be there sooner to get a jump start on the intel. Moving right along then. Ford?"

Ford droned on. "Yeah. It's come to our attention that some of you have started a game using the contractor's port-a-potties out on the runway by the stockpiles as a sort of bowling lane."

"Port-a-poppins," laughed Russ Gollywow. "Not an easy game to win."

Tuzigoot said, "Those outhouses can really fly during a high wind."

I wasn't listening to Ford reprimand the crew. I was imagining lapping away at Damon's tanned, hot as sin collarbone while running my palms down the exquisite slope of his lower back, all the way to his dimpled ass cheeks.

I wanted a new mission. For my sins I was given one.

And I never wanted another one again.

CHAPTER TWO
LOCK

It was the job of Havelock Singer's life. It would make him or break him.

And the second he laid eyes on his target, it started to look more like the latter.

In the first place, the target, improbably named Ronald Reagan, was so gay that Lock couldn't address him with a straight face. Not only was he light in the loafers—literally, he walked with a springy step—"traipsing" would be the right word for it—but he led Lock directly to the doors of The Racquet Club, Flagstaff's most notorious gay nightclub.

Well, well. What the fuck am I going to do now? I guess I have to follow him inside. I'm not exactly dressed for "gay." Maybe I should wait for him to come back out.

But you never knew. Fugitives had a way of slipping out the back doors of establishments. If Lock positioned himself in the back alley, and with the way his luck had been running lately, the fag would probably slip out the front.

He had no choice but to go in. Of course his Assassins of Youth cut was in the trunk of his Mustang. Unfortunately he could never fly his club colors when on assignment, but just knowing he was doing club work made up for it. He much preferred riding free on his Softail. His bike was his dream, and there was nothing else more important to him. Lock's club was his tribe. They had their rituals, their formalities, their rites. Things could be chaotic. They could be at war with another club. There could be backstabbing moles, intel running down the wrong channels, outsiders betraying them. But Lock knew his brothers would always go to the wall for him.

Club protocol was the glue that had held Lock together since Iraq. His experience flying combat missions hitting soft targets gave him the perfect background, the ideal personality for this sort of tracking. Havelock Singer *was* Los Toro Hermanos Bail Bonds. He had his office manager Aditya to hold down the fort, but Lock did all the hard labor, all the tracking, all the eyes and ears, all the fugitive extradition. In fact, Lock was something of an adrenaline junkie, he knew. The few times there was *not* a bail jumper to track, he felt lost, adrift. They were the Bull Brothers, but Lock usually felt like a lone wolf, operating solo missions and preferring it that way.

Right now was one of the few times he'd felt remotely uncomfortable. Just imagining walking through a club of gay men really tweaked him. He could carry out air strikes with impunity. He wore bulletproof armor when tracking fugitives, sometimes even into Indian reservations where they thought they could hide. He'd tackled women, he'd handcuffed drug kingpins to walls, and he'd tasered pit bulls to get to his targets. But the thought of walking unarmed through a gay nightclub put the fear of God into him.

What do I do to look gay? The eyebrow barbell probably helped, as much as Lock hated to admit it, and he wore small hoops in both ears, to look like a pirate. *Isn't there something about different colored handkerchiefs in your pockets?* Quickly he googled on his smart phone. He had a black bandanna in the cage's back seat. He often made a headband out of it when riding his scoot to help keep his long blond hair out of his eyes, in addition to his brain bucket. Now, he saw that a black handkerchief meant "into piercing."

Well, that's sure as hell true. I've got a few piercings. So, for lack of a better way to "gay himself up," Lock shook out the handkerchief and tucked it into the back pocket of his 501s. It made him even more nervous to have to leave his Glock in his glove compartment, but it wouldn't be worth having it discovered during a routine frisk by the bouncer.

When he exited the Mustang, he was swept along by a small knot of flagrantly gay men. They were those super-enthusiastic twinks with neat moustaches, good dental plans, and tight wifebeaters, and Lock sort of let himself be swept along behind them. He walked like a goonish Neanderthal compared to their sashaying, and it helped secure him as a man's man. He was a passive tough guy. He had to be, to move in the circles he moved in. He wasn't a bull in a china shop, crashing through knocking over everything and drawing attention to himself. He was usually quiet but lethal. Still, he felt a bit on edge because he was about to head into a giant room full of ass-grabbers.

The name of the club, The Racquet Club, could be anything, really. It could indicate fitness, health. Lock lifted weights and practiced Brazilian jiu-jitsu when at home, so he was definitely fit. But as he neared the front door, he began to get a creeping feeling. A couple of men waiting to get in wore black leather collars, one with a D ring with a little leash through it, although no one held the leash. Another guy wore actual lace-up rubber gauntlets that came almost to his elbows.

Craptastic. Fucking Ronald Reagan has to go and visit a fucking bondage club.

Lock's suspicions were confirmed when the cum fairy took money from his neoprene gauntlet, revealing it to be a wallet.

Very witty. Lock was going in, making the takedown, and getting the fuck out of there.

Inside, there were bare asses hanging out of chaps, some of them quite muscular and trim. *I'm going to go directly down this bar, scope it out, find Reagan, and take him down. He shouldn't be any problem in public like this.* Reagan had jumped bail on a kiddie porn and molestation charge, so he wouldn't be too eager to have his face Instagrammed making a scene in The Racquet Club. Those daddy Dom types usually went quietly, in Lock's experience.

Problem was, Reagan wasn't calmly bellied up to the bar. Lock was forced to check out a wide—and he meant *wide*—variety of asses while strolling up and down the entire length of the bar several times, and not one of them belonged to Reagan. There were bony asses, butts so wide they needed a highway sign, and butts that had been crowbarred into leather pants four sizes too small.

"Excuse me," Lock said after bumping into a naked torso. A few joy boys giggled at him before he realized the torso was a mannequin, bolted horizontally so patrons could park their drinks on its back.

"Tasty Don," said one of them, fluttering his eyelashes at Lock.

He tried to remain impassive. "My name's not Don." For some reason, this caused the "table" full of men to giggle even louder. Perplexed, Lock moved down the wall of red velvet drapes and antler sconces—he guessed it was a Wild West brothel look they were going for. Old newspaper style engravings of boxers and other pugilists hung from the flocked wallpaper. Stained boxing gloves were slung from pegs above the bar. He was crushed between several hairy chests where men were bottlenecked, undecided about going onto the dance floor.

Just the strobe lights alone were enough to induce a seizure, and Lock had to squeeze his eyes shut several times, hard. It wasn't going to be as easy as he'd imagined finding Reagan in this sea of latex bodysuits, nipple clamps, and harnesses. The monotonous chanting of the hip-hop racket echoed inside Lock's eardrums. When he stood on his toes to see over one harnessed guy's shoulder, he was stunned motionless by a bold hand crawling over his crotch, exploring.

Lock's eyes darted from side to side, trying to figure out who was groping him. No one made eye contact with him. He was trapped in this cloud of musk and powder, men all around him bouncing on the balls of their feet, tapping their heels in time to the music, with shining eyes wondering who their next dance partner would be. The hand zeroed right in on the cap of his cockhead, swirling a circular pattern with a thumb, pressing Lock's hot cock into his bare hip. He was petrified immobile, only his eyes shifting back and forth.

There was one guy behind him. Body heat emanating from the queer warmed the flimsy T-shirt covering Lock's shoulders. He couldn't see without turning his head, and he didn't want to acknowledge whoever was fondling him. No, much better to stand still and let the manhandling go seemingly unnoticed. Although that might be difficult to do.

Lock realized with a mortified shock that his prick was responding to the massage.

What if it was one of those wide load swishes with a hairy bare ass? Several of them wore those assless harnesses, one with a locked chastity belt feature. *As if anyone would want to get up on that.* The hand loved on his cock, squeezing the length of it almost with affection as it bloomed and elongated under the palm.

Oh God, he's going to feel that. He's going to be able to tell I'm getting hot. *Of course I am. Who wouldn't respond to a jacking like this? It's biology, only natural. The guy's good. He probably has lots of experience.* Lock's prick bulged inside his boxer briefs, straining to be let out, rising and plumping under the fag's erotic ministrations. Now a twink standing shoulder-to-shoulder with him noticed what was going on in his backyard. The guy wore one of those Village People police caps with the patent leather bill, and in the shade of it Lock could see his lustful onyx eyes taking in Lock's entire form. The guy eyeballed him shamelessly, right down to the bulging crotch of his 501s.

Lock's prick was so stiff, actually, it strained against the metal buttons of the fly. Not only was Lock not protesting the mauling, he folded his arms over his chest and ever so slightly rocked his hips, pressing his erection into the palm. The fake cop nodded his approval, even licking his lips as he elbowed his buddy and pointed at Lock's crotch.

What are you, some kind of fag, Lock almost spat out, until he realized that *yeah, I guess he is. I'm in a fucking gay bar getting turned on by another man's groping my dick.* And when the sissy behind him moved closer to cup Lock's balls in his other palm, Lock did nothing. The guy swiveled his packed crotch against the globe of Lock's ass, and Lock did nothing. The fake cop was yanking his pal by the arm, jerking his chin in the direction of the hand job action, and Lock merely set his jaw even more firmly and looked defiantly at the poofs.

"Whatchoo lookin' at?" he growled, although he doubted he could be heard over the thundering beat of the music. He gasped, though—he flinched and jumped and his eyes halfway shut—when the anonymous hand squeezed his erect length fully, and a couple drops of pre-come squeezed from his slit.

Jiminy Christmas. I hope to fuck this isn't one of those chubby harnessed bears. Worse, one of these twinks.

The twink said in a ladylike tone, "We're looking at your fine meat, Mr. Dreamboat. You're hung like a bull. We'd like to see more of that fine penis."

For some reason this plumped his dick even more completely. It was the appreciation, the admiration, that was getting to his head. With his arms crossed like this, he felt his toned pecs stand out, juicy and buff. He did nearly lose his shit when his incognito fuck buddy swiveled his hard-on against the rise of Lock's firm butt and slid a lusty hand up his washboard abs. Lock held his breath, waiting for the exquisite arrow he knew would shoot down his abdomen when the stranger pinched one of his nipple barbells between his fingers. *Yes. This guy is good. I haven't been touched like this in months...years.*

Lock sort of didn't care anymore whether it was one of the hairy bears molesting him from behind. It could be one of those disgusting ass bandits wearing a puppy play mask or rubber boy shorts. This erotic manipulation was so sublime, Lock could be as straight as a Roman road and still his cock would jump to life under this pawing. He even rocked his hips from side to side when the pervert dry humped his ass with great big sweeping undulations. He could feel through both layers of jean material that his faceless lover was thin with a nice fat cock, the mushroom head meaty and urgent against his ass. *Oh, fantastic. These fags are drooling for my dong, and they're never going to get their hands on it. I'm out of their reach. I'm beyond their pay grade. They can go suck each other and pretend it's me, but they're never getting their mouth on my meat. Look at this dicky licker. He can't put his eyeballs back in his head. I'm hung like a horse and they can all tell. His mouth is watering for my tasty spunk.*

His stiff dick was straining for release, and he didn't even care whether Ronald Reagan had snuck out the back door. He had to get this fucker to give him some relief. Slapping his hand over the other's, he squeezed it lustily, urging the hand to break more barriers of propriety. The other's warm breath against the back of his neck raised his hackles and stiffened his nipples. The guy continued toying with the barbell through his areola, shooting blissful spasms through his balls. Lock knew he couldn't whip it out and play bukkake on top of all these willing submissives. Talk about drawing attention to himself. As much as he wanted all the hungry, drooling admiration that he could get, he knew they had to cut out of here. He could pick up Ronald Reagan's trail tomorrow, or even in an hour from now.

He squeezed the hand that caressed his dick and allowed his head to sort of loll back on the guy's shoulder. The hand slid from his nipple up his throat, fondling his jaw, his short, blond beard. He had to talk before the guy kissed him and every fag on Grindr within a half mile radius was chasing after his desirable ass. Not to mention, forwarding the pictures to someone in his club, regardless of how many miles away from Bullhead City, Arizona he currently was. "Let's go," he said, almost drunkenly.

Hey. The guy was even handsome, if anyone ever stopped to think that way about another man. His heavy-lidded eyes bore down on Lock's, and he mumbled steamily, "God, you're one delicious piece of meat."

That was exactly what Lock wanted to hear. Having just split up with his old lady of two years, his ego was so low he could look up and see hell. He'd been understandably down after breaking up with the woman he thought he might marry one day. He just hadn't hurried fast enough for Ruby. Now, a hot stud was dry humping his ass like a dog, jerking his dick so masterfully he was just a cunt hair away from ejaculating in his jeans. At least three gay boys were fanning themselves with their hands and panting so heavily Lock could feel their collective wind against his arms.

"Oh, this piece of meat is giving me life!" declared one of the twinks with overly plucked eyebrows, pretending to swoon.

"This man is *everything*, Jason!" cried another.

Lock's new mystery man yanked him through the crowd like he was bass fishing, reeling and pulling him in behind him. Lock stumbled like a drunken fish too, although he was a teetotaler and a card-carrying member of the Straight Edge Movement, minus the vegan part. He did smoke weed on occasion. His dick pulsed painfully, constricted inside his jeans, scraping with every stumble he took. His balls were already pulled up high and tight close to his body in preparation for ejaculation, and he knew he wouldn't last long. It would be embarrassing, but would make his buddy feel good about his talents, at least.

This inked sex god wasn't leading him toward the front door, though. Lock followed his swinging ass toward the bathrooms. *Clusterfuck. I am not doing it in a bathroom stall.* Talk about having his face plastered all over the interwebs. However, the tanned cowboy led him to a black door that opened up on a hallway lined with curtains hanging from rods. *Aha.* Lock had heard about this type of thing, but for obvious reasons had never experienced it himself.

His heart raced with trepidation. The excitement of the illicit act and the possibility of being caught was a new adrenaline high he knew he'd want to experience over and over again. He'd finally found a new drug to replace the high of flying bombing missions with Park. It had been eight years since he'd experienced that spine-tingling, delicious high, the cortisol being pumped through his nervous system like an arrow to a splatter target. Lock felt alive in every sense of the word as Cowboy anxiously dragged him down the hallway, the scent of day-old spunk emanating from the little cubbyholes.

"In here," said his buddy. He swung Lock through the curtain, assisting with an additional shove to the chest.

Lock stumbled until he hit a wall. A greasy, oily wall. He frowned. "Hey. That wasn't necessary." He was the top around here, and briefly he wondered if there would be a power struggle.

In the light of a single incandescent bulb hanging from a wire on the ceiling, the cowboy was starting to look vaguely diabolic. Maybe it was the fact that he was wearing shades indoors. The bandanna wrapped around his head was light blue, but Lock struggled to recall what color that indicated in the gay color wheel. Placing one hand against the wall next to Lock's head, the cowboy leaned in, too close for comfort. *Maybe this was a bad idea. Nothing good can come of this.*

Intently and with purpose, the cowboy said, "It's necessary if you're serious about *this* item," and slid a hand down Lock's lower back.

Lock's hand shot out to grip the guy by the wrist. He had lightning reflexes, and he aimed to make the most of them. "*That* item was to inform everyone that I'm into piercings."

The guy looked perplexed, then smiled a relaxed, lazy grin. A mottled spot of what looked like motor oil covered his Adam's apple, and it crossed Lock's mind. *This guy's a biker too.* "Not that. You're just an innocent lamb, aren't you? You think gays still use that stupid handkerchief code?" Lasciviously he rotated his hard-on against Lock's, wiping Lock's brain free of anything that had come before. Jism surged up the underside of his stimulated prick, and he felt another few dribbles spurt from his slit. "No, I meant *this* item, baby." And he whipped something from behind Lock.

Shit! He had Lock's handcuffs in his hand! He had completely forgotten he had those—besides, any bouncer would have just chuckled at them and let him proceed. He stored them in a cuff case that was chained to his belt, and because he didn't tuck in his T-shirt he didn't think much about them.

"Besides, you had the wrong code," said the guy casually, clicking one cuff shut around Lock's wrist. He was using his smooth talk to distract Lock, and the rubbing of his stiff dick against Lock's was driving him out of his mind. Lock decided to call the guy Red Rocks after a tat on his shoulder, "Red Rocks Original." "Black means BDSM, not piercings."

Oh, God. He was a goner now. His wrists were cuffed behind his back and Red Rocks thought he was a bondage submissive! Lock could have kneed him in the groin, head butted him, and escaped. But his curiosity had been piqued beyond the point of no return. Besides, Red was sucking on his neck now and pinching his erect nipple while gyrating his giant boner against him, and what was a man to do about that?

"I'm not a fag," Lock mumbled. He was panting so rapidly he feared he might hyperventilate.

"Of course not," Red mumbled back, his mouth full of Lock's throat. "No one in this club is, aside from the guys who like Lady Gaga and Justin Timberlake."

"What I mean is..." Lock suddenly couldn't remember what he meant. "I've never been to a gay club before, and I've never done it with a stranger. I barely know who Lady Gaga is, and I'm no fucking bottom. I was here on business. I'm no damned cocksucker."

Red pulled back a few inches, palming Lock's jaw, forcing him to look into his eyes. "Of course you're not. Look. You're just lucky you put your bandanna in the correct pocket, so I didn't expect you to be a cocksucker." He punctuated this assertion with a swift thrust of his hips that had Lock gasping.

The guy had powerful muscles, maybe seven percent body fat. It was too bad Lock would never see him again after tonight. "I've got you helpless. That makes it easier for you to pretend all this is being done against your will. You're no fag, and I come along forcing you into this terrible compromising position."

Yeah. Lock liked the sound of that, and when Red kissed him, a full-on, mushy tongue lapping the backs of his teeth kiss, he reciprocated with every cell of his being. Their kiss was a manly, no holds barred, rip roaring snorting kiss. There was no affectionate loving here, just the unfettered lust of two over-the-top aroused men locking horns. Lock was enjoying the hell out of their illicit tryst, literally in the back room of a den of iniquity, a place where the bartender was buff and shirtless, pouring drinks in front of a sign notifying people of "Sperm Sundays."

So he kissed his new fuck buddy, and ground his pelvis against Red's until he was nearly out of his mind. He broke the assault of the kiss with a loud smack, panting so heavily tiny bubbles swam before his eyes. "Fuck it, you fucker," he breathed. "Get down on your knees and service me."

That's what he used to say to Park. It made him sound authoritative and masterful, even now with his own wrists cuffed behind his back. Red looked shocked for only a fraction of a second. Then that sly smile spread over his delicious mouth again, and he dropped to his knees.

Oh, Godddd. Finally. Lock swiveled his hips like a pole dancer as Red's fingers flew over his belt buckle. Lock was proud of his enormous erection, the way his balls filled the crotch of his jeans, the way his stiff prick had, over the months, made a sort of faded impression against the fabric of, well, a giant penis.

When Red lifted the heavy cock into the open air, he

groaned a dying animal sound. The puffs of Red's breath tickled his cock like tiny angel's fingers, lifting him higher and higher to ecstasy. He could pretend he was being assaulted without his consent by a man on his knees in front of him. He could imagine he was just drunk when he hadn't had a drink in years. He could play as though it had been forced on him—and what man in his right mind would turn down an expert blowjob, regardless of the gender of the giver?

No, Lock was in the perfect position right now. And already he knew he would be seeking this out time and time again.

"Do it, you fucker," Lock growled, squirming tauntingly. He could care less if he was getting several layers of Oil of Man on the back of his white T-shirt—the walls must be coated with years of ejaculate and hair products. He jabbed his cock in the direction of Red's mouth. "Suck me, you faggot! You know you want it. You've been wanting me since you started handling me in the bar."

"Oh *yeah*," Red agreed heatedly. Every syllable of his hot breath against his glans sent Lock nearly over the edge. "You're the most delicious piece of round eye I've seen in months. Being a bung hole virgin makes you even tastier."

"Do it, gay boy," Lock snarled from between clenched teeth. "Do it, or I'm gonna cry rape."

That did it. Red fell upon Lock's prick, hoovering the entire length of the member into his mouth.

It was a burning hot, slick ride. Lock had utterly forgotten how wonderful it was to be sucked by a man. They had bigger mouths, for one. Yeah, that was it. More powerful throat muscles. Waves of sheer ecstasy rolled through Lock's abdomen, through his entire chest cavity, shivering the barbells that pierced his nipples. Some ancient caveman, some fucking Neanderthal was crying out with the resonance of a wounded animal, and with a shock Lock realized *that's me. Oh my fucking God. I'm wailing away like a fucking coyote in a canyon.*

So he railed against his bonds. With a pleased shock he realized that if he struggled, if he jerked his arms futilely against the metal stricture of the cuffs, if he wrenched his arms and jutted his hips and banged the back of his skull against the slimy wall, it enhanced his pleasure. Before he knew it, obscene words were spilling from his mouth as Red expertly sucked him off.

"You'll never get away with this, you fucking fag." It shocked him how much his dirty talk spiked the thrill of the illicit act he was engaged in. "You think you can fucking handcuff me and molest me like some common dick licker, well you've got another fucking thing coming."

He thought he could feel Red smile as he inhaled his angry purplish hard-on. When Red squiggled his tongue all over the underside of the cock in an *S* pattern, Lock nearly came off. He had to do something to stop this, pronto.

"Get off of me, you queer!" he shouted, successfully jerking his penis from the hungry, hot mouth. It was shiny, harder than it had ever been in its obvious state of arousal, nearly slapping up against his own abdomen when he yanked it from the voracious hole. "You hungry for some long, fat, delicious cock? There's plenty in that bar over there."

Still grinning, Red planted his hands around Lock's hips and dove in face-first between Lock's outspread thighs. Licking, gnawing, worrying Lock's balls like a dingo at the kill, the sensation was almost unbearable. Lock's thighs began to shiver, at first imperceptibly, then uncontrollably, like a Chihuahua pooping in the snow. His inflamed dick arced out over Red's shoulder but the cowboy ignored it, centering his face on Lock's most sensitive core, taking first one ball, then the next into his scalding mouth, fluttering his tongue all around the testicles like a ballerina on meth.

"Oh, God! You motherfucker! You fucking...Motherfuck!" Lock couldn't recall later all of the highly intelligent things he shouted out during the ball-licking. "Oh God! Suck my dick! Suck my long, fat, juicy dick, you fucking faggot! Swallow my nice hot load, you big cocksucker!"

He squirmed in earnest now, dying to grab ahold of Red's skull and direct the hot mouth back to his dick. He was plastered against the wall as though stuck there by the layers of sweat and jizz, his thighs shaking like the earth about to quake. Standing on the balls of his feet in his engineer boots, his hips were thrust as far forward as possible without rupturing some internal organ. When Red nuzzled aside his ball sac and spread his ass cheeks wide with both hands, Lock truly started weeping.

Holy fuck. A tear actually squeezed from the corner of one eye. Just as it seemed frustration couldn't possibly mount any higher, the cocksucker plunged his long, wet tongue right between the globes of his ass, wriggling it right over the no man's land of his sphincter.

Holy mother of God. His entire body now vibrating like a tuning fork, Lock heard an unearthly howl coming from another cubicle. *Oh, wait. That's me. That's motherfucking me.* He was sobbing, unable to contain so much bliss in his body. Nobody had ever rimmed him, much less dared to put their mouth so close to his asshole, and the trust it showed absolutely floored him. The tongue darted in and out just ever so lightly from his sensitive hole. Lock became a puddle of emotional goo, his cock so aroused and close to spewing that a trickle of jism rolled down into his trimmed pubes.

Then his entire world caved in.

"*What the fuck!*"

The tongue abruptly stopped lapping and Red's face drew away from Lock's butt. Hyperventilating now, Lock forced his bleary eyes open. Some fucktard had poked his head between the curtains, his face askew with fury.

Lock inched his torso up the wall as Red staggered to his feet. Red faced the intruder openmouthed, his hands dangling at his sides. The stranger nodded his head tightly in acknowledgement of the juicy bulge in Red's pants.

"So this is fucking it, then?" demanded the strange guy. "Two fucking years of fake proclamations of love and you're nose-deep in some unknown fucker's asshole? It's that fucking easy for you?"

The enraged guy vanished. Red only spent a few small seconds looking helplessly from Lock to the curtains, the curtains back to Lock.

"Sorry," Red whispered. Then he, too vanished.

Lock lurched to the curtains like a drunk man on a cruise ship. Already his shoulders were aching with his hands pinioned behind his back. He stuck his head between the curtains just in time to see Red's boot disappearing behind the door at the end of the hallway.

He was the bounty hunter. *He* was the one apprehending men, taking them down, cuffing them.

Now here he was. The irony was not lost on Lock.

"Hey," he called out feebly. "A little help?"

CHAPTER THREE
TURK

"Hey. The Vietnam Veterans' Memorial Fund." Twinkletoes pointed to the booth where a few craggy bald guys with tons of buttons on their caps worked. "Isn't Duji a Vietnam vet? We should donate. That's what these runs are all about, aren't they? Make money for charities?"

"Oh, shut up." That seemed to be the watchword of the day for me. *Of the week. Of the year.* "I think the only thing Duji's a veteran of is Treasure Island where he worked as a fucking typist for two years while everyone else got their balls blown off overseas."

We meandered aimlessly down the sunny, wide Casino Drive, awash with a sea of scoots. The collective rumblings of a thousand tailpipes yearned to rev my soul, but I was dead inside. Rotten to the core. Bitter, and full of rage.

"Really?" Twinkletoes could be sort of ignorant sometimes. He was basically an IT guy, a numbers cruncher, swift with the computer and bumbling at everything else. He was prospecting for us because his loyalty was unmatched and he'd do anything, no questions asked. He had some wasting disease, multiple sclerosis I think. He was extremely feeble in a rumble and very slow to draw his piece. Maybe he'd been chosen because no one thought this would be a violent mission. I normally had more compassion, but not today. "He showed me some scars on his butt he said were from shrapnel. He said it works its way through the body. Like two decades later he was sitting in the clubhouse and a piece came through his forearm."

I snorted. "If anything came through his forearm, it was a staple he stapled himself with while filling out supply requisitions."

"Okay, here. How could you possibly say no to these ladies?"

Twinkletoes gestured at a booth that was manned by women—smiling, mild-mannered women wearing crocheted vests. They didn't look like old ladies or sweetbutts. There was nary a PROPERTY OF patch to be seen on them, but they struck way more fear into my heart than any hardass, leather-clad old lady ever could.

They were Mothers Against Drunk Driving.

"Oh, *God*, no!" I cried involuntarily, and made a beeline in the opposite direction. *Could my fucking week possibly get any worse? Those fucking vultures crying about their damned dead kids!* Once they got their claws into you, they never let go. And the fucking sob stories never ended. It was all about the fucking drunk assholes, never anything else.

The opposite direction turned out to be a booth for Big Brothers and Sisters of the Colorado River, and I dug deep into my wallet for that, throwing twenties at them. I was all about the Big Brothers and Sisters. Who could find fault with an organization that loaned kids the moms and dads they had never known? I sure wished I'd had someone like that growing up. Cropper Illuminati was a sad substitute for a guy who would take you fishing. Cropper was more like the dad who would drop you at the store so you could shoplift some electronics. He was the guy handing you some four-way Windowpane LSD before taking you on the roller coaster. Not that there was anything wrong with any of that. I was lucky to have met Cropper, or I'd be in the same boat as my brother. In the system, being shuttled from one foster home to another. No, Cropper was an improvement over that. I'd been taken under the wing of The Bare Bones MC since the short pants days. Now I was Veep of my beloved club.

I knew there was no avoiding Twinkletoes' questions, though. He was one of those sensitive souls, and blah blah blah. He was a major Klingon, though, and I'd been lucky—well, I should put that in quotes, "lucky" is all relative and hindsight—"lucky" that he'd left me alone long enough to go to The Racquet Club the other night.

I kept trying to tell myself it was a good thing I'd busted Dayton Navarro in flagrante delicto. That event had saved me months, if not years, of agony down the line. We were riding for a fall anyway, Dayton and I. We belonged to the same club. The chances of being outed together increased with every hookup. I was far from being "out and proud," but I had actually been mulling over telling Ford in so many words. He kept referring to it in indirect ways, joking, making oblique references. Or was I just reading something into something that wasn't there?

Anyway, I had a feeling people had viewed Dayton and I going hard at it before. It was just a creeping, gut feeling. Once, I had taken a break from A Joint System, formerly known as A Joint Effort before joining forces with Lytton's superb pot from his farm. Dayton had stopped by to pick up some Eminence Front, back then scarce in Flagstaff. Or was it Young Man Blue he wanted? God, already I can't recall, so maybe it's good that I'm blotting it out. Anyway, I had always been pretty sure that *someone* had spied on me smoking Dayton's dick out in the back alley by the dumpster. Dayton was a horny bastard and I always did wonder how he kept it in his pants for so long between hookups. Anyway, nobody certainly ever tried giving me a beatdown for any homoerotic activity, but I wasn't a hundred percent excellent about keeping a lid on it.

Bottom line, I probably didn't care if it came into the open. I had a hunch none of my brothers cared either, so I'd been seriously mulling over telling at least Ford. We'd come up since the short pants days, we'd stolen walkmans together, we'd pushed acid to high schoolers as a team. If Ford didn't know I was at least bisexual, well, then, I had an extraterrestrial thetan to sell him. He wasn't born yesterday. He would probably be cool with it as long as I didn't flaunt it, didn't make apple martinis, start a blog, or collect anything miniature.

Still, the shock of seeing Dayton on his knees in that shitty little cubicle, gnawing and snarling and lapping up the big prick of that handcuffed stud, well, I felt so low I could kick some Martian in the chronicles. It wasn't even the sight of that long, veined beef that put the fear of God into me. I was pretty sure my penis was just as long and thick. It was that Dayton had promised me we were exclusive. *He had promised me he wouldn't fuck around.* He was much farther away from coming out to his Flagstaff chapter, but *he had promised me there would be no sex on the side for him.*

That was the part that blew my mind. Broken promises just weren't in my wheelhouse. In a fucking world where haphazard shit was the rule of the day, where men literally leaped out from behind buildings to attack you, where you were constantly ducking from the pigs, where each business interaction was the difference between life and death—in this fucking world, promises were *everything.*

Dayton had broken that feeble-ass promise in the worst possible way. Twinkletoes had pretended to believe me when I said I needed to go to the 7-11 for smokes, and I'd left him in The Bare Bones' clubhouse. Nothing wrong with that. He was a Prospect, but I wasn't his sponsor or keeper. Dayton's brother had told me he'd gone to some tennis club to work out, so I knew exactly where he was headed. The Racquet Club, where we'd enacted many a scene, sometimes in their dungeon but usually in the private cubicles.

Dayton and I were like smoke and water. We fit together like hand in glove, or so I thought. The day I found out he was gay was etched into my memory forever. But because of the homophobic nature of our club, we'd had to sneak around. Neither one of us owned a cage, so sometimes we rented hotel rooms or went to clubs where sex between patrons was allowed. Dayton was my first real lover outside of prison, if you can fucking believe that in a thirty-two-year-old man. I'd either been faking it with girls up until then—I never failed to get it up for sweetbutts, so there must be some element of bisexuality to my nature—or having *very* infrequent hookups in filthy places. Places literally like truck stops, where I once had my horny young cock sucked by a smelly old toothless guy, just to see if it'd be any different than a woman's blowjob. It was.

Once I resorted to a glory hole in a truck stop *while on a run with my crew*. I think we were heading down to Nogales, one of those first times we picked up our new lawyer, Slushy McGill. One of those runs we coordinated with that tunnel under the Mexican border, or something like that. Anyway, Lytton, Ford, and some other brothers were literally *right outside* with engines idling when I went and stuck my dick into a hole between the partitions just to see what would happen. That time, I saw the back of the grimy trucker as he exited the restroom after me, waddling with the satisfaction of my load of hot jism warming his gut. I was definitely satisfied. Men were just hungrier than women. They were more rapacious, no holds barred about their desire. Women seemed to be going through the motions, doing what was expected of them as though acting in a porn. Men really, sincerely, craved cock. And they would near about suck the chrome right off a tailpipe to get it.

Once we were in Gallup doing surveillance on some Ochoa runner, I believe. We thought they were the ones who had jacked one of our iron trucks, I think, a load of our usual Russian ladies. Anyway, we were bored out of our skulls sitting on this one trap house of theirs. Nothing had happened for hours. I secretly posted on Grindr, telling Ford that all my texts were to my brother in Durango. It was risky posting my real photo—of course I used one where I was *not* wearing my cut, the side of my face that didn't show my ink—but I did it because I was considered a real handsome son of a bitch. People were constantly running up to me asking me to be in their television commercials or their reality show.

Anyway, I got a bite from a guy only about three blocks away. I told Ford I had to literally run to a gas station bathroom, and I went to this guy's house. Guy turned out to be a real drunk *glonni* horndog of a Navajo who wanted his bare ass and cock whipped good, so I obliged. That was how I had started learning about the world of bondage. He was upset that I had to leave so soon, so I jerked off on his ass and left. He wanted me to piss on him, too, but I drew the line at golden showers. People assume that just because you're gay you're also into all kinds of twisted things. Not so. We're probably just about as twisted as the straights. Lytton told me it was that way with bondage. People assumed because he likes to tie up his wife he's also into swinging. No, this guy had some kind of bent about being inferior and unworthy of anyone. That was also how I also learned you need to untie your partner before ending a scene.

Not to give an impression of myself as some kind of slut or cum fairy, really. I usually had my club's or a rival's eye on me, or I worked six days a week, so my hookups were few and far between. The adrenaline rush of doing something obscene just yards from the censorious eyes of my brothers or the world at large really jacked me up. My brothers thought they were bad to the bone? Well, what I was doing would top anything they could hope to do. I liked things dangerous, both my bikes and my men.

Fucking Dayton Navarro fit that bill.

Finding him gorging at the feast of that smoking hot stud was the ultimate nail in the coffin. He'd tried to follow me out of the club, but it was sort of half-hearted. He didn't run or anything—maybe just jogged. I had already straddled my ride and had jammed my brain bucket onto my head by the time he reached me.

"Turk, wait up. It's not what it seems."

"I don't know how it could possibly '*seem*' like anything else," I seethed. I turned the key and pushed the engine button just to show I was serious. *I've had it. Never again. This is it.*

"You weren't here. You were down in Pure and Easy. What're you doing here, anyway?"

"Surprising *you*, apparently."

He came forward, tried tugging on my plaid sleeve. He affected that cajoling, convincing tone. "But I missed you, Turk. I couldn't take it anymore. I was pretending that guy was you, and—"

"Let me say this in small words so you understand." I could be extremely acerbic and cutting when pissed. "You're the fucking afterbirth that slithered out of your mother's filth. They should have put you in a glass jar on the mantelpiece."

Even knowing me as he should have, Dayton's jaw dropped, and he staggered back a couple of steps. It encouraged me, and the bile rose in my chest, to see him look so aghast. It was the only revenge I could get at the moment. Fighting him would've just resulted in a draw because we were evenly matched.

I narrowed my eyes even further and revved my engine. "Does Barry Manilow know you raided his closet?" On that fine note, I burned rubber out of there. I referred to his penchant for turning up the collar of his cut like some kind of Elvis impersonator.

I was serious. *That was it.* I took a lot of abuse in my time. You had to, to belong to The Bare Bones MC. I had done a year on a weapons charge in Kingman when I was twenty. Needless to say, I was the main prey of every thuggish chicken hawk in the joint. Slushy was right. Prison was no late-night guest spot.

I was not going to let Dayton Navarro back into my life. In my rage, I even mulled over outing him, but that was an unbreakable gay code. You just didn't go there. It was up to each individual man to come out at his own pace in his own time.

So last night, I'd just partied myself blind at the Tropicana with members of The Dotards, a club we sometimes did business with. According to Twinkletoes, I'd been stuffing bills into some stripper's G-string and even sharing lap dances with the same chicks who had sat on Dotard laps. I'd made it back to my room intact and alone. At least, that's how I'd woken up, fully clothed. Right now I had that sort of black cloud of a numb hangover, that residual high where you just don't give a shit what you do.

"Turk! What've you got against MADD? How could anyone

possibly be down on an organization that tries to curb drunk driving?"

"Oh, someone *can*, all right," I said, handing the Big Brother another twenty. I was stuck rolling with a guy named Twinkletoes. If that wasn't flaming, I don't know what was. Actually I think that was a cruel road name suggested because he limped, and he certainly couldn't dance.

I needed to change the subject, and I was running out of twenties to give out. Stepping away from the Big Brother awning, I put my hands on my hips and faced the ocean of bikes in the parking lot of the Colorado Belle, a fake paddle-wheel steamer built right on the Nevada bank of the river. It was a bizarre sight in the middle of the desert. "Let's go check out this steamer. Have a drink in the bar."

"Yeah," said Twinkletoes skeptically. "Because you didn't have enough drinks last night."

"Hair of the dog," I said heartily, clapping him on the back and causing him to nearly pitch face-first into a big-titted gal wearing a PROPERTY OF patch. I was spoiling for a fight, but when the old lady took note of Twinkletoes' wasted condition she just smiled indulgently. That happened a lot with ol' Twinkletoes. He got a lot of mercy fucks. "So how was that skunk stuff we bought last night? I don't remember."

"They didn't call it Eminence Front," said the Prospect as we started weaving through the lake of scoots. "It was total schwag, but it wasn't the bunk crap we're chasing down. Listen. We can't be buying and sampling weed from every person in Laughlin. There's got to be a better way to do this. Something more methodical. Tyke McCarthy from Vegas has a line on it, and our Flagstaff brothers are here, so they should be sniffing it out for us. Literally. All we have to do is ask for some Eminence Front, find out it's not ours, and boom, we've got our man."

"Fuck our Flagstaff brothers," I said hotly. I nodded at a guy I thought I had partied with the night before. "They wouldn't know schwag from dank. I suspect Papa Ewey of those Assassins of Youth. Find him, we find the ersatz schwag. They control that Highway 95 corridor down to Yuma and into Sonora, where I'll bet it's coming from. I can taste that putrid dry crap a mile away. It comes in the shape of bricks from Sonora and gives you a fucking headache."

"Well," said Twinkletoes, carefully picking his way between two Sportsters, "you might not have to look too far. Isn't that Papa Ewey right there?"

I looked, but all at once I didn't care so much about Papa Ewey, the Assassin's President. Because standing right next to him was the self-same guy I had witnessed at the Racquet Club in Flagstaff…receiving a blowjob from my boyfriend.

Yes. That's the guy. There was no doubt about it.

I'd recognize that snobby, impudent face in a fucking police lineup. That smug, self-satisfied upturn to the perfect blond-haired god of a nose. That simpering half-smile that said "Look at me. I'm a blond-haired god. I know I'm God's gift to women—or to men, in your case. I can swing both ways because I just want to fuck whoever is going to piss someone else off the most, just because I can. I'm a buff weightlifter with no jailhouse tattoos. Come suck my cock. I dare you to, because I'm a hedonist who lives for pleasure…and for pissing people off."

Or something of that nature. That's what this fucktard may as well have been screaming at me, he set off so many of my triggers simultaneously.

It must have been instinct, that old fight-or-flight in me, but suddenly I found myself practically surfing across the parking lot. I seemingly bypassed about ten bikes that had been in between us. How I did that, I later couldn't figure out. It almost seemed like I had flown with Superman-like intensity, because the next thing I knew, I was issuing a balls-to-the-wall uppercut to that fuckwad's jaw. Now *he* was the one flying through the air, his stupid torso hitting someone's Softail in the handlebars, and he crashed to the ground like the Tin Woodsman, all clunky and clumsy, one arm hanging off the front fender.

"Well, check that out!" I bellowed, shoving the sleeves of my lumberjack shirt up past my elbows. "Looks like the best part of you ran down the crack of your mother's ass and ended up a brown stain on the mattress!"

Several Assassins actually chuckled at this, as though maybe they had wanted to give their brother a beatdown for a while, too. They seemed to want to know more about the reason a stranger from another club had just whaled on their brother. One guy called out,

"Looks like he's got your number, Lock."

Naturally, rage soon filled Lock's face, and he gathered himself to stand, brushing off his arms, his cut. "What the fuck's your problem, asshole? There'd better be some reason why you've come out of nowhere to attack me."

I stepped closer to him. "Oh yeah? Think harder, motherfuck. You're disgusting with your fucking tanned crocodile skin like some fucking suitcase. I'll bet you punch just like you take it up the ass!"

Lock's crew issued a wave of "*ooo*s," but that was all Lock needed to hear. I'm still not sure if he realized who I was, but no self-respecting biker—or any *man*, for that matter—would stand there listening to that. Lock executed a lightning left jab that I easily ducked from, having long expected it.

"I've got your back," shouted Twinkletoes as I popped back

up like a jack-in-the-box and pounded Lock's face with a series of alternating cross-punches. His stupid skull jerked like a bobblehead on his turkey neck. Now I'd seriously pissed off Lock's brothers, because one of them grabbed Twinkletoes from behind and held him in a nelson. Not that Twinkletoes would've been able to fight anyone, anyway. But the guy, a giant bruiser and probably the Assassin's enforcer, had my Prospect's jaw in his giant palm as though threatening to twist his neck.

That threat only enraged me further. When Lock recovered from my brilliant series of jabs—blood already trickled down the impression at the center of his bowed angel's lips—he attacked me head-on. It was plain from the start that he'd had martial arts training, the way he slipped and dodged my blows, the way he managed to land several punches directly to my chest, knocking me off balance.

Now that he had a grip on himself, he was whaling on the offensive moves like a purple belt. I got in a straight left to his jaw again, knocking him back against that Softail. I knew I was a lean, sinewy fighting machine and I could easily take his more pumped-up musculature. I didn't cut him any slack for being down, but pummeled him in his stupid iron man stomach, gratified at the sound of the air being expressed from his lungs.

But he threw me off with a violent shove, sending me stumbling back into the powerless Twinkletoes. I even stomped on the Prospect's boots, giving Lock enough time to advance on me brutally, tossing his stupid blond tresses out of his eyes as he growled at me,

"I remember you now. And you seriously need to grow the fuck up if shit like that surprises you in this world."

He bent at the waist, completely taking me by surprise. He ran at me like a bull, executing a perfect takedown when his hard head went under my armpit, his hands encircling my biceps.

He had me in the air, pinwheeling me around like some fucking wrestling madman before tossing me to the ground like a sack of shit, practically making an indentation in the asphalt. No one had ever gotten the jump on me like that. Besides feeling as though every bone in my body was broken, I was mentally in shock. Suddenly my world was upside-down and I was looking up at a ring of bikers all hovering like doctors around an operating table. Their stupid black silhouettes loomed large like angels of mercy or death, and suddenly Lock was tearing them apart to get at me again.

He must've been watching too many WWF performances to go jumping on me that way. Like a flying squirrel he soared, but I wasn't born yesterday. I easily rolled out of his way, leaving him to hit the asphalt like another sack of shit. In a flash I was on my feet again, hands like talons ready to take him on. But like the utter weed he was, his beefy arms encircled my knees, and I toppled over again like a falling redwood, like someone running a sack race.

We grappled in earnest now. Over and over we rolled. Men were moving their bikes out of our way as we went head over heels trying to get a grip on each other. I'd have my hands around his throat, thumbs digging into his windpipe, and he'd break the hold with his massive forearms. Then he'd get a handful of my ponytail, practically breaking my neck as he headbutted my forehead, sending red and black sparks shooting from my skull—or so it seemed.

Then I'd break that hold and would get him pinned. Straddling him, I planted myself squarely down on his hips and gripped both his wrists in one hand over his head so tightly my knuckles were white. He thrashed and snorted and flopped around like a beached fish, even spitting in my face.

Of course I couldn't wipe it off, so I snarled, "I hope that fucking blowjob was worth it, asswipe."

With a sudden shock that wasn't entirely unpleasant, I realized I had wedged my ass crack directly over his dick. And *his prick wasn't totally flaccid.* It pulsed like a direct challenge against my asshole, which was cemented solidly against him. *He was getting an erection because it turned him on to fight.* With this realization, blood surged through my own dick, and I could feel it lengthening inside my 501s.

He growled, "Why would I stop to question a free blowjob? Especially when it was the best I've ever had."

Like Flash himself, I released one of my hands and drew back so far, I knew my direct slug to the nose would break it. I could tell by the dull but satisfying *crunch* that he'd had his nose broken before. But again, this asshole Lock roared like a cornered animal and found the strength to totally throw me completely off him, and we were once more rolling, grappling, him dripping blood on me every time he managed to pin me.

It was becoming quite exhausting, actually. After my dissipated night of drunken revelry, I wasn't in top form. It must've been during one of these holds when we were locked in a standoff with our thighs straining against each other that I first smelled the unmistakable scent of schwag weed.

Fake Eminence Front. He's got some. It's in his cut pocket.

But of course my hands were occupied either holding him or pummeling him, and I had to wait until I had the upper hand. I was on top this time, again straddling him, almost luxuriating in the full sensation of his stiff dick in my ass crack. I even rocked my hips ever so slightly in a victor's arrogance as I sneered down at him. I needed to address the elephant in the room.

"Makes you hot to give a guy a beatdown? Go to The Racquet Club often?"

Knowing that would throw him off guard, I risked releasing one of my hands that pinned his wrists, and I flicked open his cut pocket. Now that an actual *cut* was being threatened, at last his crew closed in around us shouting things like,

"Hands off the colors, asshole!"

"Never touch a man's cut."

Lock's dick was clearly throbbing now between my ass cheeks. I was the pumped-up, superior victor pinning him helplessly, my own erection filling my jeans with the ego boost of triumph. Between index and middle finger I easily withdrew a rolled-up Ziploc of pot, sneered some more, and stuffed it in my own cut pocket. Then I leaped off him and backed off toward Twinkletoes, to indicate I was done.

"Enough!" I shouted, hands in the air in the universal gesture of surrender. "Release my Prospect," I directed the enforcer. He did so with a giant shove, and I had to catch Twinkletoes in both hands.

"I've got your back," gasped the poor Prospect.

Lock was getting laboriously to his feet. Never taking his eyes from me, he wiped his bloody face as though the back of his hand was a giant hankie. He huffed and puffed like some overblown Hulk, but he didn't try to get the jump on me. It was their President, Papa Ewey, who squared off with me.

"I don't know what your beef is with Lock, probably some snatch, but I've got a few words for Ford Illuminati next time I have a face-to-face with him."

Lock and I both had the same secret we wanted to keep from the world. We would both agree to pretend it was over some gash. "Fine," I spat, hoping that wasn't a tooth that went sailing to the asphalt. "This beef is strictly between me and that sleazeball. I've got no beef with your club and neither does

Ford," I lied. Ford and Lytton had been the ones to suggest the Assassins and their Bullhead City clubhouse might be the source of the schwag weed.

Papa Ewey poked me in the chest, and I let him. "I don't want to see you again during this rally, scumbag. You got that?"

"I get that," I agreed amiably, and with Prospect in hand, began ambling toward the fake riverboat.

CHAPTER FOUR

LOCK

That damned Ronald Reagan was on the move again.

Lock was working in his Los Toro Hermanos offices in Lake Havasu City when Aditya got the call from one of their informants.

"Lock!" cried the excitable Punjabi. He wasn't an Assassin of Youth patch holder due to his many phobias—of heights, crowds, open spaces, enclosed spaces, ladders, pockets, vomiting, blood, England, atomic explosions, flutes, ventriloquist's dummies, thunder and lightning, beautiful women, dancing, chopsticks, bicycles, knees, handwriting, and being infested with worms. The fear of blood and atomic explosions stood in his way of patching in, but it was the fear of bicycles mainly that kept him from prospecting. A motorcycle was just a glorified bicycle, Aditya said, with the same two wobbly wheels.

"Bob Inflorida saw someone with Reagan's plate pumping gas at his store in Topock. An '03 Lexus, right?" They employed businesspeople and other sleazeballs all up and down the major highways of Arizona to keep an eye out whenever they had an ATL, an attempt to locate, on someone.

"Right." Lock was already on his feet, grabbing his leather barn jacket from the coat rack. He never wore his cut while hunting—it stood out too radically, and he drove his brown

Mustang with no identifying paint or stickers, keeping an overnight bag loaded with necessities in the trunk. "Was he heading toward Needles?" It wouldn't make it any harder to extradite Reagan because Lock's badge gave him the ability to transport fugitives across state lines as long as he informed the local PD. It might even help if Reagan was slowed down declaring his fruit and firewood at the border protection station.

"Inflorida said he definitely went south on 95."

Lock paused, frowning. "Huh. In other words, heading this way."

"Right. Maybe you just go out to the highway and wait."

Lock shrugged. Sometimes it had been as easy as that. He had once caught a wife beater who had skipped bail by waiting at the McCullough Chevron for the guy to come out of the London Bridge Resort. The guy needed gas, and Lock just calmly walked over and slapped cuffs on him.

Lock had already punched Inflorida's number on his speed dial by the time he backed his Mustang out of the spot in his warehouse's parking lot. His office window looked out over London Bridge Road, the landscape past that, the sand and sagebrush beach backed by the blue-green waters of Lake Havasu. It had been a madhouse during spring break two weeks ago, but now the waters glimmered placidly, blinding him with diamonds until he donned his wrap-around Oakleys.

Inflorida had, as trained, written down the time he'd seen Reagan. One-oh-eight in Topock. Lock calculated it would take Reagan twenty-eight minutes to get to the intersection of Kiowa and 95. That gave Lock nineteen minutes to sit in the Circle K parking lot waiting for the Lexus to cruise by.

Cigarette smoke stung his nostrils when he lit one up. It was difficult to even breathe through his nose now, with it being busted again and filled with dried blood. His mind drifted back to the impossibly good-looking fucker who had broken it. *That fucking cocksucker.* Visions of that fucker had been rolling around in his head like sneakers in a dryer for days now. He'd even started taking his PTSD meds again in an effort to clear the images from his brain. Up until now, he'd thought they were working.

They weren't. Turk Blackburn had come out of nowhere in front of that riverboat casino, blindsiding him. Lock was in such shock at first, he hadn't responded immediately. Looking back, Blackburn was fucking lucky Lock hadn't taken out his switchblade and ventilated him. Or his Glock, which nearly every self-respecting outlaw was packing in that town.

But he'd left his Glock back in the hotel room, as most casinos had metal detectors during the rally, and Lock loved feeding cash into those one-armed bandits. So he'd been attacked by his pickup's lover, fair enough. He couldn't really blame the guy, as Red had apparently had some kind of exclusivity agreement with Blackburn. But surely Blackburn would take his rage out on Red and not Lock, the innocent bystander in the whole affair?

Maybe a switch just flipped when Blackburn saw Lock again. It probably just set him off. Lock had asked around discreetly, casually, and Blackburn didn't seem to be an "out" outlaw. He was just as deeply undercover as Lock himself. Lock now knew "Red" to be a Dayton Navarro of The Bare Bones Flagstaff charter—what an asshole, if he had really made a promise to Blackburn.

And the fight. Once Lock had woken up to what was happening and got his shit together, it became apparent he was equally matched with Blackburn. Fighting was an oddly intimate activity. Tussling, wrestling, grappling with that long-limbed beauty, once Lock had realized they were evenly matched, became a sort of erotic sport.

He'd been on top of the fucker, his hand splayed against the crown of his skull, the better to grind that pretty face into the fucking asphalt. But he'd been cinching the asshole's upper thighs with his own powerful thigh, and that's when he'd noticed. The curve of the biker's strong lower back fit perfectly against his hipbone, and the beautiful rise, the sexy swell of the buttocks shaped by the tight jeans was crying out for a squeeze.

That's when Lock's penis had, embarrassingly enough, started to stiffen and plump. He took pleasure out of simultaneously shoving the beautiful face against the parking lot, and grinding his aroused tool against the shapely ass. Nobody would notice—it just looked like the typical arrogant male domination of two men wrestling, although the idea that Blackburn had felt him rubbing his hard-on against him turned him on again, even now.

And it *had* turned on Blackburn, there was no bones about that. When the rival biker had straddled Lock, he'd inadvertently ground his asscrack directly over Lock's hard-on. *That* was almost a bigger turn-on than pinning him, Lock discovered. Up until now he'd been an unapologetic total top—at least that's how it had been with his Air Force buddy Park. He reasoned that if he lacked the tiniest shred of effeminate behavior that marked a bottom, a twink or a pup, that somehow made him less gay. The more macho he was and felt, through and through, the less he was a serious fag. The less danger he was in from being outed.

As Blackburn pinned Lock's wrists above his head, Turk's curvy asscheeks massaged Lock's hard dick, sending thrills shooting through his groin. Lock spat in his face to deny him the pleasure of his erection, and that's when Blackburn broke Lock's nose, but the whole damned thing had been worth it.

A DANGEROUS REALITY

The whole thing had been worthwhile because now Lock had images and visions to fantasize about when he jacked off. He'd made casual inquiries, like any guy would do about the man who had just broken his nose. "What do you know about that Turk Blackburn asshole?"

He was Veep of The Bare Bones based in Pure and Easy, Arizona. He ran a pot dispensary, and before that, he'd run an army surplus store. He'd been present the year before in the desert down by Nogales when *someone* had hit the Bare Bones' former president, Cropper. Turk knew what had gone down but he wasn't talking, and shortly thereafter he'd been promoted to Veep. The gloss and shine this myth had put on his rep was worth its weight in gold. It had earned Turk his bones, and Lock had to grudgingly admit, it elevated the guy in his estimation. Turk didn't wear a "Filthy Few" patch like his Prez Ford had sported since the age of seventeen, but then not every outlaw who had killed chose to advertise it that way.

Lock had definitely cranked his love pump several times since the Laughlin beatdown, drifting and dreaming about the luscious pot pusher's long, fat dick. The guy was simply model-perfect in every way, with his stylish man bun twisted at the back of his neck, the long bangs that were growing out slipping out of the bun and framing his ravishing face. He had those long swinging arms Lock had come to love, not those stumpy things that waved around near a guy's hips like a thalidomide baby. Blackburn didn't just walk, he *loped* like a mythological creature, his long-limbed beauty turning male and female heads wherever he went. His neatly-trimmed Vandyke facial hair was just perfect enough to cry "gay," but on Turk it was more an actorly affectation, like he just happened to stop by the barber that day before shooting a soft drink commercial.

It had been enough of a risk that Lock had accidentally

received a piston job from Blackburn's lover. If Blackburn had had nothing to lose too, he could've taken out a billboard to advertise *that* juicy tidbit of blackmail. But he hadn't. The snarled remarks about blowjobs had been under the breath, and even if anyone had overheard, they'd think it was a skank they were fighting over, not another man.

But why did he take my weed? Lock had shrugged that part off. Maybe he thought Lock had stolen the pot from him. The whole incident didn't make any sense, so he dismissed it.

He'd also discovered, in his discreet research, why those gays had called him "Don" at the BDSM club. They weren't. They were calling him a "Dom," a Dominant male. It was sort of flattering—and true. He'd kneeled for *no one*, and he was proud of it.

And now Reagan's Lexus was stopped in front of him at the stoplight.

Lock lost valuable seconds in reverie of that night at the club. His lightning reflexes more than made up for it as he put the pedal to the metal, maneuvering the Mustang onto 95 just a couple car lengths behind Reagan.

Reagan quickly got up to sixty-five once out of city limits. The barren Mojave Mountains rose to Lock's left, rust-purple and treeless, capped by Mount Crossman. Lock's home was out there in an older subdivision called Rough and Ready, a town that had been started by unlucky miners in the nineteenth century. Lock enjoyed his home, the few times he was able to get out there and spend the night. Between club business and the bail bonds agency in town—where he also sometimes had to sleep—he felt that he rarely got home, and it was starting to irk him.

He really wanted a dog, a large, furry dog. He knew most dogs freaked at the sound of a motorcycle's pipes, but he'd seen photos of dogs in sidecars wearing goggles. It must be possible. He thought if he got the dog when a small pup he could do some aversion training on her, so she wasn't gun shy of bikes—or guns, for that matter. He could take her to the outdoor shooting range.

His old lady Ruby hadn't wanted a dog. She had decorated his sparse, minimalist mid-century modern house with tacky, frilly, "country" stuff, like ceramic pigs wearing chef's hats. Various witty wine bottle holders were scattered about, like roosters or pirates actually "drinking" from the bottle—or the worst, a pig in a chef's hat guzzling Chablis. Lock didn't even like white wine.

Ruby had taken a lot of that stuff with her, thank God. Now his house looked more appropriately like a pathetic, loser bachelor's home with none of the frilly comforts of a woman. It had been in the back of his mind to marry Ruby for a while, but his procrastination, and the fact that he was gone much of the time, had worn on her. She was young and hot, and knew she could find someone much better in "the city." In fact, he suspected she'd already done so by the time she moved out. She had cleaned their long Formica kitchen counter of every scrap of dirt, yet she'd carefully placed a photo of some fucking cowboy on a horse in the center of it. *Thanks. Nice subtle symbolism. I literally get the picture.*

He'd never told Ruby about his military dalliance with Corporal Langham. He had thought that was just a minor deviation from his regular, normal hetero life. He'd just done Park because of the danger they experienced together. It bonded them to go on missions together, facing the enemy side by side. Also, being alone in an Islamic country, there was no access to women. It was natural he'd want a warm mouth around his cock now and then. There was nothing wrong with it. They were like explorers in the Wild West. No women around, so what was a guy to do?

He'd imagined coming back home he'd just go back to his old ways, banging women. And he'd been right—until recently. Ruby leaving him had flipped some kind of perverted switch in his brain. He'd been thinking about men again, and not just Park's smooth beauty. Other men. Any man. Cock in general. How much tighter and firmer men's asses were than women's. It was starting to worry him.

He needed to get with one of the club sweetbutts pronto. *That* would tell him what was up.

They crossed over the Colorado River. California was literally one glimmering turquoise ribbon away to the right now, but 95 stayed strictly on the Arizona side. Reagan had fled from the charge in Needles, so Lock had expected him to return home after jumping bail. So far he hadn't. Now Reagan turned off the highway at the Bluewater Resort. *Thank God. Now I can grab him and take him back to Needles. Might even get to sleep in my own bed tonight.*

But the douche monkey didn't even get out of the Lexus at the casino. He just circled around in the parking lot, making Lock stand out like a fucking sore thumb as he followed. *Maybe there aren't enough kids around here for his liking.* Reagan got back onto 95 and continued south.

They drove through the dismal, dust-colored landscape, bypassing a big trailer park. Instead of taking the bridge in Parker that would take him to California, though, Reagan hung a left as though heading toward another Circle K. Lock was completely mystified until Reagan hung a right at the Colorado River Indian Tribes Fish and Game office. He saw the sign in front of an industrial-looking building. *Parker High School. Aha. That explains it.*

A DANGEROUS REALITY

They were already on Rez lands of the Colorado River Indian Tribes. The tribe owned the Bluewater Resort. Naturally many dark-skinned young men of the combined Mojave, Hopi, and Navajo tribes walked the corridors of this institution, some in football jerseys, and Lock tried to recall who exactly had been Reagan's prey when he'd originally been arrested. Reagan was parking the Lexus among other typically teen vehicles, in this case the battered trucks and Chevys of the underprivileged Native American kids.

Lock had every right to just walk on over and arrest Reagan. He didn't even need to Mirandize the fuckers he apprehended. As bail jumpers, they'd already been informed of their rights. Lock was just remanding them back into the custody they had ostensibly never left, so he wasn't restricted by a lot of the laws arresting officers were confined by. But now he was curious to see what the pedophile had in mind.

So he parked around a corner by some dumpsters. It looked like the back door to the band classroom, as some nerds were hanging out with their tubas smoking cigarettes. Aditya would have freaked at the sight of the wind instruments. When Lock got out of the Mustang and peeked around the corner, he got a good view of the perv just sitting in his Lexus watching students, so he texted Aditya. *Which ethnicity was Reagan's victim/s?*

For lack of anything better to do, Lock lit a cigarette. He knew he wouldn't blend in with most of the kids with his longish dishwater blond hair kept out of his face with a bandanna headband. Leaning his shoulder against the wall like the drug-dealing thug of the school, Lock even crossed his boots and dug the fingers of his free hand into his front jeans pocket. Trying to inhale the smoke reminded him his nose was broken. And that reminded him of the reason.

That damned fucking model-perfect asswipe. I can't get that fucker out of my head. Oh, great. This'll look real great, lurking behind a school smoking a cigarette with a hard-on—

A hand caught his bicep and twirled him around. His lit cigarette went flying.

"Pushing pot to kids now, is *that* your game?"

Lock gasped with horror. He was face to face with the cocksucker who had broken his nose.

Reflexively he cringed back against the building. As Blackburn's words sank in, he sneered. "Pushing pot? Sounds like you've been *smoking* a bit too much."

The good-looking asshole was on the offensive again. He just would *not* let up. The guy had stick-to-itiveness, Lock had to hand him that. "That's why you're not wearing your cut. You don't want anyone to know you're pushing weed to underage kids."

Lock was aghast. It was like Blackburn was speaking Esperanto. That was how small of a clue Lock had about any of this. "Why the fuck would I be wasting my time with small potatoes like a fucking high school? I've got bigger fish to fry, asshole. And I see you're not wearing your cut either. What you got to hide?"

Lock had to admit. Even loathing the fucker like he did, the guy was stunningly handsome. With his thumbs hooked in the front pockets of his 501s and the loose locks of hair framing his fine-boned face with the jailhouse teardrop below his eye, he was set to star in a show about…well, bikers. "Didn't feel like advertising the brand while sleazing around corrupting high schoolers."

Lock folded his arms tightly and stepped up to the Bare Bones Veep, lifting his chin arrogantly. "That's not where my mind went. Why does your mind keep going there? Why are you so fixated on pot?"

A DANGEROUS REALITY

Rage flooded the handsome face. Anger only made Turk prettier, if such a thing was possible. His voice became low and menacing. "You fucking know why, asshole. The Assassins are the ones who've been running around selling bunk weed—now I find out to fucking kids—with *my* strain name on it. How do you think that looks to me? Looks like you intend to profit off all my years of hard labor building up my strain brand, and associate it with *children*. I run a legal fucking medical dispensary, not some fucking back alley head shop."

What the fuck? "Is that why you took that pot out of my pocket in Laughlin? What the fuck? I don't call it anything—I just call it 'pot' and put it in a fucking pipe."

Blackburn sneered with disgust. "Yeah. And you call yourself a Straight Edge member."

What in the name of Isaac Newton…? Lock was getting seriously fed up with these strange accusations. "How the fuck do *you* know I'm a Straight Edge follower?" Now he really did poke Blackburn in the chest. "Been shadowing *me*? You follow me all the way to Parker just to accuse me of some fucked-up copyright infringement? Man, you seriously need to get a hobby."

Later, Lock didn't know which part had pushed Blackburn over the edge—advising him to take up fishing, or poking him. But all of a sudden Blackburn's face was twisted with fury, and his palms shot out in a flash, striking Lock's chest with such power he went flying back against the band room wall.

"Fight, fight!" chanted some of the tuba-playing kids.

Lock reacted with a brilliant right cross that whipped Blackburn's skull completely back on his neck. Satisfied he might've given the fucktard whiplash, Lock followed through with a one-two uppercut to that handsome jaw. Blackburn crashed back against a dumpster with limbs splayed, and Lock knew he had the upper hand. He felt pumped up and superior.

That lasted all of one second.

With a giant roar, Blackburn came at him. Lock dodged, but Blackburn was only feinting. The Bare Boner hit him head-on with his shoulders, low in the abdomen, carrying Lock like a football tackling dummy until he smashed against the band wall.

Blackburn pinned Lock with the power of his hips. Stomping on one of Lock's boots didn't help, either. He grabbed one of Lock's wrists and slammed that against the wall, too, but Lock's other hand was free. He could've easily pasted the Veep with a left hook, but his curiosity got the better of him. Why was Turk plastering him to the wall with nearly his entire body? He must have something important to say.

Turk was so close Lock could feel his breath against his face. "There's some energy between us, some game we need to play out. I know you felt it in Laughlin. I don't blame you for fucking my boyfriend. You probably didn't know. What I *do* blame you for is selling this knockoff weed, giving me a bad name, and tantalizing me with your hella fine body."

Turk spoke so low and fast, that last part nearly went right on by Lock. Lock was achingly aware of the pressure of Turk's hips against his, the warm rush of energy emanating from the Veep's lean body. Lock's dick even began to plump and lengthen just at his rival's proximity. He was still thinking about the strange case of the ersatz marijuana when Turk kissed him.

CHAPTER FIVE
TURK

I swear I didn't plan that kiss. It just happened.

I know that "it just happened" is the world's lamest excuse for things like shootings, extramarital affairs, and One Direction. But I'm telling you. I didn't shadow Lock Singer from Laughlin all the way to Parker just to kiss him.

Not that it hadn't occurred to me. Since our fight in the parking lot of the Colorado Belle, I'd been thinking about it a *lot*. I mean, what self-respecting gay *wouldn't?* The guy was a banging hot blond god, and no, it *wasn't* his fault he'd been taken in by the smooth moves of Dayton Navarro. It had happened to me, too. I no longer held it against Lock that he'd done that. But I sure would like to hold something *else* against him.

I knew it was impossible. We were in rival clubs, for one. It had barely been possible with a guy from another Bare Bones charter. For another, Lock belonged to the club we suspected of dealing this knockoff weed. I'd been following him from his Laughlin hotel ever since, trying to catch him in the act of doing something weed-related. I doubted he would bring anything like that around his bail bonds office, and I was impressed by the heft and power of his business. Twinkletoes ran a Dun and Bradstreet on the business, and they were quite well-respected and highly rated.

But I became more suspicious when he left Los Toro Hermanos and sat in a gas station parking lot for ten minutes, waiting for someone. Then I knew I was onto something. He'd taken off his cut before getting into his Mustang, so I knew he was about to do a run for the club—something that involved driving a cage and not his scoot. It became obvious he was following this shady-looking guy in a Lexus, so I knew this was the weed contact.

When I realized he was selling to high schoolers, I just lost it. I might've smoked pot when I was twelve. Okay, ten. I probably had done LSD, cocaine, and all the usual suspects by the time I was twelve. But fuck it, you know? *My childhood was different.* I lost my parents and was being raised by a guy who thought education was the Playboy Channel and protein was a bukkake session. No wonder Ford wore the "Filthy Few" patch by the time he was seventeen.

This didn't mean I thought it was a *good* thing, handing drugs to kids. If given an option, if I could go back, I probably would've been a lot more circumspect about everything I ingested. For instance, and no one believes me, but I rarely smoke weed now. I only do it on the occasions it's called for as part of my job, like when I have to taste test a new shipment, or if someone asks me for my opinion. But really, as I get older and more serious about life, as the things I used to think were fun start to look more like one giant hassle, I toke less and less. It's a demotivator, really. I hate to think of all the years I wasted sucking on a bong, eating Doritos, and waiting for the leaves to turn color.

Well, I guess I was grabbing the gusto by the horns right now. After being slammed into a dumpster and laughed at by a bunch of dipwads who should be off tooting their clarinets, I was a raging mass of inflamed hormones. Still, I hadn't planned what I did. Honestly. One second I was pinning Havelock Singer to the wall with my pelvis, and the next second I'd clamped my open mouth down over his.

Maybe I wanted to taste what Dayton had tasted. Maybe I wanted to find out firsthand what had attracted Dayton to Lock—what had made him choose Lock out of the presumably hundreds of guys he could've banged that night.

At first, he squirmed and resisted. This only served to stiffen my penis, and I luxuriated in rolling my hips against his, massaging my burgeoning glans against the buttons of his crotch. He pressed his free hand against my shoulder, first urgently, then just insistently. Pretty soon he was barely pressing at all.

I sucked on his sweet, luscious lips, nibbling on his lower one the way a dog nibbles on ice. His mouth softened as he surrendered to my assault. Soon he was extending the tip of his tongue to meet mine, shyly tickling me. I let loose an erotic little groan that vibrated our mouths against each other, and I lapped at the underside of his tongue as though it was honey. Which it was, to me.

Over the sound of our panting against each other's faces, I could hear the high schoolers giggling.

"Fags!"

"Can you believe it? They look too macho to be fags."

"Why are fags selling weed at our school?"

"Faggots! Fairies! Homos getting their rocks off!"

I had forgotten how homophobic and cruel teens could be. As much as I didn't want to pull back, I had to. I gave his tongue a few last thorough licks. He reciprocated, nibbling anxiously on my lower lip, as though his teeth shivered with cold.

He ran his free hand down my chest before we broke the kiss. His fingertips lingered for a split second at my nipple, rubbing the very tip with his thumb. Erotic pangs shot straight from my nipple into my groin. But then he twisted the flesh almost viciously, and this time he really *did* shove me away violently. Our lips parted with a loud smack, and I staggered back like a weak zombie.

But I was chuckling. I know, it sounds weird to say, but I was actually *chuckling.* That's the best word for how I laughed with self-satisfaction. To see this virile, macho biker glaring at me, his lower lip sticking out indignantly, as though I'd mauled him against his will. Because as we knew—Havelock Singer would *never, ever* allow another man to kiss him. Furiously, he wiped his mouth off with the back of his hand. His hypocrisy made me chuckle.

"Total fags!" a couple of Navajo teens were yelling. To their credit, a few of the girls seemed to be trying to pull the boys back into the classroom.

"*Boo-yah!*"

The sudden streak to the left side of my vision turned out to be Twinkletoes. True to his name, he leaped out from where he'd been hiding around the other corner of the band room. Like a bogeyman with undulating arms and bug eyes, he threatened the rude teens. Because he still wore his Prospect's cut and both his arms were thoroughly inked with tribal and biomechanical tattoos, I'd probably be scared too, if I didn't know him.

"Who you calling a fag, *fag?* Those Merrell slip-ons make you look like you're about to say 'let's go clubbing, guys!' And that shirt makes you look like the First Lady of Myanmar."

The teens were dumbstruck. Most of them hid in the classroom and peeked out from behind the shoulder of the one boy who was the boldest. Lock and I shared amused glances and stepped toward Twinkletoes to back him up.

The bold teen bellowed, "They're *fags* because they were *kissing*. That equals *fag* in my book."

Twinkletoes continued his rant. "Hey! If I wanted a joke, I'd follow you into the can and watch you take a leak! You think you're as cool as us? You're not like us, motherfucker, you're a punk. We're *made* people, connected, hopping businessmen. Why don't you get out of here and go snatch a purse?"

Lock and I were chortling aloud now, but I had to put a stop to this potential beatdown. Twinkletoes would get the worst of it, and it would draw unwanted attention to us. I clapped him on the shoulder.

"That's fine, Twinkletoes. Thanks for the backup. Let's get out—"

"You're nothing but a pack of homos!" yelled the Native American.

"He's a regular wit," murmured Lock.

But Twinkletoes wouldn't take it lying down. "Oh, yeah? Well, your birth certificate is an apology from the condom factory!"

"Oops," Lock uttered.

That was it. Twinkletoes had just accidentally insulted the boy's heritage. It was the sort of insult you'd make at anyone regardless of their ancestry, but I knew that for the Navajo that sort of joke went over like a lead balloon. Being a brother to two half-blood Pretendians, Ford and Lytton Illuminati, I had learned to police myself so I didn't accidentally make cracks such as this.

I muttered in Twinkletoes' ear, "All right. That's fine, Prospect. Let's just move along now."

But the John Redcorn teen now had to defend his mother.

"That's fucking *it*, fag!" He came forward in a boxing stance while the doorway behind him filled to overflowing with eager, excited faces.

And Twinkletoes didn't know when to stop. "Your family tree is a cactus because everyone on it is a prick!"

Lock caught my eye. He nodded at the student. "You two bail. I'll handle this."

As much as I wanted to fight the guy, the school might have cameras back there, and the last thing I wanted to do was wind up on tape assaulting an underage kid next to someone flying my club colors. So I took Lock up on that offer, gripping the Prospect by the shirtsleeve and dragging him away.

We couldn't resist, though, peering around the corner and watching what went down. Twinkletoes kneeled below me, the big cowlick over his forehead trembling with excitement.

"I really got some good ones off at him."

"You know, you're kind of a loose cannon. Did you know that, Prospect?"

He laughed. "I aim to please, boss. *Ooo, ooo!* That asshole is whaling on that kid!"

I already knew that Lock wasn't just "that asshole" anymore. He might be ripping off our trademark, but I was certain I could convince him to stop using our brand name. Meantime, I wasn't too sure what Twinkletoes had seen. I'd told him to hang around the corner and keep an eye out, and so he had, until the student had started slinging mud at us. I had to hand it to the Prospect. He definitely stood up for his club.

The band nerd wasn't so nerdy after all. He had muscles, probably a football player just taking band for the credits. Lock approached him with palms up, facing the teen in the universal "let's talk" position. But the kid was enraged, and sucker-punched Lock in the jaw. The blow glanced off thanks to

Lock's quick reflexes, but part of it must've caught Lock's nose, which looked to have been recently broken.

A veritable crimson flood of red spurted from that perfect, crooked nose. Lock was mad now. Grabbing the idiot by the front of his First Lady shirt, Lock dangled him from his powerful left arm as he pummeled him with a flurry of right jabs.

Teenagers flooded out of the band room now, surrounding the fighters, and I didn't know whether to stay or go. Lock wasn't a brother. He was our enemy, allegedly. We owed him nothing. Then again, he'd gone to the wall for us after my Prospect went and instigated a gang war.

I said, "Let's get out of here. If a security guard nails Singer, he's gonna find that weed on him." I was actually surprised that a professional bondsman would risk his badge by doing something as frivolous as selling weed to high schoolers—to *anyone*, actually. As he whaled on the homophobic teen and his T-shirt hiked up, I could see his iron stuck in the back waistband of his jeans. I knew that no bondsman could have a felony conviction on his record, especially one where he'd carried a deadly weapon. He was risking his entire career just to defend us. Defend Twinkletoes, actually.

"*Ooo!* Beatdown, beatdown!" Twinkletoes chanted.

"What's going on around here?"

My Prospect and I spun around to face some older authority figure, a school counselor of some sort. I held Twinkletoes back with my palm flat against his chest so his colors would be to the wall.

I wasn't fast enough on the uptake. It was Twinkletoes who declared earnestly, "It's some punk from Lake Havasu High School!"

"Is that so?" said the athletic lady, instantly buying it. She must've been used to goody two shoes students narking to her.

I fell into step with my Prospect. "Yeah! He started calling our football team fags—"

"—and said he was going to open up a can of whoopass on our team!" finished Twinkletoes. "He told us to burn our trashy uniforms, and said we'd only make it to the playoffs if there was an Ebola outbreak and everyone else died."

"Oh, he did, did he?" The woman thumbed her hand-held radio. "Agent Beale, to the rear of the band room immediately. What? No, by the dumpsters where we go to smoke."

Lock had pummeled the loser into submission by now, and I waved my arms around the corner, gesturing for him to bail. I marveled at the way he stood still, the bloody-faced kid writhing on the ground beneath his feet. Lock was stock-still, his hands dangling at his sides, and he was barely breathing any harder for having issued that beatdown. His chest rose and fell, the protrusions of his nipple jewelry standing out under his tight wifebeater. I could practically *see* the blood pounding in the prominent tornado-grey network of veins in his arms as he clenched and unclenched his fists.

And he *smiled* at me. It was that sort of shit-eating grin that guys give to each other after they've participated in a good rumble. A sort of "hey, that was fun" grin. "Let's do it again." It was probably just wishful thinking, but it gave me the impression we'd been through the wringer together, and had emerged the other side.

Then we ran off in opposite directions.

CHAPTER SIX
LOCK

"You made me lose my mark."

Lock tried to remain as calm and impassive as possible. The fact of the matter was, this slender, long-legged stallion sitting across from him in the coffee shop was specializing in busting his concentration.

To his credit, the guy looked sheepish. Turk Blackburn toyed with an empty aspartame packet on the table. "I didn't know you were tracking someone." Now he looked up at Lock, his long lashes flickering with accusation. "But I still don't believe that you're not involved in trafficking this bogus weed."

Lock guffawed and pounded the table with a helpless fist. "What, because I happened to have some stuff that smelled like skunk in my pocket? This is an automatic indication that I'm the culprit infringing on your trademark?"

Turk's response was swift. "It is, when you and your club were the main suspects to begin with. It's obvious the weed has been travelling up and down the Colorado River corridor, turf controlled by you."

Lock had to give this thing a second thought. It could very well be true that his club was running around calling their weed something it wasn't. They'd been known to do that. And Lock *had* heard of the wide fame obtained by the Eminence Front strain. He just hadn't known it was grown—and *only* grown—on Mormon Mountain in the Bare Bones' backyard. He sipped his manly black coffee. "I could look into that for you. I could reach out to a brother based here in Parker. He deals with the reservation head honchos."

Turk looked confused. "I didn't think it had anything to do with any Native Americans."

Lock shrugged. "I'm not saying it has to do with any featherheads. But we run a lot of stuff through the reservations to clean it—Fort Mojave, Colorado River, and Cocopah. We control that whole network of private docks through the Rezes."

Turk nodded with admiration. "Smart. No one ever questions the natives, and it takes a whole Supreme Court injunction to gain entry. This shit weed is obviously from Mexico, I can tell by the look, smell, and shape of the brick. It'd make sense if it came up through Cocopah from Sonora."

Lock was flush with pride that Turk was admiring him. He liked to be admired, and he knew that the Assassins of Youth's turf extended farther and wider than The Bare Bones' did. "I'll do it, but listen. I was about to nab that pervert when you busted in. He's been slipping through my fingers ever since Flagstaff, and fugitives *do not slip through my fingers*. I arrest *every single one of them*, so this does not happen to me. You get me? I'll go talk to Stumpy, but if my fugitive pops back up on my radar, I'm out of here."

"That's understandable. That's your job."

Now that they'd figured out their next step, there was an uncomfortable silence. Turk had posted that arm-flailing, undisciplined Prospect outside of the coffee shop after Lock had given him the plate number of Ronald Reagan's Lexus. It was a Prospect's duty to constantly be on guard and not be privy to the inner doings of patch holders, but Lock was glad to be alone with the lean, sinewy Veep.

"Where will you be, so I can get ahold of you once I find out the lowdown?"

Turk shrugged. "I'll stick around, I guess. Maybe this shitty Motel 6." There was a Motel 6 right next to the café.

Lock wanted to ask about the kiss. Fighting was one thing. That could happen every day without anyone questioning it. But it seemed that they'd been using physical violence as a substitute for the lust they both felt for each other. That sultry, erotic kiss had been on Lock's mind ever since tear-assing out of that high school's parking lot. He'd been kissed by another man behind a high school band room, and the lewd implications of that had been rousing him to even greater heights of stimulation. Turk's lips were so soft, an unexpected feature of such a nasty, hardened biker. Their tongues had twined intuitively, as though they'd kissed hundreds of times before. Turk mouthed him as though he loved him, his kisses laden with affection that could hardly have been there. And when Turk had pressed his own erection against Lock's, unescapable waves of arousal had swept through Lock's groin.

The fact was, he currently sported a hard-on so firm he was afraid to stand up from the little bistro table. If Turk got an eyeful of that, he would know Lock's next words rang hollow. "Look, I just want you to know, I'm sorry about what happened with your boyfriend."

"That's okay. I know you had no—"

Lock barreled ahead, having practiced the speech ten times already. "I'm no homo. I was in that nightclub tracking the same guy I was tracking this morning, some child molester. I just broke up with my old lady. I was with her for two years."

Turk tilted his head intelligently. "You were at The Racquet

Club for work. Just how did that work necessitate going into a private booth and having my boyfriend eat your dick? Especially, you know, seeing as how you're not gay."

Lock shifted uncomfortably. His dick was throbbing to the beat of his heart inside his jeans. *Think about baseball. Better yet, think about soccer. That's even worse than baseball.* "Your boyfriend is very…persuasive."

Turk had the ability to raise one eyebrow only. "So persuasive he convinced a straight man to be handcuffed by his own cuffs and allow a hungry wolf to gorge on his vitals? My, my. I knew Dayton was persuasive, but that really takes the cake."

Turk was understandably skeptical. Lock didn't fully grasp it himself. Did he want it to happen again with Turk? Most of his soul did, but the majority of his brain was screaming *No, no, no! No flaming gay boy is getting near my dick again! I'm all about the sweetbutts. That's it. Pussy, pussy, and more pussy—that's my middle name!* For lack of any more valid arguments, Lock resorted to being obtuse. "I don't need you to understand. That's your business if you want to leer at a bunch of big boners." *Oh, God, I just said "big boners." That indicates I care about the size of the boners.* "I'm certainly not about to out you to anyone."

Turk narrowed his eyes now. "That's mighty white of you. Especially since if you did, I'd just out *you*."

Lock shot to his feet indignantly. But he'd completely forgotten about his *own* big boner. He couldn't very well yank his tight wifebeater down over it, so he grabbed his paper coffee cup and held it before his crotch, completely ineffectively. But he had a good argument. "Listen here, you Boner, *I'm* the one doing *you* a favor, tracking down this knockoff weed for you. If you want to bring it to your club's table that you couldn't find the source, fine. Leave me out of it." And he stormed off, pride intact.

He was barely through the door when he already regretted his actions. Already, he missed Turk. The few encounters they'd had together had been a clear display of their compatibility, both personality-wise, strength-wise, and sexual-wise. Already the cells in his body were crying out for the balancing act of Turk's cells. His yin was crying out for Turk's yang, or whichever of those two was the more macho.

"Hey!" cried the Prospect. "You're already leaving? I haven't seen your guy drive by…"

Relief washed over Lock when he heard Turk's engineer boots stomping down the sidewalk after him. He slowed his pace enough for Turk to catch him, but not enough to show he actually *wanted* to be caught.

Turk grabbed a handful of his wifebeater and spun him around. Lock allowed himself to be shoved back into the entryway of a used bookstore. *Good.* A place where no one ever went.

"Listen," Turk said huskily, placing one palm on the glass next to Lock's head. "You know that's not what I want. I'm not the most experienced gay-about-town either, Lock. But I think I can tell a man who wants another man a mile the fuck away. You can go around pretending you don't want me, or the next guy's juicy ass, or the next guy's long dick, but you're never going to get around the reality of it. I know because I tried. I faked that I liked girls for years until I did a year in Kingman, where nobody bothered faking it."

Turk stepped closer, so close Lock's prick twitched as it caught the scent of the Veep's body heat. Turk went on lazily. "Dayton was my first real boyfriend after that, so you think I want to dive right back into some gut-wrenching, soul-busting relationship with another dude?"

"No," said Lock. It came out more like a rat's squeak. He

realized he was holding his breath. "I wasn't suggesting anything like that."

Again, Turk gathered a handful of Lock's wifebeater. This time his fingertips brushed the silver barbell that pierced his nipple. Was it intentional? Either way, just that brief touch sent shockwaves resonating through Lock's stiff cock, his full testicles bulging urgently with seed. "That's the last fucking thing I want, to be backstabbed again by someone who can't be true to his own nature. You want to run around in a fantasy land pretending to be straight, humping women with a half-hearted dick, that's your own business. But the man I saw fucking my boyfriend's mouth with his wrists bound behind his back was *this fucking close*"—Turk held his forefinger and thumb apart as though describing a miniscule penis—"from shooting a giant load of bull gravy into another man's mouth. And *that* tells me all *I* need to fucking know."

Before Lock could exhale, Turk had gently shoved him in the chest and was striding off toward the Motel 6. Turk was so fast, in fact, that Lock barely had a second to step onto the sidewalk and yell as loud as he dared,

"I'll let you know what my guy says!"

Turk raised a hand in acknowledgement, but didn't look back.

Suddenly there was a void in Lock's life he hadn't known he had. He felt incredibly empty and bereft watching that graceful stallion loping away. A beauty like that should be staying in a McMansion, not a Motel 6. Or at the very least in Lock's mid-century abode. He could clean it up, take out all the recycling, stick an air freshener on the wall. No one would ever miss those goofy scarecrow wall hangings that said "Harvest Thyme."

Lock knew from all his intel-gathering that Turk *did* live in a McMansion—Ford Illuminati's McMansion to be exact. He shared the three thousand square foot house with Ford's wife Madison and a toddler, name unknown, Lock had never cared for children so he didn't bother finding out. That was one thing that had caused Ruby to dump him. She wanted kids, and pronto. She was nearing thirty and past her prime childbearing years, she often liked to shriek. He genuinely hoped she could find someone to provide her with a kid. This fact let him know that he didn't truly love her, because if he did, that idea would burn him up inside.

He got in his cage and headed out Mohave Road, not bothering to warn Stumpy he was coming. Stumpy Meadows, the Assassins' sergeant-at-arms, was a weird, hermit-like guy, probably a meth addict. He was a great sergeant-at-arms because he was definitely willing to shoot anyone at a moment's provocation. Lock guessed he was sort of a doomsday prepper and general all-around white power guy, judging from his jailhouse tattoos of Woody Woodpecker, an Iron Cross, and spider web Lock had been unlucky enough to see once in Stumpy's underarm.

Stumpy had an alfalfa farm here that Lock had visited on a couple of occasions on his way to or from collaring a fugitive. Boy, if Lock thought his 1960s tract house needed sprucing up, he only had to go to Stumpy's ranch house. Lock's house was a palace compared to this ramshackle clapboard wreck where you expected to find dead bodies under the floor boards. Oddly, Stumpy held an attraction for women. He'd nailed almost all of the Assassins of Youth sweetbutts, and they just kept coming back for more.

In fact, there were a couple on Stumpy's front porch draped in various stages of undress. Even sweetbutts had their limits, and they were probably too skeeved to go inside what with the cockroaches and pillow cases for window curtains. Lock didn't know why Stumpy couldn't afford a better place. Between his farm and his trafficking through the Rezes, he must've made a mint.

"Hey Dahlia, hey, ah..." Lock couldn't remember the second sweetbutt's name so he just lifted his chin at her in acknowledgement.

She sure knew *him*, though. Stroking his shoulder, she practically plastered her nearly-nude body to his. Sweetbutts were a strange creature. They mostly came from broken homes. Obviously if they were heading for a college degree they wouldn't derive most of their ego boost from which grade of patch holder they could bag. Lock didn't hold any particular office with the club. He was no Veep or even a road manager. His Air Force buddy Tim Breakiron had sponsored his prospectship when he'd been honorably discharged with a slight PTSD problem, a slight traumatic brain injury. The brain injury must've been responsible for him currently forgetting he'd been vowing to get up on any sweetbutt he could see. He just asked her,

"Stumpy around?"

She pouted with disappointment that he hadn't come to the middle of the desert on the Colorado River Indian Rez to see her. "He's tuning his bow."

Shuddering because now he'd have to pull open the holey screen door and enter the kitchen, Lock steeled himself. Stumpy almost always had his crossbow. He was always out there bagging duck, deer, turkey, and even the odd rattlesnake or two. To Lock's disgust, today's bill of fare was a Gila monster splayed on its back with arms akimbo on the butcher block table in the center of the room. Its forked tongue flopped out of its mouth like a "pull here" tab. Its skin was really very beautiful, like coral and black petroglyphs.

Stumpy sat at the table waxing his bow strings. He barely glanced at Lock from under his curtain of hair. Between the hair and the beady eyes, Lock didn't know how Stumpy ever saw anything. But he did. He rarely missed a shot.

Ignoring the dead reptile, Lock sat, too. "Hey, Stumpy."

"On a mission?" Stumpy mumbled. He was one of those guys who talked without moving his mouth, like a ventriloquist.

Lock lit a cigarette. *I need to quit smoking. Especially if I'm going to keep getting this damned nose busted.* "Yeah. Only something new came up. Guy from The Bare Bones is accusing us of selling some bunk weed under his trade name, Eminence Front." He fingered a sample from the top pocket of his cut and tossed it on the table next to the lizard.

Stumpy barely glanced at it. "That fag who beat the crap out of you in Laughlin?"

Lock's blood ran cold in his veins. *Fag?* When had Turk come out of the closet? Stumpy was the first person Lock had heard term Turk as a homosexual in all of his investigative interviews. He tried to laugh casually. "What makes you think he's a fag? He was pissed because I'd gotten a head job from his favorite fender fluff. But yeah, if you noticed him patting me down for weed, that was why. I know you control the traffic up and down the Rez, down the river into Yuma and Cocopah, and this shit is definitely Sonoran. He wants us to cease and desist using his trade names of Eminence Front and Young Man Blue."

Stumpy finally set his bow aside and looked at the weed. "Eminence Front, eh? Yeah, that looks like my shit. I've been using those names to boost interest."

"Well, uh, can you *stop?*"

Stumpy finally grinned. There was nothing stumpy about him that Lock knew of, and it was a fact he'd dated a few supermodels in his time. Lock didn't see the attraction. Maybe he was the "strong silent type." "So that fag wants me to stop using his product brand?"

Lock squeezed his eyes shut patiently. He spoke in measured tones, knowing it wouldn't behoove him to piss Stumpy off. "I don't know why you keep referring to him as a fag, Stumpy. In addition to not using his brand name, maybe you could stop spreading false stories about him."

Stumpy frowned. "Since when are we in bed with the Bones? Or I should say since when are *you* in bed with Turk Blackburn?"

That was fucking *it*. Slamming the table with his palm so the Gila monster did a little jig, Lock shot to his feet and pointed a stiff finger at Stumpy. "Just where…the fuck…do you get off slandering him with these names. I did a background check on him and there's nothing like that in his 411."

Now Stumpy guffawed incredulously. "Relax, *gabacho!* I'm just referring to the rather large and obvious hard-on he got when wrestling with you. Keep your shirt on." He giggled. "Or maybe you'd like to take it off…"

"Listen," roared Lock, "am I going to have to give you a beatdown? Because I will, in order to defend my fucking honor, *brother*. I can tear your head off barehanded if you'd put that bow down for one second. I came here asking you a simple fucking request—to stop infringing on the Leaves of Grass trademark. Now you seem to be accusing me of being some kind of joy boy—"

Holding up his hands in surrender, Stumpy shot suddenly to his feet, too. Lock hated to admit it, but he did jump a little, got a little defensive, put up his dukes. But all Stumpy apparently wanted was to defuse the situation.

"Relax, brother. Here. Let me get Danielle outside here to

give you some comfort. That'd prove you're not interested in poppin' it in some Boner's toaster."

"I don't need to prove nothing..." Lock mumbled. But it *was* a good idea, anyway, to push up on the sweetbutt. It would prove to *himself* that he didn't have any interest in being tongue-fucked by the loping pot pusher.

So he took Danielle into one of the little shabby bedrooms. The sheets probably hadn't been changed in ten years, so Lock stood while Danielle kneeled. She took his flaccid dick out and mouthed it for a bit. Lock started panicking that it wasn't getting stiff. Panicking, of course, made it even worse. Danielle withdrew and looked clinically at his dick from all angles, as though it would turn purple or fall off.

He tried talking nastier. "Do it, bitch. Suck my dick." He was glad he didn't say "suck my *big* dick" because that was painfully, obviously, not true at the moment. So she kept trying, and Lock filled with despair. This had *never* happened to him with a woman!

At last, in desperation, he hit on an idea that filled him with delicious, lewd arousal. He would pretend Danielle was Turk. If he closed his eyes, threw his head back, and drowned out her tiny feminine sighs, he could pretend it was Turk's tongue swirling around his penis, doing indescribably obscene things to make his prick harder, longer, plumper.

Lock realized with a sick thrill that he was doing the exact same thing Stumpy had just accused him of. But if he was only doing it in his *head*, and there was a live, female sweetbutt on her knees in front of him, what difference did it make how he got off? Men took Viagra to achieve an erection. They fantasized about all sorts of perverted things while jacking off. If it made him hard to think of Turk Blackburn's teardrop tattoo and his mouth hungrily suctioning his dick, then whatever worked, right?

That's when it started flowing. "Oh *Goddddd* yeah!" His sudden enthusiasm rattled the windowpanes, echoing so loudly he was sure Stumpy could hear him. *Good.* "Oh *fuck* yeah, keep sucking me, bitch. Use your tongue. *Yeah,* that's it. Oh *Goddd,* you love sucking cock, don't you? You just can't get enough of it. You want your mouth filled with a nice long, fat dick. You want to gulp that tasty, hot jizz—"

His orgasm was unexpected, racing up out of his very depths, giving him no warning. He was suddenly spending in the hot, sucking mouth that swirled around his glans, pleasuring him so acutely the hairs on the back of his neck stood out. The bare skin of his ass shivered with delight, his balls like two boulders pressed up tight against his perineum. *Oh, Lord. The only way this would be better is if something was sliding in and out of my ass.*

"That's it," he gasped, cradling the silken head to his groin. "That's it, God, don't stop."

When she gulped and cried out, the fantasy of Turk was broken. Lock pulled away with a gasp. Ignoring the girl as she sat on the floor, he went into a dilapidated bathroom and washed up. Out the window he could see a Super Glide with the Assassin's logo displayed on the gas tank rumbling up. That would be Papa Ewey, the President. Since Lock had last left him in Laughlin with plans to continue the week-long party another week, he was surprised to see Papa. Shortly behind him was Lock's sponsor, Tim Breakiron, on his classic Panhead ride.

"What the fuck?" Lock mouthed, and made a beeline for the kitchen.

"Wow," drawled Danielle as he breezed past her. "You sure dropped a load on me. How long's it been since you came?"

He didn't have time to go back and sneer at her. But it had

actually only been about twelve hours since he'd whacked off, again thinking of Turk. His guilt and shame over these incidents caused him to be more respectful than usual when Papa Ewey and Sergeant Breakiron entered the kitchen.

"Sir," he said to them both. Breakiron had literally been his CO in the Air Force, so it was a natural holdover for Lock to refer to him that way. It continuously struck fear into his heart that Breakiron may have once or twice been aware that he had been butt fucking his copilot, Corporal Park Langham. Breakiron had never mentioned as such, of course, and he wouldn't have sponsored Lock as a Prospect if he'd thought he was a homo. Breakiron must not have known. Or, like in the Wild West, he just thought it was collateral damage to the whole Iraq environment.

"Have a seat, Singer," said Papa Ewey.

Having a seat was never a good sign. They all sat around the butcher block table that still held the bloated Gila monster. Stumpy stuck a Bowie knife a half an inch into the table next to the lizard, as though Papa Ewey was just keeping him from butchering it for the grill. Stumpy's beady eyes flickered at Lock, and Lock glared back at him. Breakiron crossed his massive arms in front of his stomach. Now *there* was someone who should've been called Stumpy. With arms like redwood tree trunks and the ever-present beanie giving his long, lank hair a bad case of "helmet head," he was the epitome of what most people probably pictured as an outlaw biker.

Ewey started out. "It's come to our attention that a kilo of Golden Triangle White has gone missing."

Stumpy was expressionless, as always. "Which shipment did it go missing from?"

"When that boat the *I Love You* reached the slip at Hidden Valley Road on the Rez yesterday, it was light the kilo. Somewhere between the hand-off at the Bighorn slip and the Hidden Valley slip is where it went south."

Lock was familiar with those parts of the river. He'd had to chase many a fugitive down into the Rez, where they liked to hide because it was much more difficult legally for a skip tracer to follow onto Indian lands.

Stumpy made a sound. "Hm. Well, it's pretty obvious it's either one of the workers loading it at Bighorn, or one of the ones unloading it at Hidden Valley."

"We thought of that," said Papa Ewey with no trace of sarcasm. "That's why we're reaching out to you. You know your crew. I'm putting it in your wheelhouse to figure out which dope boy pinched that H. Lock, you're an expert sniffer. Makes sense if I put you on the trail of the courier who's been pinching it."

"But I'm on a job," Lock tried to protest. "I've been chasing this fucking chomo for three days. Any second now I could get a text that someone saw him, and I'd have to leave."

Papa Ewey and Breakiron fixed him with accusatory glares. Club business always came before business business. To Lock's surprise, Stumpy stood up for him.

"I don't need Singer," said the sergeant-at-arms. "I know my crew like the back of my hand. If anything, it's one of those fucking blanket-asses that help me transport it through the Rez. They don't get their fucking subsistence checks until the first, so the last week of the month they get real desperate. I've got them all jonesing for more of it, but some of them can't budget their green properly. Ain't my fault if they don't make it till the end of the month."

"All right," said Papa Ewey, "then do you know these maize-munchers well enough to figure out which one did it? I didn't think so. Lock, you stay close to Stumpy until you get your text about that diaper sniper."

That was an order, and Lock knew it. "Yes, sir," he said sullenly.

The Prez and Breakiron stayed another interminable hour at Stumpy's ranch. They did a little target practice at some bottles out back, tested out some anti-personnel IEDs Breakiron had been devising. No one would question an explosion on an Indian reservation. Time crawled for Lock. All he could think about was speeding back to that fucking Motel 6 on the pretext of telling Turk he'd solved his Eminence Front dilemma. If he just texted him his answer, Turk would leave. Stumpy didn't want Lock here, but they'd have to at least pretend to be looking for the missing heroin. By then Turk would be long gone. Turk had no other reason to hang around Parker, Arizona.

Lock was lovesick.

CHAPTER SEVEN
TURK

Kissing Lock behind the band room had brought some fierce memories rushing back to me.

I had lunch with Twinkletoes at some greasy spoon, but these memories would *not* let me alone. The high school incident was a primal, formative one, one that Freud would blame as the catalyst for my homosexuality, no doubt. I know Freud has been massively discounted these days, but you know what? I *don't* recall having many urges toward boys before this incident. I was ambivalent, I should say. I could have gone either way. And yeah, as you've probably guessed, it took place in a locker room.

I had to return to my motel room to whack off, instructing poor Twinkletoes to stay alert for any texts or calls. He had to sit out front in case the Lexus went by again. I had prospected just like anyone, even Lytton Illuminati, and I recalled those sleepless months sitting in painful positions waiting for shit that never happened. Anyway, it was luxurious to frig my dick in quiet, picturing Lock's impudent, arrogant face as one of the football players.

My first actual hands-on experience with boys was in my junior year at Pure and Easy High—I didn't go back for my senior year. I got my GED. I usually tried to fly under the radar in PE, but I was very tall, and good at basketball at least, so I shined there. I tried to remain aloof from most everyone, especially the jocks. Since Ford wasn't in my PE class, I tried to stay a loner. That could be difficult sometimes with the typical adolescent teasing and towel-snapping that happens. Especially when you've got a full, long, fat dick, such as I was blessed—or cursed—with.

The jocks liked to call me things like "donkey-rigged" and "miracle meat." It would be thought of as gay to *touch* another man, but I guess looking at his meat and commenting on it was acceptable. "Blackburn, why don't you get up on Ashley Holt?" I remember that one. They always wanted me to get up on this cheerleader for some reason. I guess it was better than being tormented by them—they seemed to want to draw me into their circle. "She's always eyeballing your junk when you're playing." "Yeah, she could take that donkey dick." Implying that my man meat required a slut and might tear asunder a virgin. Their moronic banter irritated the crap out of me, and I always showered and dressed as fast as possible.

This one particular day, I guess I wasn't fast enough. And there was a new guy, a transfer student I couldn't take my eyes off of. He was dark, delicious in a smoky way, as though you could lick his neck and he'd taste like a sooty Greek grill. He resembled Ford, it occurred to me with a forbidden thrill. The flared nostrils in the proud Roman nose, the eagle's profile, the long fingers like talons. He never said a word, but they were recruiting him for the football team because of his long limbs. I could tell he had a nasty and twisted side. I couldn't stop thinking about it. Especially when we wound up showering next to each other.

His eyes flickered at mine, his eyes as though lined with kohl like a Middle Eastern Nautch dancer. More than once his gaze flashed over my face in some kind of recognition. I hoped beyond hope at its meaning, but I'd been disappointed and threatened too many times to trust in that. So I turned my back on him and stalked to my locker, proud that I hadn't fallen for his flirtation. I knew I had to get out of high school—and beyond the limits of my motorcycle club's backyard—to even begin to indulge in the sorts of taboo delights that I wanted so badly to taste.

I was drying my hair when the corner of a wet towel bit into my ass. Stung, I cringed in automatic response and spun around with fiery eyes.

"Blackburn." It was the toolbag who harassed me the most, Chris Baumgardner. Looking back on it now from the sage perspective of my thirty-two years of experience, he probably was a latent homosexual.

"Hey Troy!" yelled Baumgardner to the fullback with the enormous buck teeth. "I caught Blackburn giving Tognozzi the eye. He was looking at his dick!"

Which was correct. I had been eying that delicious, creamy slab of beef. But to hear it shouted out in a locker room full of adolescent boys wasn't a dream come true. It was pretty much a nightmare, and at least it was guaranteed to deflate my cock that had stayed at half-mast since I'd ogled—what was his name? Evo Tognozzi, that's right, the Greek god with the sooty eyes.

"Tognozzi, really?" guffawed Troy. "Hey Tognozzi! Guess who's got a crush on you! Hey, now we fucking know why he never wants to get up on Ashley."

"Yeah," guffawed Baumgardner. "He'd rather get up on *Asher* than *Ashley*."

It was halfway witty, at least, and I chuckled, trying to lighten the mood. But Troy, Baumgardner, and several other jocks including Tognozzi now closed in on me. My heart started racing, and not in a good way. A few months ago a boy had been hoisted up the main assembly flagpole because he wore pants that made him look like he was waiting for a flood, and the other teens were bored.

"Listen, guys. You fucking know me," I protested, hands up. "I'm no fag. I'm in a fucking motorcycle club. That's the least gay thing you could possibly do." I wasn't actually *in* the club because I was only sixteen, but I rode a hog, some hand-me-down from Cropper. It was cooler than most of the other boys' clunky muscle cars.

"Fags can ride bikes," said Troy, his lower lip jutting self-righteously. "I saw a parade in San Francisco once. Lots of fags on bikes."

Tognozzi took center stage now, the flimsy towel wrapped around his waist betraying the sad fact that he had no erection whatsoever—and I could still view the erotic outline of his massive dong. "Why don't we find out once and for all? Lock the door," he shot at a lackey, a wannabe football player. He whipped my underwear from my hand that I'd been hoping to step into and tossed it into my locker. Instead he withdrew my sweaty jock strap, and he shoved me until my bare ass hit the hard metal bench.

"Now, this isn't necessary," I protested feebly. "You fucking know I'm no homo. I dated Kelsey Washington, and everyone remembers the vortex party where I was banging Britny Krabbenhoft for all eyes to see." Speaking of eyes, I was eyeball-to-cock with about ten hefty, beefy, and hormone-riddled teens. It was difficult *not* to admire their flaccid pricks, and I thought I detected more than a few plumping up as Tognozzi wrapped the elastic of the jock strap around my wrists several times behind my back.

"Beards," sneered Baumgardner. His eyes became darker

and full of portent as he loomed over me. Funny, for such a beefy guy—he had no chest hair whatsoever—you could tell that his little dick wouldn't get very long even when hard. They say all dicks are the same size when hard? Not. No, they are not. Not even close. "Those chicks were your beards."

Troy seemed confused. "How could Britny be a beard if he was really banging her? I saw him doing it."

"Fags can fake it," Baumgardner asserted, reaching behind me to grab something else from a locker. It turned out to be a cheerleader's pompom, and Troy and I became even more mystified when he shook it. "But you know what fags can't fake? They can't fake getting all turned on when a guy touches them. Real straight guys wouldn't get hard no matter what another guy did to them."

Which, as any student of Biology 101 already knows, is completely untrue, but I guess that's beside the point, because Baumgardner was now tickling my penis with the plastic tentacles of the pompom, and yes, it was lengthening, filling with seed. The more I struggled against my stretchy jock strap bonds, the more my pectoral and abdominal muscles strained, making it look as though I *wanted* to be admired, drooled on, looked at.

"Yeah!" urged other players. "Do it, Baumgardner!"

"Let's watch him gay up!"

"Watch his dick get all hard!"

Baumgardner guffawed like an ape as he tickled my prick and balls into attention. He slithered the dainty plastic arms of the instrument up and down the length of my cock as though he took delight in arousing me. Indeed, the scent of boyish excitement in the room was rising. My nostrils flared at the tangy odor of full testicles as a few boys even dared grab their own dicks and squeeze.

A DANGEROUS REALITY

"Look!" Baumgardner hollered. "He's living up to his name. His donkey dick is getting stiff because another *guy* is touching it."

Troy clung to Baumgardner's shoulder. "Huh, he's hung like a bull," he catcalled, echoing nothing new in the way of taunts for the past several months.

"Listen," I tried to tell them, controlling my voice so as not to betray my excitement. Truly, Baumgardner was giving me the thrill of my lifetime, a thrill more erotic than any of my most twisted dreams. I was being stimulated by a muscled stud *in front of a crowd of boys*. It was a sea of shining, leering eyes, teenaged boys licking their lips, wafting their hands over their own cocks *because they were ogling* me. Their heartbeats were accelerating, their testicles were filling with seed, their cocks were swelling *because they were looking at my penis*. "This is only natural. Who the fuck hasn't gotten a hard-on when accidentally brushing against something?"

"Not like *this*," breathed Baumgardner, serious in his work now. He squiggled the pompom all over my penis almost with affection, making sure to tickle my perineum, the sweet spot behind my ball sac. "Your dick is all purple and shiny like a racehorse's because you *like* being touched by another guy. Admit it!"

I spat out without forethought, "Your dick is hard too!"

It was. His little winky dink jutted out like a beak. It was just so small, it was hard to tell that it *was* hard. Several other boys were trying to hide their arousal, too. Some stuffed their hard-ons into their jocks ineffectively. Some were carried away by the gang bang aura of the scene, and clutched their boners, squeezing and choking the lives from their tools. One boy's eyes even rolled up in his head with lust, as though he didn't care anymore what the others thought. If anyone bothered looking at him, since all eyes were so fixated on me.

It was the scene of my life, beyond my dirtiest fantasies. The stakes were raised when Baumgardner snorted with rage and tossed away the pompom. "I am *not* hard!" he yelled, contrary to all evidence. He whipped out a stiff arm and commanded someone to "give me that!" A ruler was slapped into his hand, and my prick twitched with anticipation. At that stage of my life, I had never dabbled in the world of BDSM. I had watched porns with Ford and Cropper and their crew where a girl was tied up. I knew it excited me to see the way her nipples poked out through the strands of rope, how helpless she was, how she secretly loved the "torture."

All hell broke loose when Baumgardner slapped my dick. I jumped and gasped, of course, but kept my thighs spread wide to show I could take it. It stung, and pain radiated through my groin, but after the first few seconds it became a pleasant tingle that erected my nipples and sent shivers up and down my back. Gooseflesh was raised on my butt, and it seemed my cock bounced, yearned, straining for more. Gritting my teeth, I looked my tormentor directly in the eye, challenging him to escalate.

"You can't hurt me, you goon," I said, low and seductive. "This is just basic biology, and I think it turns you on, too, getting me all hot like this."

"Fag!" Baumgardner cried. Now when he slapped my penis with the stick, it seemed to upset him. His eyes shined with what looked like tears. It was difficult sometimes to tell anger from sorrow, I'd learned from watching The Bare Bones in action. "It does *not* turn me on! I want to out you for the homo you are!"

"Admit it," I said slyly, seemingly unruffled by the beating. "You're a sadist. It turns you on to strike my giant pole. You wish you were on your knees between my thighs right now, sucking my big old wang down your throat, gulping my hot jizz, lapping up every last single drop—"

"*Oh, God!*" cried out one of the football players. "I can't fucking take it!" For the first time, all eyes turned to this boy as he fully stroked his own erection now, making no pretense at choking his boner or stuffing it in his jock. Jaws dropped all throughout the steamy aisle of lockers as this one boy just said fuck it and frigged his flute from stem to stern.

Boys made way for him, too, when he stepped up to me, obviously intending to splatter me with his juice. He frigged himself assiduously, jerking off as fast as he could while a drip of drool shined on his lower lip. He had eyes only for my big purplish beaten hard-on. The sight wasn't repellant to me, and I think I smiled a little. Other boys around him took his cue and began furiously fondling their own woodies.

"Bukkake!" cried out one boy. I didn't know what that word meant at the time. But I was about to find out.

The brisk knock on my hotel room door was like someone tossing a pail of ice water over me.

I leaped about a foot off the bed like a cartoon character. Clutching the sheet to my naked crotch, I stared at the locked door as though Mommy Dearest was waiting behind it with a coat hanger.

"Turk!" called Twinkletoes.

"Oh, Jesus," I whispered, leaping off the bed and grabbing my boxer briefs. Even the sudden fright hadn't deflated my cock completely, I was that close to coming. *Damned fucking fugitives. Always popping up at the worst times.* I could shove my half-mast cock up against my hip, and my jeans would cover the rest. "What the fuck?"

"Lock is here."

Oh. My clothes practically flew back on my body now as if by magic, although I didn't completely button my plaid shirt before I swung open the door to greet Lock.

He seemed about as happy as I was. We were two happy-go-lucky guys. He looked even more beautiful than I had recalled, his hands buried deep in his pockets, and he even looked sort of sheepish. Different from his normal arrogance.

The right thing to do would've been to suggest going back to the coffee shop, but I just didn't feel like it, and since when does an outlaw biker need to explain himself? I yanked Lock by the arm into my room, slammed the door shut behind him, and locked it.

I shrugged into my cut—respect for the colors and all—and got a Bud from the little fridge.

"No thanks," said Lock. "I don't drink."

It made me wonder whether he'd had a former problem with it, but I didn't know him well enough to ask, so I sat at the round laminated table. He wore his cut, too, and it felt like we were at a bargaining table. Which we sort of were.

"I just came to pass the news along that Stumpy admitted to having used your brand name to sell weed. He promised to stop doing it." He shrugged. "That's all there is to it. I'm really sorry that we infringed on your turf. What can I say? You've got an excellent product that's widely known and imitated."

I knew that Lock could not betray a brother by calling him an asshat or douchemonkey, as much as he might want to. From what I had seen of Stumpy Meadows, at rallies, Great White and Lynyrd Skynyrd concerts, he was a shady guy who kept to himself and couldn't be trusted. Since that described pretty much every outlaw biker in the Southwest, I hadn't paid much attention.

I took a gamble in what I said next. "You didn't have to

come out here to tell me that. You could've just called." He could still just get up and walk away. Our business was done. I'd achieved my mission and could return to Pure and Easy now, report back to the club.

"I know." Lock sighed, his features pinched as though he were in pain. "I just didn't feel comfortable the way we left things."

My heart literally jumped with hope. "Oh yeah? Why is that?"

Lock reached his hand around the small of his back. I tensed and probably half-stood a couple of inches. He put his free hand out, palm facing the table, silently telling me to calm down. "It's nothing. This thing is just digging into my back."

Lock slammed a pair of handcuffs onto the table. I instantly knew he was lying, because he'd left the cuff pouch clipped to his belt, and that would've been the part that was digging into his back. Not to mention the forty cal Glock he kept shoved into his waistband. *Interesting.*

"What didn't you feel comfortable about?" I prodded.

It was clear one of the things he was uncomfortable with was discussing shit like this. He shifted around in his chair and looked everywhere but at me. Rubbing the sparse beard on his chin, he mumbled something.

I leaned forward across the table. "Excuse me?"

It looked as though it irritated him hugely to spit out, "I wanted to see you again!"

Interesting indeed. Now, I am a switch—mostly a skilled power bottom. I like topping from below, and yes, I like a big juicy prick as well. I knew this was the perfect moment to take submissive charge. Lock was giving me an in to his heart, his psyche, his soul. He had surrendered already to me just by coming to my hotel room. I had done my job—I had reeled him in mentally and made him anticipate making love with me. With my sexual confidence in my own skill and the art of seduction, I had enticed this delicious biker. I had the power.

But Lock was the sort of man who needed to maintain the *pretense* of being the dominant top, always in control, dictating what happened and when. I knew he was nowhere close in his gay odyssey to begin outright admitting he wanted to explore anything with me. Since I was already leaning across the table, I stretched one arm out, palm up. He looked at it as though it had leprosy.

I didn't withdraw it. "I wanted to see you again, too. I can stay a couple more days if you'd like. Tell my club I need more time to find the scumbag. You intrigue me, Lock. I've been fantasizing about having a session with you since—well, I admit it, ever since seeing you bound at The Racquet Club. I put myself in Dayton's shoes and I'd do the same fucking thing. You're a juicy, delicious hunk of man, Lock. I'm not anywhere near ready for a real relationship since being betrayed by Dayton. But I wouldn't mind a few hot, healthy rolls in the hay with you."

Lock squeezed his eyes shut. It sounded as though he said, "*Chupa mantequilla de mi culo.*" I wasn't as good at Spanish as our resident linguist Knoxie, but I knew it had something to do with butter and his ass, and that was an encouraging sign. I scooted my chair around the table so we were sitting knee to knee. My mouth watered at the growing bulge in the crotch of his jeans as he sat with his thighs splayed, making no motion to hide it.

Now I picked up his hand, encircling his erotically-charged thumb in my fist. He looked at our hands with mild, almost childlike curiosity, like some show-and-tell exhibit. "You're going to have to admit your inner nature, Lock, be true to yourself. You may have gone into that nightclub to track some kiddie pornographer but you wound up in a fucking sleazy cubicle with an experienced Dom licking your hard-on. You let him cuff you and I'll bet you've never let any fugitive get the drop on you like that. You wanted it, Lock. You wanted it bad." I lifted my chin at him. "Say it."

He repeated obediently, "I wanted it bad." Gathering more courage, he squeezed my hand and even looked me in the eyes. His eyes were dazzling, intense, like sky-blue celestite. With conviction he said, "I wanted a man sucking me off because they do it better. They eat dick better 'cause their mouths are bigger or something. Or maybe they want it more than chicks."

That was weird, because that had always been my theory. Lock's openness encouraged me to slide a hand up his thigh and boldly grasp his erection in my palm. Oh, Great Caesar's Ghost, it was like his dick was made to fit in the cup of my hand. His eyelids fluttered when I lightly squeezed the succulent tool, and I gasped louder than him when I felt it twitch and pulse in my grasp.

"They *do* want it more, Lock. Only another man knows the turn-on and the thrill of gulping another man's prick down his throat. Only another man knows how to work it just right, how to tongue the cockhead, how to finger the sweet perineum."

To demonstrate, I slid my other hand under and between his ass cheeks, thumbing the seam in the jeans that bisected the globes. His eyelids slipped almost completely closed, his nostrils trembled with excitement, and I was this close to losing my composure too. When I thumbed the pulsating cockhead I was gratified to see a drip of pre-come darkening the denim fabric, and I knew I had to act fast.

"Men *know* men, Lock." I was panting heavily by then, like some kind of degenerate dogging it in an adult video arcade. I literally had this studly biker's manhood in my hands, my mouth watering for a taste of what Dayton had enjoyed. Already I was afraid I was falling deeper and harder for this tough bounty hunter. I was in no position to be laying myself wide open for more pain and sorrow—and Lock Singer was a good candidate for that. But you know how you tell yourself you'll "just" screw around with the person, have a little fun, then forget them? I was in *that* delusional phase. "Men appreciate the flavor of a nice load of spunk sliding down their throat."

"Mm."

Lock's little grunt of agreement was all I needed. With his eyes shut now and his face tilted toward the carpet, he was as close as he'd ever get to crying out "Take me." There was a lot Lock couldn't bring himself to admit, and it was up to me to read his mind, to intuit what his body language told me. That's one of the innate traits of a good power bottom. I whipped the cuffs from the table, fell to my knees next to him, and in a flash had him cuffed behind the metal chair.

He nominally resisted, just enough to show he didn't make this a habit. "Hey," he protested weakly, testing the restraints to make sure I'd done it right.

As for me, I crawled around till I sat between his powerful thighs. Lunging forward, I grasped his hips and mouthed the heavenly dick through the denim. I breathed out a hot, sultry breath to warm it, knowing it was stiffening his nipples, shivering the barbells that pierced them. I gummed the savory penis, saturating the fabric with my drool, even tonguing the delicious glans, feeling the stiff ridge of the corona with my tongue-tip.

Lock bucked and snorted like a caged beast. His gyrations only served to press his cock against my mouth more tightly.

"Look," he grunted, his voice a full octave lower than normal, and full of gravel. "I don't do this. I told you I'm no fucking fag, and I'm no fucking fag. *Ah!*" He snapped his head back when I withdrew my mouth. Covering him with my torso, I yanked the bottom hem of his wifebeater up to reveal his taut, rippled abdomen. I slimed circles with my tongue around his navel, following the oily line of hair that arrowed down to his belt buckle.

I needed this. Now.

As my fingers flew to release the buckle—a giant custom thing with his Assassins logo—I panted up at him. "The safe word is 'tennis.'"

I doubted we'd need to use it. I was right.

CHAPTER EIGHT
LOCK

Lock was nearly immobilized with fear.

True, he was immobilized because he was cuffed to a chair. But he was also petrified at what was happening seemingly *to* him, without any action on his part. All he'd done was slap the cuffs on the table because they were hurting his hipbone. With all the other crap he had to wear on the duty belt—cellphone, wallet chain, Taser, sometimes a radio—the cuffs just weighed him the fuck down.

Plus, even *he* questioned why he'd returned to the Motel 6. He really *didn't* need to give Turk the news in person that he'd put a stop to the knockoff weed. He was just impulsively driven, unable to get Turk out of his head, and that hadn't happened since Park had left him on R&R for three weeks, and he'd begun to suspect he was actually in love with the pilot. Lock had never been this obsessed with Ruby. She could come and go as she pleased and it barely affected him, part of the reason she eventually dumped him. "I'm not important in your life," she had said.

Now, having known Turk only a few days, and having fought with the guy way more than he'd loved, the biker from a rival club was already the most important thing in his life. How the fuck had that happened? When Turk kneeled and stripped off his cut, his plaid shirt, and bent to lick the diamond patterned shrap metal scar on his abdomen, a patch of sun fell on Turk's shoulder. Lock longed to touch his mouth to it. He knew it would feel like a sun-warmed piece of velvet. Turk had fine skin the tone of olives, not quite Turkish but maybe Spanish or Greek, and Lock's mouth watered to taste him.

But he couldn't even caress the ponytailed head, couldn't feel the strands of fine auburn hair slithering through his fingertips, couldn't direct the mouth where he most wanted it to go. He'd come just hours ago with Danielle, pretending she was Turk. Already his ball sac plumped with a fresh load of seed, filling and fattening his sac almost to the bursting point. When Turk mouthed his penis through the layer of jean material and exhaled hotly, the heat spread like an atom bomb directly to his erect nips, his throat, and the backs of his eyes which filled with tears. He was experiencing such bliss it was making him cry. *This* was where he was meant to be. *Jiminy Christmas*, his arms were bound and he had no way of casually wiping the damned tear away! And that was *not* just Turk's spit darkening his jeans where the cockhead bulged. Lock's prick was so ready to explode, a few drops of clear fluid had already spurted. And Turk hadn't even taken his dick out of his pants yet.

Lock still felt the need to protest. In a way, the idea that he was being innocently assaulted heightened the eroticism of the scene. Turk was definitely what he'd heard called a "power bottom," a man who lives to give pleasure to the other by being submissive, but a man so secure and confident in his own sexuality he actually wound up controlling his partner. Lock refused to be controlled. "I'm not a fucking fag," he tried to say again. But he was panting so rapidly it sounded like he'd just run a mile.

Turk glanced up at him, his eyes devilish, the long lashes

fluttering seductively. *Lord, this is one good-looking man. Even a man's man would fall for his beauty.* "I'll pretend to believe you're not a fucking fag, Mr. Singer." Lock gasped reflexively when Turk massaged his hard-on. Turk's long tapered fingers knew just where to push, squeeze and fondle. He was much more experienced than Lock, that was evident. With his looks, he'd probably had hookups with men in every fucking alley and porn theater in Arizona.

"You just want the best cocksucking of your life, that's all. Who wouldn't want that? Let's see here. Let's see exactly how it doesn't arouse you to be caressed by another man. My, what's this?" Standing to exhibit his own donkey's dick pulsing in his tight jeans, Turk took a few steps to a nightstand and grabbed something. Lock was so fixated on the long, thick length of meat displayed so arrogantly, he didn't notice what Turk had grabbed until the sexy, lanky budtender stood between Lock's outspread thighs and single-handedly whipped open his belt buckle.

Now Turk's eyes darkened like the sky right before a tornado. "You're a magnificent stud, Mr. Singer." One, two, three buttons popped open as if by magic, and Turk slid his hand over Lock's pubic mound, squeezing lovingly, rustling the crisp hairs beneath his palm. "You're more exquisite than a statue of David. You drive men wild with your taunting, your seduction. You show off your sculpted body, make men want to be fucked by you, screwed by you."

Turk's admiration pumped Lock's ego almost as much as his prick. Turk wrapped his fist around the root of his cock now, every squeeze wringing another few drops of jism that widened the dark stain on his jeans.

"You're a virile stud," Turk continued in his seductive, syrupy voice. He lifted Lock's giant dong into the air, and Lock nearly lost it when he swiped his thumb over the slippery slit. Lock gasped and bucked, gritted his teeth and snorted like a roped stallion. But Turk wasn't going to give him any such release. He brandished what looked like a feather duster in his other hand, and as he fell to his knees between Lock's thighs, he released the cock and just tickled it with the duster. Ever so slightly with just a whisper of the ostrich feathers, he tickled Lock's penis, laughing almost like a schoolboy when it jumped and twitched. "This is one delicious, beautiful horse cock."

"What are you doing?" Lock snarled. "Are you going to make me come or not?"

Turk replied leisurely. "Orgasm denial is one of my specialties."

The fucking bastard even leaned his face against Lock's thigh and watched with amusement as the wand bobbed and darted this way and that, touching his engorged, sensitive cock with the most feathery of touches. It was beyond embarrassing the way his stupid, purplish cock jumped and twitched at every slight whisper of the wand. A pearly bead of spunk glistened at the slit. Turk dipped his head ever-so-slightly, flicked that pearl from the cockhead with his tongue-tip, and Lock roared.

He could feel his eyeballs bulging in the sockets as he threw his head back and howled. It sounded unearthly, like it was coming from somewhere outside on the dusty highway. A lone wounded wolf bellow vibrated in the pit of his stomach, but it sounded like an enraged coyote out on some distant plateau. And when he opened his eyes, that bastard was *grinning*! Sure, Turk looked like some billion dollar billboard model any sane guy would give his right nut to fuck. But he was *grinning* as though it was some ultra-hilarious game he was playing.

Lock yelled, "What the fuck is the idea, Blackburn? Just take my dick in your mouth and *suck!* You fucking know how to do that—you've done it hundreds of times in fucking back alleys and truck stop bathrooms and filthy cubicles in gay bondage clubs and—"

There. That flash in Turk's eyes, that churning hurricane look in his eyes. Turk was all over his cock, sucking like the slut Lock knew he was. The hot, ravenous mouth was hoovering away like there was no tomorrow, the tongue squiggling big snake trails up and down the underside of his bulging dick.

Now the howl that seemed to emanate from Lock was one of purest ecstasy. Now he was freed from his sexual bonds, his cock allowed to rampantly take pleasure in the expert sucking of another man. He hadn't been sucked like this in years, and the semen surged like a waterfall up the length of his prick.

"Do it, you fucking slut!" he commanded. "You know you want a bellyful of hot male spunk—so *suck it! Oh God, yes!*"

Lock teetered on the edge of orgasm, this close to shooting his enormous, eager load. That's where Turk's sly, devious nature came back into play.

Turk backed off. He squeezed his fist around the base of the prick like a hot, fleshy cock ring. His talented thumb pressed the channel right under the glans, effectively stopping the flood, keeping Lock poised on the edge, on his tiptoes, his hips shuddering for release. Lock struggled so fiercely against his bonds the chair lifted off the floor. It was his only tiny sense of satisfaction to bang that chair on the shitty carpet like some crazed lion tamer, so he did it over and over, rat-tat-tatting like a machine gun.

"What the *fuck*, Blackburn? What do you want from me? What do you want me to fucking say? That I'm a flaming fucking homo? That I *want you*? I'll say anything you want. I'm a flaming fruit who wants another man's mouth around my junk. I fucking crave you like a heroin addict. I'm a fucking homo who wants your dick in my mouth as much as I want your— *Ah!*"

Something long, hard, and slick, something deviant Lock had been eternally craving probably since a fucking adolescent, slid up his rectum. His sphincter clamped down automatically around the slick tool, accepting it at the same time that he felt violated, raped by it. Turk wielded the instrument with precision, massaging the inside of his asshole, first sensuously, then savagely.

Lock found he enjoyed the brutal thrusts almost as much as the sensuous caresses. Turk alternated between loving and vicious. Lock calmed his bucking, not wanting Turk to accidentally injure him with the object he figured out was the handle of the feather duster. He found himself fascinated with the sight of the bare-chested beauty, the way his pecs rippled as he impaled Lock's most sensitive core with the expertise of a surgeon. Turk's upper lip would lift into a snarl when he invaded Lock rapaciously. Then his eyes would fill with affectionate tenderness, and he'd stroke Lock's gland with love.

Meanwhile, Lock's shiny, bursting cock pulsated against his belly. He felt imbued with machismo, being admired by such a smoking hot stud. Looking down, even he admired his own bullet-hard nipples, the luscious, rich, realistic owl tattoo that spread out fiercely over one pec. He had thought it symbolized his craving for freedom, and now for the first time it stood for his actual freedom. He was *living* freedom, acting on it, taking steps toward it.

He admired his own taut abs, the neat Brazilian wax of his pubes he'd maintained even after Ruby had left. He had other shrapnel scars, scars from fights that toughened him, made him his own man. He mentally challenged Turk to find a more carved, ripped bastard than him, and he knew his cock was longer and thicker than most, having spent hours—days, months—looking at delectable nude men on the net. He suddenly didn't care that being fucked up the ass was a passive gay thing to do. That yesterday it would've struck fear into his heart that another man was reaming him deliciously with a fucking inanimate object, while his own pounding hard-on remained securely snug inside his tantalizing 501s.

Lock was bared for all to see, almost buck fucking naked, the baldness and transparency of his craving just laid wide the fuck open. Turk now knew him more closely than anyone ever had, maybe even Park. Corporal Langham had never dared to tie up the bossy, controlling Dom, much less shove anything up his ass.

And Lock was loving it!

When it was Turk Blackburn wielding the tool, Lock hungered for more. Another round, one more scene, just one more spear and thrust.

Now Turk was saying something. Lock had to shake his head to get it on halfway straight and make out what his lover—*my lover!*—was saying.

"You like that? I can tell you like that. You like being fucked by this handle. You like being fucked by *anything*, don't you, because you're a twisted, bent motherfucker who likes it hard and rough and—"

"*Yes I like it!*" Lock roared. "I like being fucked by you, I like being sucked by you, so get down on your fucking knees, you fucking slave, and *do it!* Make me come with your mouth while you fuck me up the ass with that *thing*, and make sure you rub it against that sweet spot that's going to make me explode into your sucking—*Agh!*"

He'd finally gotten to Turk. Turk fell upon his groin, his broad shoulders lifting up the backs of Lock's thighs so the tips of his boots barely touched the carpet. He inhaled the entire length of Lock's dick like a manic beast while diddling the blunt end of the wooden handle directly against Lock's prostate.

Awareness of the room around him shut down, as though someone had decked him and he was blacking out.

All sensation gathered in his groin—unbearable, intense. Turk's gulping, swirling mouth was the center of his universe as Lock unloaded down his lover's throat. What felt like pints of cream shot from his dick, all sensation heightened by the devoted, earnest ministrations, and the sure coordination between Turk's mouth and hand.

Turk stroked Lock's asshole, coaxing out jets of spunk that Lock didn't know were possible. He was seeing stars against a black, satiny night now, and he heard himself sobbing, begging Turk to stop. Or was it to keep on? Either way, he was fucking *begging*, and Havelock Singer *did not beg*. Just as he didn't kneel— he *did not beg*.

He was crying some shit like, "Jesus H. Christ, you bastard, just finish me off! Oh, God! Oh, God! *Just do it*, you fucking slave!"

Lock was half-unconscious by the time Turk detached his mouth from his used, drained penis. He was like a beached dolphin just flopping around bonelessly on that fucking chair. His dizzy, dry eyes were looking at the ceiling, but he could *feel* Turk grinning like a fucking Cheshire cat. Turk's smug self-satisfaction just filled the room. Lock could picture the biker sitting back on his boots, balancing with one hand on the carpet while gazing upon his handiwork.

Yeah, you succeeded, bitch. You got me. Maybe I'm your slave now. Because I sure as fuck know I want me more of that. Again. And again.

Panting like a lathered racehorse, Lock finally dared to look at Turk. Turk was exactly as he'd imagined, his eyes roaming over Lock's body, assessing, as though seeing him clearly for the first time. From Turk's delighted smile, Lock reckoned he liked what he saw. He wasn't embarrassed to be in such a compromising position anymore.

"Beautiful," murmured Turk, gently squeezing Lock's pubic mound. "Just beautiful."

And for the first time in years, Lock really *felt* beautiful.

CHAPTER NINE
TURK

I just lived in the moment for about five minutes, soaking up the beauty of all I'd seen, felt, and tasted.

You know how various practices and religions instruct you to "live in the moment"? And you never fucking *do*? Your mind is always wandering, thinking about the next chaos and disaster looming around the next corner. Who you are is so shaped by past experience and future dread. Who the hell has time to "live in the moment"? Well, I was actually *doing* it.

Just drinking in the sensations, all five of them, really. The crinkle of his strip of pubic hair under my palm—yes, he was a real dishwater blond. The sight of his tight pec, his heartbeat tinkling the little barbell that pierced the pebble of his nipple. The musky scent of buckets of semen mingled with sweat just wafting from his crotch. The sound of his hoarse panting. And Great Caesar's Ghost, the tingling, slightly acidic sting of his spunk, still coating my tongue like a deranged person's.

He just looked at me, panting, licking his dry lips. His look was challenging, as though he was saying, "So what if I succumbed to you? Who the fuck *wouldn't?* It's no big fucking deal. You want to make a big fucking deal out of it?" But somehow, I knew it *was* a big fucking deal to Lock Singer.

Eventually I knew I had to unlock his cuffs. Lock had the

pen type of cuff key clipped to the pouch on his belt. Kneeling between his thighs and unlocking the cuffs was the first time I'd ever had my arms around his body. His cells seemed to cry out to me. Our pheromones were compatible, a perfect balance of good and bad, hot and cold, black and white. My body practically hummed with the buzz I received, my bare chest mashed against his. We literally had good chemistry. I slipped the key in the lock, but I wouldn't miss this opportunity to feel close to him.

I tilted my head so I faced him subserviently. "Master."

As predicted, his face suddenly went blank with shock. He looked so appealing, so naïve, so innocent of the cruising and rough trade I was used to. A flood of what seemed like love rushed through me so fast I had to act, or risk feeling it more intensely, so I kissed him.

He was rigid at first, but he soon plunged himself into the kiss. Our tongues lapped together. Lock could no longer pretend he was just being assaulted by some perverted horndog. He was giving himself fully to the kiss, and he didn't even stand to gain anything from it. He'd already orgasmed, deep inside my throat.

Yet here he was, stroking my tongue with his almost lovingly. I slowly unlocked his cuffs, knowing his arms would be sore from the uncustomary position. Plus, I wanted to keep nibbling at his lips, sucking the sweet Cupid's mouth between my teeth. He even tickled the backs of my incisors with his tongue tip, nipping back at me like a tired dog.

As I released him, I dropped the cuffs to the floor and massaged his arm as though wringing a wet shirt out. His satisfied moan vibrated deep inside my chest, resonating through to my solar plexus, my abdomen, my stiff, neglected cock.

But he soon yanked his arms away from me and broke the kiss. He rubbed his own arms now, and I sat back on my heels.

I said, "'If we could read our enemies' secret histories, we'd find sorrow and suffering enough to disarm all hostility.'"

Lock glanced at me skeptically. I didn't figure he was much of a literary guy. I was only literary due to the influence of Ford Illuminati, who read voraciously like a Promethean vulture. Over the years living with Ford, I'd just naturally picked up various books he'd left lying around. But Lock snorted. "Who the fuck said that?"

"Longfellow," I said, now sheepish. "It means you're not my enemy anymore."

He grinned adorably, still rubbing his bulging, muscular arms. "You've sucked my jizz down your hot throat. I'd say we're not enemies."

"At least we don't plan on killing each other anytime soon."

He looked at the nightstand when he said, "I like being called 'Master.'"

"Well, you *are* my Master, right? You've mastered my desire. I'll stay here another couple of days. Maybe we could do something discreet up at Lake Havasu. What do you do in your spare time up there?"

"Fish." It really struck me that he would fish. It made him more of a whole person in my eyes, less of a two-dimensional icon that I adored. I could see him fishing, I really could. I hadn't had much of a fishing upbringing—it was one of those unfamiliar things I admired in other people. Lock finally looked back at me askance, his gaze sweeping up and down my bare chest. "Not that there's ever any spare time. I'd like to see you get at least one of your nipples pierced."

That idea made my prick jump. The idea of Lock's eager eyes on me as some other man handled my nipple caused a surge of lust to sweep through my belly. But I had to go check on Twinkletoes, who had been mighty quiet the past half hour. Usually I could hear him chatting amiably with whoever happened to walk by out front. Although I hadn't been the one savagely used, I had to go piss out the beer I'd drank.

I came out of the bathroom intending to head to the front door and check my Prospect. But someone was already knocking.

Of course at first I assumed it was Twinkletoes. But the way Lock had backed up against the wall, his eyes round with fear, made me think twice.

His hand was slowly going for his Glock. Mine was in the nightstand drawer, so I headed there. Twinkletoes was arguing with someone outside.

"You can't interrupt him!" protested the loyal Prospect. "He's resting. And who the fuck are you?"

"I can interrupt whoever I damned well please," said the unknown redneck. I knew he was a redneck due to his country twang and, well, because I hated him. Anyone who would bust in on my romantic interlude was a fucking colossal asswad, and I slid back my action to chamber a round and aimed my barrel at the closed door. I had no compunction whatsoever about blasting whoever directly through the door. It wasn't like I hadn't done it before. "Come on out, you cocksucker!"

I frowned fiercely at Lock and whispered, "Do you know this guy?"

Lock was already replacing his piece in his waistband. "Yeah," he sighed, "unfortunately."

I wasn't quite as relaxed as my lover, and I did *not* replace my iron as Lock strode to the door. He swung it wide open and stood with hands on hips as though to block the beady-eyed shrimp trying to peer around his shoulders. The guy had an

Assassins cut on, so I knew he was no rival of Lock's.

"What do you want, Stumpy?" Lock asked. "Something that couldn't be said over the phone? Did you find out which bow bender jacked your H?"

Stumpy had the sparse, weedy facial hair of the guy who would never be mature enough to grow a proper beard. I hated him on sight, and kept my piece at my side. "Yeah, but that's nothing compared to what I just saw through these damned curtains."

"I'm sorry, boss!" Twinkletoes piped up from the back row. "I literally went to take a shit after eating all of that supreme burrito, and that must've been when this douchebag showed up!"

"You don't need to be so literal," I said, striding forward to back up Lock. I didn't blame Twinkletoes. I knew from untold hours sitting security on various other criminals that one couldn't constantly be on guard duty. Over Lock's shoulder I said, "Excuse me, who the fuck are you?" Stumpy had a sergeant-at-arms patch on, so it was pretty obvious, but I just didn't like being accosted on my own turf.

Lock turned and pushed his palm against my chest. He said in a low voice, "Just some job we were doing—I'd better go—"

Stumpy shoved into the room through the gap Lock had left vacant. Twinkletoes tried to shove in after him, but Stumpy slammed the door in his face. Normally I would have defended my Prospect, but I was getting a sneaking feeling Stumpy was going to say some shit I didn't necessarily want Twinkletoes to hear. Not that Twinkletoes was too ignorant to get what we'd been doing in the room, not at all. Just that the devoted Prospect would never be so rude as to bring it up, like this asshat was doing.

Stumpy poked Lock in the chest. That got my goat. I wanted to slam the runt, but so far, this was Lock's business, and he was letting the guy poke him. "I knew you were gay for this Boner but what I just saw and heard takes the fucking cake. I heard you shout out that you're a flaming fag who wants this guy's mouth around your junk. I heard every gross, disgusting word the two of you fairies exchanged. I heard you yell like you was at a rodeo that you're a fucking homo who wants this guy's boner in your mouth."

Lock and I were both frozen silent, both probably for different reasons. Yes, Lock *had* yelled that he wanted my hard dick in his mouth. I remembered that now. It had been a surprising admission but I'd glossed over it in the frenzy of the moment. *That's right, Lock did say that. That was abso-fucking-lutely delicious. I'll bet he's never had another dick in his mouth. And he wants mine.*

Stumpy raved on, slowly taking steps toward Lock, his chest about four inches from Lock's, backing him up into the dresser. "And my eyes can never unsee the putrid sight of this weirdo reaming you up the ass with some fucking feather duster. I got a fucking *picture* on my fucking *camera*, so don't you try to deny it."

Lock finally spoke when his butt came up against the piece of furniture. "You got a fucking twenty-pixel grainy-ass photo on a cheap cell that isn't even a smart phone, Stumpy. In other words, you got nothing." He held his hands up as though surrendering.

Even without a decent photo, we both knew we may as well be surrendering. Just the accusation of sodomy in the MC world was enough to at least have the participants removed from their clubs in good standing. That was a possibility within my club. I'd long been pondering it. Ford was The Bare Bones' president. He'd joked with me several times on a light level about the possibility I might be bi, or something. Of the others, it was hard to tell in general on which side of the issue a guy might come down on. Russ Gollywow, for instance, had just shocked the hell out of me by making a sort of racist black joke. And he even *sang* in a Philly Soul sort of group in his spare time, wearing a sparkly suit, snapping his fingers and stepping in tune with other guys. You just never knew.

But it was pretty obvious where the Assassins of Youth landed on this subject. Stumpy was broadcasting that loud and far. He would burn off Lock's back pack personally with a blowtorch. And from the looks of that Papa Ewey Prez and his hulking Veep, Tim Breakiron, they would sit back and sell tickets.

Stumpy didn't back down an inch. "Whose word they gonna take, Singer, mine or yours? The word of a guy who's got gay porn in his browser history, or the word of an old school dyed-in-the-wool member with so many Filthy Few patches I could make a chess board?"

With his jaw grimly set, Lock was at least attempting to push back. "What fucking gay porn on what fucking browser?" I could tell by his expression and stance, though, that he was guilty as charged. As a guy with so many daddy Dom and Kinbaku rope torture videos I had crashed about twenty computers in a row, I knew that look.

Stumpy poked him again. "Seely Buxton told me you were looking at fags humping on your cell phone when you were sitting surveillance on some fugitive in Yuma."

Lock sneered. "You sure are interested in all of this 'gay' stuff, for a guy who pretends that he isn't."

Stumpy stepped so close he practically bumped chests with Lock. "You want me to bring it to the table, gay boy? You want me to put it up for a vote? You want everyone in the club knowing what a dickie licker you are? Never riding with your brothers again will be the *least* of your fucking concerns, you fucking queen."

I was about to butt in and inform Stumpy that a queen was a transvestite who liked to wear women's clothing, but of course that would have only confirmed Stumpy's suspicions. How else could I possibly have known that, unless I was one, too? This was Lock's battle, and I wisely remained mum.

Lock said, "Of course I don't want you flinging your slander all over *my* club."

"So you fucking *admit* it?"

"Of course I don't fucking admit it, you nozzle! I was just here telling Turk that you agreed to stop selling your crappy rubbery schwag weed using his strain name. You're lucky he doesn't give you a beatdown for smearing the good name of his pot all over the southwest!"

Lock glared self-righteously at me. It seemed as though the same thought was occurring to us at the same time. We could easily pop off this Assasshole and dispose of the body using Lock's cage. The hotel was on a busy street and there was a chance no one would hear the gun's report. From the fucktard's demeanor, it didn't seem like anyone would miss him much. The club could always find a new sergeant-at-arms. And I was still gripping my iron.

But eventually I suppose we decided not to. That was a fateful decision that led us down a winding, tortuous pathway from which there was no return. Looking back, I don't know if things couldn't have happened any other way. Without Stumpy's threats, I probably would have sucked Lock's dick a few more times, maybe even let him fuck me, but we would've parted ways sooner or later. I had to get back to my dispensary and club, and he had to find his child molester. I might've already been in love with Lock, but since when do you get to be with everyone you're in love with?

Not very fucking often.

I'm not at all religious—that was another class that was never in Cropper Illuminati's color wheel—but being allowed to be with the one you love is a blessing, a privilege, not a natural right. Especially when you're a man who has to sneak around and keep your true self under the wraps of night, it's not a right by any stretch of the imagination. I was seeing my chances of being with Lock dwindle before my very eyes, and I had every reason to want to hit this sergeant-at-arms. I'd put down less rabid dogs in my time, and for way less reason. But something in Lock's demeanor made me hesitate—and you know what they say about hesitation.

I was lost.

Stumpy pointed at me. "Not only is he not going to give me a beatdown"—he sneered at me—"as if he *could* give me a beatdown, I'm going to give you rear gunners the chance to make this right. I promise not to use my photo and everything I can never unsee to out you to the club."

Lock put his hands on his hips. "In exchange for?" We had to be careful where we landed on this. We were admitting nothing, yet we were going along with his game. Someone with nothing to admit wouldn't even want to hear any asinine plan.

Stumpy knew this, and he chuckled with glee. You could tell he rarely ever genuinely laughed, the way his face crinkled like a gift-wrapped box. He was one of those gritty, old school bikers who live the hard life because it's all they know. I guess all of us Boners were that way, too, but Stumpy probably had never had any other options, like most of us had. It was a choice, with us. Ford had been a SEAL, just as Lock had been in the Air Force. Going back to the biker life wasn't our only option.

"All right. As you guessed, I figured out who the blanket-ass is who stole our H. He's one of the morons I got hooked on the stuff and he can never make it until his subsistence check arrives to get more. My problem is, I have no proof. I'd have to have some iron-clad proof to bring news like this to the table."

Lock and I looked quizzically at each other. *Why? Why would he need iron-clad proof? Since when did an outlaw MC require proof beyond the shadow of a doubt before taking out some featherhead?* The answer was *never*. I knew right then and there that Stumpy had stolen this heroin in question himself, and was trying to frame a Native American. Then again, *we* had no proof Stumpy had stolen any H. We kept our mouths shut.

Stumpy continued, "I was able to buy back a little bit of the same batch just in case Carmine's men want to test it, to make sure it's the same stuff before punishing the dirt worshipper."

Lock nodded, his arms folded tightly. "What do you want me to do about it?"

"I want you to get inside the Rez and plant it on the guy. I want to stay out of it. This way I've got plausible deniability, an alibi. I'll be up at our clubhouse in Bullhead when you make the call and get all the glory for finding the guy."

Again, Lock and I shared skeptical looks. Why else would Stumpy be giving Lock the credit for the collar unless the Injun was innocent and Stumpy was guilty? Still, we knew the alternative. Us being stripped naked, tarred, feathered, and lynched from the highest branch of an ancient saguaro. So we listened.

"All right," said Lock. "No problem. The Colorado River Rez, right out here? I've been in there plenty of times. Just tell me who the guy is and where to find him. I'll plant it somewhere in his sorry little shack. Who'll make the discovery? Look pretty shady if I do the planting and the discovering."

"You let me worry about that. You just let me know when

the stuff is hidden. And take this gay boy Veep with you. You can get some more cocksucking in that way, and it gives me one more impartial witness to the guy's guilt." No one said anything, so Stumpy said, "All right?"

"All right," Lock said reluctantly. They both looked at me.

"All right." I actually *was* looking forward to more cocksucking opportunities. I honestly didn't care too much that we were framing a possibly innocent man. It was a dog eat dog world we ran in, and such things were par for the course.

"Okay," said Stumpy. He withdrew a plastic package from his cut's pocket and handed it to Lock. "Here. The guy's name is Kwahu Johnson, some Hopi or Navajo blanket-ass—I can never tell them apart. Go south on Mohave Road until you hit Poston."

"I know Poston," said Lock.

"He's at 1399 Poston Road, near the aqueduct. If you go to that giant dick-shaped war memorial, you've gone too far." Stumpy sure was obsessed with dicks. "If he's in the house, lure him out with some molly or party favors. Blanket-asses love that stuff. Here's some MDMA."

Lock nodded, took the tiny dime bag, and glanced at his cell. "Good enough. It's two now, so we can head on down there pronto."

Stumpy was walking to the door. "Give me a good head start, about four hours, to get to the clubhouse. That'll give you time for some more rimming and fisting."

Lock and I rolled our eyes at each other as Stumpy opened the door. Twinkletoes was standing right there, angrier than I'd ever seen him. His eyes bulged even more than normal, his weak little hands clenched into fists. He barreled right into Stumpy in his efforts to get inside my room, and this time, Stumpy let him.

But the sergeant-at-arms, standing outside the room, had to shout a last caveat. "Leave the nerdy Prospect here. I don't want any more potential witnesses to our mission."

Twinkletoes slammed the door on him. He was practically teary-eyed with rage. "What an asshole."

I replaced my piece in the waist of my jeans and asked him, "Did you hear?"

"Every word."

"I want you to do something. Put a tracker on my scoot."

"You got it." Twinkletoes went to the window and peered out to see if Stumpy had gone. All Twinkletoes' cyber equipment was in his room next door.

Lock asked, "You've got GPS trackers? That's supposed to be my game."

"Yeah. It's a hobby of Twinkletoes', and it does come in handy on some runs."

Lock sighed deeply and took me by the upper arms. "I'm fucking sorry about this, Turk. This was none of your beef and you got roped into it because you were with me."

"Hey. You wouldn't even *have* a beef if you hadn't of been—"

Lock quickly said, "Yeah, I know," and withdrew his hands from my arms. He didn't want Twinkletoes to hear anything untoward—even though the Prospect already had. "Still, this beef with that dickwad has been a long time coming. He hates pretty much everyone aside from Papa Ewey and Breakiron, and of course he's got his nose glued to their assholes. He's hated me since Breakiron sponsored me as a Prospect. It's like he's jealous—like everyone else is rivals for his daddy's love or something. Anyway, just a numb nuts theory."

"It's not numb nuts. I like how psychological you are."

Lock grinned. "Yeah, it's Psych 101. He's also obviously a classic case of antisocial personality disorder. Hey, I was in the Air Force. I've had psych debriefing. Anyway, let's go grab a bite. *With* Twinkletoes. We don't need to give that motherfucker a four hour head start. One is fine. People can do the math, figure he wasn't involved."

"He's gone," declared Twinkletoes, cheering up as he headed for the door.

I headed there too, grabbing my plaid shirt from a chair. But Lock held me back as my Prospect disappeared out the door. He held me from behind, my bare back pressed to his chest, and he bit my earlobe as his hands ran up my abdomen.

"I want to see these delicious nips pierced. Pierced with a lock. Lock's not just my name. It's for the lock I've got on you, and I'm the only one with the key."

The shiver that raced down my spine was beyond belief when he actually tweaked both my stiff nipples. We were standing right in the fucking doorway where anyone going down the highway could feasibly have seen us, which sort of added to the thrill. I've always been something of an exhibitionist, thus the dangerous interludes in truck stop restrooms. The idea that Lock already wanted to claim me, to brand me, had my cock plumping with arousal before he even slid one hand across my crotch to grab a handful of it. I gasped as a tiny jet of precome spurted from the tip of my penis.

He held me so tight his arms trembled. He thrust his erection against the cleft of my ass and whispered in my ear. "I'm going to fucking take you, slave. I'm going to fuck you until jizz pours from your eyeballs. I'm going to grease your cock and jack you until you shoot on the fucking ceiling. You're a delicious stud, Turk. I don't want anyone else touching you."

He tweaked my nipple, slapped my ass, and I was stumbling out the door with an enormous erection for the entire world to see.

CHAPTER TEN

LOCK

It didn't start out being the fucking worst thing that'd ever happened to Lock.

There could be worse things, he was thinking as he blazed down the highway toward Poston. He'd been hit by several IEDs in his time in Iraq. That was way fucking worse. He'd had shrapmetal that had gone into his stomach work its way out his wrist years later. He'd seen a guy recovering chemical munitions drooling, puking, and shitting due to exposure to sarin gas that his own country had secretly placed in the eighties. He himself had hit a woman with an automatic grenade launcher because the big bag she carried looked suspicious. It turned out to contain groceries. He had dropped weapons on unarmed bodies to make it look like self-defense—as instructed by his superiors.

So running down to Poston to place a few ten sacks behind some Hopi's—or Navajo's—eighteen inch television set with rabbit ears was no big deal. He'd just slap it into the toaster oven, leave, and call Stumpy to tell him it was done. In the meantime, he got to ride behind the juiciest piece of ass he'd seen since he'd sobbed over a few pieces of Corporal Park Langham's body in Diyala Province. He had not even recovered Park's dog tags and had wandered for a couple of days aimlessly, dazed, as though his brain was bruised—which he later found out was true. Now he finally had something more cheerful and uplifting to think about. He wouldn't even let the fact that he was stuck riding Twinkletoes' white Dyna get him down. Twinkletoes even had a "gremlin bell" on his handlebars, and Lock pretended to believe it warded off evil road spirits.

Simply put, Turk Blackburn was the most banging hot piece of ass he'd enjoyed in years. Turk was—what had those Twinks in The Racquet Club said to him?—a delicious piece of meat who was giving him life. Turk was *everything*. Lock was only sad this run wouldn't take longer, actually. It was only a twenty minute shot down to Poston, cleaving the litter-fringed highway without much to look at other than sorry shacks, emerald squares of alfalfa, flax, and a few trading posts. Just thinking about the cocksucking Turk had laid on him was making his prick expand as he rode. Turk's skill with that improvised implement of pleasure was enough to get him off within seconds, and it was a good thing he'd used his fingers as a cock ring to prevent an untimely explosion.

Lock had never been drilled up the ass like that. Although he'd done it, what seemed like hundreds of times to his former lover, it was a whole different scene having it done to him. The thrill was so intense it seemed to clutch at every innard he possessed, wrenching his stomach, lungs, heart. He'd never allowed himself to be violated like that before, but being handcuffed like that seemed to eliminate all the guilt from it. He was cuffed, so what the fuck else could he do but submit to the well-oiled manipulations of the experienced slave?

Mortified at first that he'd shouted something about wanting Turk's dick in his mouth. Not that he'd ever *do* it—that was far too subservient for his macho tastes—but fantasizing about it wasn't as gross as he'd imagined. It reminded him that he'd even dreamed of sucking Park's dick a few times. He'd always been relieved he'd never told Park any of this, but now, for the first time, Lock sort of regretted it. He was in a barrier-smashing mood this week, hooking up with the lean, ponytailed Veep of The Bare Bones. Turk called him "Master," and he felt like Master of the Sonoran Desert as he blazed past the shoddy warehouses and water towers.

Maybe we could go fishing. Nobody would see them if they took his boat and motored into some of the coves on Lake Havasu. Suddenly the idea of fishing with the exotically beautiful biker meant the whole world to Lock. It meant normalcy, a ritual that gave at least the illusion of stability, permanence, security. He'd never known he craved these things before. Maybe he was getting old too fast. It hadn't bothered him much when his only security symbol, Ruby, had walked out on him. Why was the idea of cooking in his kitchen with Turk suddenly tantalizing him at the back of his brain?

He knew a good tattoo artist in town, a guy the club often used, who could pierce Turk's sweet nipples. Lock longed to nibble and tongue the delicious nips, just as Turk had done to him. He realized that getting pierced was a lot to ask of a guy he'd only just met, but somehow with Turk it felt right. He even entertained the idea of getting similar tattoos—where no one could see them, of course. Motorcycle clubs were a primal form of alliance, Lock knew. That's why their colors—their symbols and rituals—were so important. The Assassins' colors were a big "fuck you," emphasizing their separation from the rest of society, an influential and exclusive macho club. Their colors set them apart from every civilian on the street. Tattoos could do that for Turk and Lock, because they couldn't let anyone else know who they really were.

The turnoff on Poston Road was marked by an adobe-styled gas station, so Lock took the white scoot around Turk's flank and signaled for him to head toward the aqueduct. They rode slower here. A few alfalfa fields later, and Lock began to get a bad feeling. *What the fuck?* The only buildings out here were the remains of some World War Two barracks where thousands of Japanese had been interned. Lock had been through Poston enough times to have read the memorial markers. He knew these barracks had been built over the objection of the natives, who didn't want a hand in doing to others what had been done to them. They had helped build the dick-shaped Japanese internment war memorial that Stumpy was so obsessed by.

They rode to the end of the street. Nothing.

"What the fuck?" yelled Turk, echoing Lock's sentiments. They were incognito so they'd removed their cuts. Turk had zipped up a plain black hoodie he'd purchased at Walmart, but he looked just as fine and dangerous as always.

Lock shouted back, "All I can figure is he's somewhere in those old barracks. Let's go back."

Hanging a left into the barracks compound, Lock felt like he was on an abandoned movie set. He passed row after row of dilapidated barracks, some with caved-in roofs, some with no roofs at all. Twenty thousand people had lived here at the camp's peak, in three camps the Japanese named Roastem, Toastem, and Dustin. Now, of course, Lock was amazed to see people at all. A few old timers, women and children stared expressionless at the bikers. *How the fuck do they live out here?* Lock had a partial answer when he saw a few more able-bodied men listlessly moving around bales of alfalfa they had stashed in a barracks.

Lock parked his ride and waited for Turk to do the same. Putting his brain bucket on his seat, Lock slowly lifted an arm in greeting to the Hopi warehousemen. They were definitely Hopi,

Lock knew from having lived nearby for so long. Hopi had thinner, more cynical lips that made them look skeptical of everything. Men were more likely than women to speak English, and the younger, the better. These guys must've been in their thirties. Lock wasn't too sure about being able to entice them with "party favors," though. They looked pretty agricultural—total countrymen. Ironically, Lock and the two farmers wore identical black bandannas round their skulls.

"Good afternoon," said Lock with what he hoped was a friendly tone. "I was looking for a friend of mine, was wondering if you knew a Kwahu Johnson."

Turk came up behind Lock. "We came from Los Angeles to see him."

The farmers looked at each other. One finally said, "Kwahu went to Phoenix for a couple days."

"Yes," agreed the other. "To protest the name of the Washington Redskins at a football game."

Lock frowned. "At the draft rounds at the university stadium? The last round was yesterday."

"Then he should be returning soon."

"That is not our mascot," intoned one of the farmers.

"Oh, I couldn't fucking agree more," said Turk amiably. "The team owner says it honors Native Americans. He's never going to change it."

A farmer spat air onto the ground. "Bullshit."

"Total bullshit," agreed Turk.

Lock ventured, "Where does he live? We could leave a note on the door."

"He doesn't really have a door," said one Hopi, but the other lifted an arm to indicate they should follow him.

They went around the back side of the decrepit barracks. Clotheslines were strung over rock kilns that spewed smoke.

Goats, chickens, and pigs roamed seemingly freely, and children played with lousy toys that looked worse than the secondhand toy bin at the Goodwill. Lock noted kids finding amusement with a chewed rawhide dog bone, a frayed and stained Pound Puppy, a Parcheesi game board, and a bendable policeman with wire poking from its joints. It was the most depressing thing ever, and Lock shared a glance with Turk. *Let's do this and get the fuck out of here.*

Turk said, "I didn't have the most prosperous upbringing living in The Bare Bones clubhouse, but it was a damn sight less dismal than this." A toddler held up a plastic baggie that looked to contain a Whitney Houston cassette tape and a lone Blizzard Blue crayon. Turk pretended to admire it. "Ah, very nice."

Lock asked, "Why'd you grow up with the Illuminatis?"

Turk's barely noticeable pause instantly made Lock sorry he'd asked. "My parents were killed in a car crash."

"Oh," Lock whispered weakly. "Fuck me. I'm sorry. Both in the same crash? I can't think of anything fucking worse."

"Yes, both together." Turk sighed. "It wasn't like we were so much better off than the Illuminatis to begin with, though, before Cropper started all of his businesses. But these children make us look like the fucking Cosby kids."

"Drunk driver?" Lock ventured. It was always a drunk driver.

"No," was all Turk would say.

It was like an entire self-contained post-apocalyptic town back there, with women hauling jerricans of water, slapping corn tortillas around on filthy surfaces, and even making wind chimes out of empty cans, as if they somehow managed to wring a shred of enjoyment out of that place. Lock half expected a few slow zombies to come crashing through the ruined stucco walls, and he was relieved when the farmer led them under the shade of one of the barracks.

But here, people had made walls from boxes of old library books. The walls separated them from their neighbors, Lock supposed, and the farmer led them to the cubicle of Kwahu Johnson.

"Great Caesar's Ghost," whispered Turk. "Everyone can see everyone."

The farmer gestured at what looked like a dollhouse setup with table, chairs, couch. Items of furniture that would have filled a normal house looked like a stage set here because the walls didn't go all the way to the ceiling. Apparently Kwahu's prized possession was an old spray painted sign that said COLORADO RIVER INDIAN TRIBES LIBRARY MUSEUM ARTS & CRAFTS. The Indians had started out protesting the internment of Japanese here, but now they were living in the ramshackle shadows of those prisoners.

"Have at it," said the farmer, and started to walk away.

Lock couldn't fucking stop himself. It may have seemed patronizing, but he couldn't stop his hand from going to his wallet and handing the guy a Benjamin. "Thanks for all your help," he said sincerely, feeling uncomfortable as hell.

"Fucking glad we didn't wear our colors," Turk muttered. "I'll pretend to write him a note. You hide the stuff."

The guy did, indeed, have a toaster oven plugged into a dangerous Medusa snake of an extension cord. Lock threw the heroin in there and slammed the door shut as Turk wrote on a paper towel, this time with an Electric Lime crayon that didn't show up too well. It didn't matter, since they weren't writing a real note. Turk left his shopping list or whatever on the Formica table and they did the James Brown out of there. Lock couldn't wait to put the whole creepy thing behind him. He even planned to invite Turk and his Prospect to spend the night at his Rough and Ready house. He had a guest room Ruby had set up for her niece. Twinkletoes could stay there. It would be nice to sleep in his own bed again.

But instead of going back to their rides, Lock grabbed a handful of Turk's sleeve. "I've got to call Stumpy before we split, let him know it's done."

So they headed toward a building stenciled as having been a GYMNASIUM, heading out of the worst of the doomsday scene and into something resembling a place they might have played as kids. Here, squares of sunlight through wooden windowpanes warmed up dusty wooden floors, and they found a small uninhabited room that might've been the coach's. A metal desk was covered with an inch of dust but had been otherwise undisturbed for years, if not decades. It had a stillness and a sense of security that pleased Lock, reminded him of his high school in Brentwood, Los Angeles.

Lock said, "That fucking Sonoran cartel is just using these poor bastards as mules. I know, my club's doing it too. And we're giving them an income they wouldn't normally have. They have a long history of moving contraband like guns, prescription drugs, and cigarettes up and down these waterways."

"But does it look like Kwahu Johnson's doing well by *any* standards?" Turk asked.

"Good fucking point. What the hell is Stumpy paying that poor bastard, fifteen cents an hour? No wonder he stole some H."

"If he even did it."

"If he even did it," Lock echoed, just as Stumpy answered his phone.

"Hello?"

"It's done," Lock said simply.

"Okay. Where'd you hide it?"

"In the toaster oven."

"Stay put. I'm gonna send some guys around to tell you the next stage of the plan."

Lock's heart sank. "Wait. There's another stage to this fucked-up plan?"

"Right. I didn't want to tell you before or you might not have wanted to do it."

"Well, damn *right* I might not have wanted to do it, Stumpy! That's usually why you tell someone the entire fucking plan! I was kind of hoping to finally hit my own fucking sheets for the first time in a blue moon."

"With your boyfriend," Stumpy said, reminding Lock of the hold he had over them. "Are you gonna stay put, or what?"

"Do I have a fucking choice? What am I waiting for?"

"Bald black guy named Roland. Don't worry, you'll be heading back up toward Lake Havasu. Might even be home in time for a midnight delight." *Click.*

"Fuck this," Lock fumed, angrily shoving the phone in his back jeans pocket. "We're supposed to wait for a bald black guy now, Turk."

Turk snorted. "Like *he* won't stand out in this environment?"

Their disgusted expression evaporated when they realized they might have a few minutes. Together. Alone. The same new sly expression spread over Turk's painfully handsome face, telling Lock they were both thinking the same thing.

It was idiotic to do it again in public. They had just had their entire world dangled over a cliff just because some moron had seen them kissing. But Lock couldn't stop. He was about to do it again, because Turk was *that* good. *That* delicious. Lock approached his lover and took a handful of his well-marbled butt. Touching the tip of his nose to Turk's, he said in a low and salacious tone, "Tell me, slave. Was Dayton Navarro your first real lover?"

"No," whispered Turk. Lock tickled Turk's bottom lip with his tongue-tip, and Turk sucked on it. Licked it back. "I did a year in Kingman on a weapons charge when I was twenty. I had a daddy there to protect me. We all did. You had to."

For some reason this aroused Lock even more. He swiveled his burgeoning erection against Turk's, and a thrill went from his balls up his front, stiffening his nipples until they stood out sharply against his thin T-shirt. When he rubbed his nipples against Turk's chest, gooseflesh rose on the globes of his ass. His testicles drew up hard and tight next to his body like bowling balls. He was so horny he was light-headed. As much as he wanted to hear sordid details about the state prison near Kingman, Lock had to say, "But he was just your daddy Dom, right? I meant *real* lover. Someone you were in love with." That was at the root of his question. He wanted to know how often, and how easily, Turk fell in love with another man.

It was sheer luck that the prison story *was* a story of love. "Fender *was* the love of my life, Lock. At first, of course not. At first it was just survival to have this giant hulking white power guy protecting me. But the longer he humped me, the closer to him I became." Lifting the bottom hem of Lock's shirt, Turk slid a hot hand up his smooth abdomen. He made burning concentric circles with that talented thumb. He only had to barely touch the barbell piercing with his fingertips to have Lock's now ramrod-stiff dick twitching inside his jeans.

Lock tried to regulate the trembling in his voice. He bit Turk's lower lip and murmured, "Did it turn you on, being fucked by a big snarling brute?"

"Yes," Turk said, with passion. "Fender became quite talented through repetition and he began to pleasure me too. He didn't want to just fuck me all the time. He started to really develop feelings for me. I know he was just a shallow, racist, violent motherfucker, and no one would believe me if I said he could be quite tender. He loved to kiss my entire body, suck on every inch of me."

Lock diddled with Turk's nipples, too. He loved to hear the hitch in Turk's voice when he thumbed him just right. He dared to slide one hand down Turk's rippled abdomen, under the massive, chunky Bare Bones belt buckle, and tentatively weave his fingers into the moist, humid bush surrounding the rigid base of his cock. *This cock*. Lock had seen it only in the bulging, impressive outline it had worn in the denim fabric of Turk's jeans. Was it gay to want to touch it? Suddenly he didn't care. "Did he suck your dick?"

He licked at Turk's mischievous smile. "He did. Of course he pretended to be straight on the outside. He had an old lady waiting for him, kids, all that. But he was a prison wolf, and his favorite thing was to suck and lick my cock. I was just a punk at first, and he raped me heartlessly for the first couple months. It was a violent thing, not sexual. But it turned sexual."

The vision of Turk on his back being pounded by some bruiser with a shuddering ass who just wanted to get his rocks off quickened Lock's pulse. He wanted to *be* that bruiser, minus the racist part of course, and probably minus most of the racist ink. Turk was a delectable morsel, a treat for all of the senses, any man's wet dream. There wasn't much room in Turk's sultry, tight jeans, but Lock managed to wrap his fist around most of the fat, beefy dick and squeeze. It was juicy, and steamy, and made his mouth water to grasp it like that. He urged Turk on with his story because he knew he wouldn't last long. "But you came to love it, to love him."

"Right. I guess because he was my protector, the Stockholm Syndrome or something, but I soon came to genuinely care about him. He was a pit stop mechanic for Indy race car drivers."

Lock didn't care about any of that shit. Already he had his

cuffs in one hand, flipping them open with a snap of the wrist. "And you loved his cocksucking."

"And I loved his cocksucking."

"Just as you loved sucking his cock."

"Yes, I loved sucking his big, veiny, grey-haired—"

That was it. Lock clicked the cuff around one of Turk's wrists and shoved him into a metal, upholstered chair. The dusty seat created a mushroom cloud of tiny, sparkling dust motes. Turk was living in a Disneyland of fairy dust as Lock leaned over him, yanked his arms behind his back, and secure him to the chair.

In the twinkling of an eye, Lock's belt popped undone. His cock was like a deviant satyr's erection, so full and hard it seemed to have grown to unheard-of proportions. Angry and scarlet, it jutted forth in his fist, aimed directly at Turk's luscious mouth.

"Take my dick, baby," he commanded. He shoved it so deeply down Turk's throat he probably hurt him. "Pretend I'm that veiny, horny old man if you want. Just eat all of me. Swallow every drop of my jizz until you fucking choke on it, slave."

Lock had come home. With his hard-on seated deep down the windpipe of a handcuffed man who lived to suck cock, he had truly come home.

He was never giving this up. Never.

CHAPTER ELEVEN
TURK

My Master was fucking my mouth.
    I had never been luckier in my life.

I mean, Lock was *going* for it, balls-to-the-wall, just going all out. His defenses were mostly down. He'd tossed aside any aversion to me, any fear that gayness would rot him from the inside out.

He was still the dominant top in control, of course. He'd seen to that when he'd cuffed me, when he'd plunged his throbbing penis into my mouth. He was humping me like there was no tomorrow, swiveling his hips like he was grabbing a wham, bam, thank you ma'am with a sweetbutt, jabbing his cock in and out of my hungry mouth.

Only, I got to taste his prick. I got to lave the juicy length of it with my tongue, got to suck, lick, gnaw, and chew. I sounded like a pig at the trough giving him that head job. And his bent language only enhanced my arousal.

"That's right baby, take my dick in your mouth. Take all of it. You know you want it. You know you live to eat dick. I'm hung like a bull and you're a cum slut for it. I'm everything to you."

How did he know that? He already *was* everything to me. He had just been turned on by my telling of the Fender story.

My talk about sucking the hulking older man's cock had stimulated him so heavily, he had even stuck his hand down my jeans and grabbed my hard-on. That was a new, bold thing for him to do, to display that he was an active participant in a homosexual union, not just some guy who happened to like blowjobs like ninety-nine percent of all men. Possibly it even aroused him to imagine Fender sucking on my young, fat dick. I could imagine, couldn't I? No, his actions told that he was turned on by *me*, that he craved *my* cock too, and I sucked him with gusto.

He pulled it out a few times to hump my face, to slap his ball sac against my chin. Inhaling the bulbous sac, I snarled and worried it like a dog with a rag. Up and down my head bounced, like one of those cheerful smiling bobbleheads, eagerly mouthing the full sac. He parted his thighs as far as he could with his pants round his knees. Holding his sac up with one hand, he allowed me access to his sweet, sensitive perineum. I smashed my face against his crotch, my tongue darting out to bathe the slick mound of flesh with expert precision.

"Jesus Christ," he murmured, "you're good. Do it, Turk. That's it. That's perfect. Lick my asshole. Suck my asshole. Tongue-fuck me."

I needed no encouragement to tickle his beautiful hole with my tongue. Instantly he groaned like a dying beast, and I could tell by the slapping of his testicles against the side of my face that he was jacking himself while I rimmed him. I bit his ass cheeks as I skimmed my tongue around his hole, and I did as he instructed, tongue-fucking his hole. It turned me on that it turned him on, and not being able to touch him was driving me over the edge of the fucking abyss. Did he know he was inadvertently practicing orgasm denial on *me*?

His grunts now became less intelligible. He was a primal

caveman of a beast now, stroking himself off while I blew his ass. I felt the balls smacking my cheek grow higher and harder, his grunts coming closer together as his pumping became more furious. I only wished the coach had thought to install a mirror in his office. Maybe it was my overactive imagination, but I thought I could hear his jet of jizz striking the wall, and his asshole contracted with sheer ecstasy as he shot.

I pleasured him with my tongue while he continued jerking himself. I knew the point at which bliss would shift to pain, so I slowed my tonguing, retreated to slipping my tongue over the ridge of his perineum. He shuddered, and the insides of his thighs trembled with exhaustion and delight. When I slurped a ball into my hungry mouth, he groaned like a bear and catapulted himself off me.

"*Damn!*" he roared. Normally I would've laughed at the silly way he staggered back, his hand blindly reaching out for a surface to prop himself on, pants down, the silken knob of his aroused penis shiny like a doorknob. But this was some serious business. I lived to pleasure Lock Singer. "Jiminy Christmas! That was some fucking rim job! *Jay-sus!* I think I'm still coming."

I tried to wipe my mouth off on my collarbone. "I think you still are, too."

He had fallen back into a bookshelf. Dust from the tops of encyclopedias or wrestling textbooks showered his shoulders, and he had this utter look of disbelief that melted my heart. He slapped his own chest. "Fuck me dry, Blackburn. You are...you are...*fuck!* I can't even think of the words."

"The most amazing piece of ass on the entire face of the fucking planet? Even more awesome than an extraterrestrial thetan? Better than a sex cake or a hallelujah or a chick who says yes too soon?"

Lock laughed, openmouthed. "I was gonna say 'better than having a boyfriend.' But yeah, I'll take those other things, too."

"Except maybe the girl."

"Yeah," he agreed amiably. "Forget the girl."

Maybe remembering how he'd been abandoned handcuffed in The Racquet Club, he seemed to gather himself up. Springing off the bookshelf with his dick still bobbing out at half-mast, he came to me, straddling my thighs, sitting himself lightly onto my lap, ass planted on my bulging erection. His eyes glittered as though struck with a handful of stars. It was as though joy spilled over him and he was unable to contain it all. Like I had done with him, he took his sweet time unlocking the cuffs. He touched his nose to mine. "You're some kind of a fucking power bottom. You know exactly how to get me off. I don't think I want to let go of you."

"Then don't," I suggested. "Am I really better than having a boyfriend?"

"No," he said lazily against my mouth. "I think you're *exactly* as good as a boyfriend."

Hope and glory surged through me to hear this. It was his roundabout, indirect way of saying that I *was* his boyfriend, and I think he might've even kissed my ass mouth then, had not some fucking imbecilic stooge of a toolbag come crashing through the coach's door.

He was Roland, the bald black guy we'd been told to expect, only he had two losers flanking him like blinged-out zombie pets carrying assault rifles. These were hyenas, young men with no commonsense, paid by the cartels to hunt people down and murder you in cold blood while laughing. Roland himself was so badass he didn't need to heft a weapon to scare the living shit out of us. He was slick, with a black T topped by a raw silk jacket that had probably been custom-tailored to fit his Vshaped bulk. The diamond stud in his earlobe was probably a billion karats. Lock sprang to his feet like he wore ejector boots and in one fluid movement had grabbed his Glock that he'd placed on a desk. He held it aggressively with two hands in the Isosceles stance, unsure who to point it at—or why.

Luckily, he'd finally turned the cuff key far enough for me to unleash my aching arms, but I was a bit slower on the uptake to draw my own piece from my waistband. Without getting up, I aimed the barrel straight at the bruiser's shiny knob, so now we were evenly matched. But the guy was laughing, that sort of evil chortle I thought only moustache-twirling cartoon characters did, nodding in acknowledgement of Lock's now limp dick.

"I see," Roland said richly, as though set to narrate a credit card commercial. "Stumpy was right. You two douches *are* cornholing each other. My, my." Slowly he began unbuckling his own belt, and sudden dread and doom sank its tentacles into my bowels. *Great Caesar's Ghost!* Why the fuck did everyone assume that gays were deviant, adored punishment by strangers, and wanted to be manhandled in general? Rape was fucking rape no matter *who* it was perpetrated by, and us sodomites enjoyed it about as much as the average person.

Lock yelled, "If you're sent by Stumpy, why the fuck are we pointing our pieces at each other?"

Roland slapped his own palm with his belt, as if testing it out. "We're pointing our irons at you *because* Stumpy sent us, that's why." He nodded at his henchmen, who got into proper gangland shooting stance with their choppers, one aimed at Lock, one at me. It was a Mexican standoff true and proper, and Roland advanced on Lock. "Put down your piece," Roland said calmly.

"Why the fuck should I?" Lock's voice was high and frantic. "I don't even know why the fuck you're doing this. Stumpy said you were going to show us the next part of the plan."

Roland said, "We get it, you're a rough and tough outlaw, but I am going to shoot off your little boyfriend's dick if you don't put down those pieces."

Slowly, reluctantly, Lock and I both did. I stuffed mine back into my waistband. Lock started to reach for his fly to cram away his bared prick, but Roland had other ideas.

"Hands up!" Roland barked. As Lock obeyed, Roland whacked his limp dick with the belt. Roland's eyes shined with the zeal of the professional sadist as he whacked, then backhanded, then whacked again. "You like fucking that sweet angel's mouth? See how it feels to have your dick whipped hard—and I mean *hard!*"

What the fuck? I'd never seen this guy before in my life. Why was he calling me a sweet angel? Why was he taking his ire out on Lock? That leather belt was thick and snapped loudly like a firecracker, making me cringe, though I was sitting eight feet away. Even with an AK pinning me to my chair, I couldn't stop myself from leaping up. Lock shielded his face with his forearm and was taking the pounding like a man, but I couldn't sit and watch.

"Fucking stop it!" I roared, my voice practically vibrating the dust from the books on the shelf. "What's the point of all this if we don't understand why the fuck you're doing it? We were just here doing a job for Stumpy."

To my surprise, Roland actually paused, belt in hand. "Good point. Better leave some for the boss."

As confused as ever, I kept shouting. "What's your beef with us, man? We fucking did what Stumpy told us to do."

Roland slapped his own hand now with the belt, as Lock was finally allowed to angrily put his poor abused cock away. "Oh yeah? I heard different. I heard *you* were the ones stole the

H from Mr. Rojas and were trying to frame that downtrodden Injun."

"*What?*" seethed Lock.

I was aghast. Looked like Stumpy was doing a bit of the ol' double-cross. For whatever reason, homophobia or other, he *really* disliked Lock and wanted to send him up the river.

"That's *bullshit*, man!" roared Lock. "Stumpy's the one who stole the dope! He's blackmailing us to frame that poor fucking Hopi who probably didn't have a fucking thing to do with it."

"Yeah," said Roland. "I presume Stumpy was going to out you for your little manhole-inspecting activities. That would absolutely *not* fly in our world, now, would it? As for your little innocent teepee creeper, maybe he's not so fucking innocent after all." He lifted his chin at one of the hyenas with the gold grill in his mouth. The guy stomped out of the dusty coach's office.

Lock and I shared fearful glances. This was not going our way at all. Any crazy idea we might've had about enjoying a peaceful night together eating cheese and crackers and drinking wine went right out the window. Our expressions turned to panic when we heard some dull thuds coming from outside, exactly as though someone was being beaten. Strangled cries backed up this theory, and soon the grill-faced hyena appeared rattling a poor heap of a guy. Kwahu Johnson must have returned from protesting the Redskins name yesterday. The blood on both his cheekbones and around his mouth wasn't fresh, and the purple-green general swelling of his face wasn't new, either.

The Grillmaster half-carried, half-dragged the guy. When he saw new white men, Kwahu wailed, "Why are you doing this to me?"

"You know why." Roland gave Kwahu a swift kick to the

shin. The shinbone might've already been shattered because the guy absolutely crumpled into a heap.

Maybe I was accustomed to living and working hand in hand with two brothers who were half Navajo. I had already gotten many earfuls about the horrible living conditions of the Native Americans. I doubted that this poor fucktard had stolen any H, and now we were being framed as well. Whatever the case, I suddenly found myself in the fray, hauling back and just belting that fucking Roland asshole in his square, sturdy jaw.

He probably didn't expect it, because it connected with a satisfying sock. From the get go, I was fighting a losing battle. I must have decided *fuck it, let's just go for it*, because when that Roland fucker stumbled back into a bookshelf, I whaled on him again. And again.

I didn't have the time or energy to utter any epithets. Soon Lock was joining in, pummeling one of the guys who had been leashed to Roland. Roland must've been so unaccustomed to being hit that he just lay there against the shelves like a piece of tissue paper. I'll never forget his surprised, round eyes as I walloped him in the gut, in the chin, the throat.

But he finally got his shit together. Ducking from my next punch, he swooped down and swiped up the chopper the hyena had dropped. He whacked me good with an overhead swing of the gun stock, catching my shoulder and bringing me to my knees. The remaining thug covered me with his barrel, and I stopped fighting.

Roland yelled, "You want a fall guy for the heroin? You've got a fall guy. But you're still gonna have to answer to Mr. Rojas. I'm not going to hurt you because Mr. Rojas would be angry." He swiveled to shoot his evil pinpoint gaze to Lock, who had paused in his pummeling of the other guard. Lock looked at him like *What?* That was when Roland made a quick bash with the gun butt, smashing Lock directly upside the head.

The blow had so much power behind it, Lock was actually swept off his feet. He actually went flying a couple feet in the air, landing face down on the dusty floor.

Roland was breathing heavily. "But I can hurt *you*. So don't think I won't, you fucking fairy punk." He kicked Lock in the hip for good measure, but my lover wasn't moving. Roland turned back to me. Blood trickled from one nostril, and he stuck his tongue out to taste it, as though loving the flavor of metal. One eye was all bloodshot, I remember that. I must've broken every vessel in that eyeball.

"Now you. I think it's in your best interests to play along with me. I can't leave any lasting marks on you, but I can sure as shit do a lot of other things to you. Zip tie him," he instructed the guard who hadn't been whaled upon.

CHAPTER TWELVE
TURK

I knew that once we got into that Cadillac with the blacked-out windows, it was all over.

I've seen enough true crime shows. Hell, I've *participated* in enough true crimes to know that once you get into the cage, something spectacularly gruesome is about to happen. If you can somehow avoid getting into that damned Cadillac or windowless van, let me tell you, *do it*.

Worse, they shoved Lock into a separate Caddy so we couldn't even see each other, much less talk. It was something, to go from the intensity of harsh, gritty lovemaking to the white leather back seat of a Caddy. Before they put the hood over my head—yes, they actually fucking did that—I saw blood stains on the seat. I wondered why they didn't get a darker shade of leather for the seats. They shoved poor Kwahu Johnson in there with me. He was in much worse shape, still oozing blood from his face, and the front of his *guayabera* shirt was absolutely caked with it. Kwahu glanced despairingly at me out of his one good eye. He added more blood stains to the seats before they stuck a burlap hood over his head, too, and then we were both in muffled darkness.

I knew a baby gangster was driving, with Roland in the passenger seat, as we pulled onto the highway and hung a left.

Okay, so we were heading toward Lake Havasu. Now that we were on the straightaway, I had the confidence to speak up. I had the distinct impression they didn't want to harm me, although the same couldn't be said for Lock.

"Look, Roland, why are we in your crosshairs? I'm not even an Assassin. I just went along for the ride."

"Oh, I'll say you went along for the 'ride,' all right," chuckled Roland. What a fucking wit. "All Stumpy did was track down the thief of that H. Once he told us it was you and that jackoff bounty hunter, Mr. Rojas became interested. He wants to see you. Just you. Not the jackoff."

I persisted. "But why the fuck does Mr. Rojas even *care* about me? This isn't my turf. I'm with The Bare Bones out of Pure and Easy, south of Flagstaff. You must've heard of us."

"Never heard, don't care," said Roland smoothly.

"Oh, *come on*! Eminence Front weed? Young Man Blue?"

"Now *that* I've heard of. That's your stuff?"

"*Yes!*" I cried, relieved. "We grow it and sell it in my medical dispensary."

"Good stuff," Roland allowed. "You're a fucking ganjier?"

"That's *all* I am. I'm the Veep of The Bare Bones, and I wouldn't even be *in* your backyard if I wasn't trying to track down the fucker selling crap weed using my strain name. Which turned out to be Stumpy Meadows, by the fucking way. That guy is a jack of all trades of pure evil. He's the guy who lifted your dope, not us. We just got roped into his game."

"Dope on a rope," goofed the hyena.

"Oh, I think you're more than that," Roland said calmly. "Mr. Rojas is interested in you."

What the hell was everyone *talking* about? What were these obscure references, and why the hell did a kingpin I'd never heard of before want to see me so badly? Obviously not for my pot, because Roland was acting like he'd just learned I was the proprietor of A Joint System. "Look. Where the fuck are they taking Lock? What's happening to him?"

"Don't you fucking worry about that bounty hunter. You just worry about your own sweet ass. Now shut the fuck up, pretty boy."

Roland mumbled to himself as he apparently read a text or something. I knew how many minutes it took to get from Parker to the Japanese barracks, and I thought I had a pretty good sense of timing. And I had timed how long it took for me to follow Lock Singer from the gas station parking lot in Lake Havasu down to the reservation high school. Thinking of the high school made me think of Lock's quarry, that kiddie porn guy named, hilariously enough, Ronald Reagan. I knew Lock had an impeccable rep for collaring every single bail jumper he'd been asked to follow. If this sleazebag was the first to slip through his clutches, his guilt would be compounded by the fact that it was a chomo, the lowest vermin on the planet.

When we'd dismounted upon arriving at the barracks, I'd checked my texts. In addition to one from Carrie Gunslinger wondering where I was, and a few from my club and my assistant August, there was one from Twinkletoes.

The Gipper is on the move again heading W on 10 toward Palm Springs.

The enthusiastic Prospect had only informed me he'd put a GPS tracker on Reagan's Lexus just as he was placing one on my scoot. He'd done it while waiting for us behind the high school band room. While Lock and I were busy fussing and fighting, Twinkletoes had, true to his name, tiptoed over to the Lexus, after ascertaining it was the target of Lock's interest. At the time, I had more important things on my mind. I was just hopping on my ride to follow a sex god down into the Rez on a relatively simple run. There were twenty things higher on the priority list than some creepy bail jumper. I probably would've remembered to tell Lock eventually. Now, I was glad I hadn't. Knowing where Reagan was but being unable to do anything about it would've pissed Lock off more.

We started to slow down for a series of lights, so I knew we'd entered Lake Havasu City limits. After that, I was so unfamiliar with the city I only nominally tried to keep track of our turns. I hoped Lock was doing a lot better in the other Caddy driven by the other baby gangster.

The Caddy went over a bump. The crunch of gravel under the tires told me we'd entered some kind of driveway. They tried to leave our hoods on as they yanked us from the car, but I guess Kwahu kept stumbling, what with that shattered shin and all, and finally Roland said with disgust,

"Oh, just take the damned hoods off!"

Bright daylight was revealed to me, and we were shoved up a ramp that led to a hallway. It looked like an Italian villa, with scrolled ironwork on the double doors, and stone archways. It became evident Kwahu couldn't walk, period, so the hyena brought a rollaway chair and rolled him into another room.

I tried again. "Where's Lock?"

Roland was inscrutable. It was impossible to tell what lay behind his words. "Your boyfriend will be fine. Mr. Rojas just wants to meet you."

I figured he wanted an inside line on my weed, I really did. But then why had Roland seemed surprised I was proprietor of the famous strains?

The house looked as though some realtor had staged it for sale, that's how immaculate it was, like some Ethan Allen showroom. We passed by an office where a woman in her forties wearing glasses was glued to a desktop computer. She had a view overlooking the swimming pool. Mrs. Rojas? Or the office manager of his empire, whatever the hell it was? I wasn't impressed by the glamor. I'd been living in Ford Illuminati's brand new southwest style mansion for over a year now. I had my own damned *wing*. I was used to grand foyers, fire pits, and butler pantries.

The home office Roland led me to even resembled Ford's—at least superficially, at first.

Roland whipped out a switchblade and cut the zip ties off my wrists. I massaged my arms.

"You wait in here for Mr. Rojas," said Roland before shutting and locking the door.

Of course, the first thing I did was look out the window. Yup, there was the fire pit, the entertainment area with built-in gas grill, bocce ball court, and if I stood on tiptoes, a tiny bit of putting green. So the house was on a golf course. And we were up high enough that I could see a few flashes of Highway 95. I knew we were not far from London Bridge, for whatever good that did me. Lock—if he was fine, okay, cognizant—probably knew exactly where we were.

Of course they'd taken my piece from me first thing. But they hadn't frisked me very well, and I still had a little switchblade of my own stuck inside my engineer boot. I knew cameras would be on me, so I didn't check it. I snooped around the office casually instead.

A framed photo of who I presumed to be Carmine Rojas was on the credenza behind the desk. He stood next to the woman I'd seen in the office, both holding wine glasses, so she must be his wife. It was my experience that cartel kingpins like this married ridiculously young trophy wives, so he must have been married to this Mrs. for quite a while. I didn't give him any credit for looking beyond age and seeing any depth to the woman. Being married for a while was the only answer. She even looked like she had natural, God-given tits.

Rojas himself was the bald-headed, craggy thug I'd expected. In the pinstripe suit he could've been a CEO. But I knew that the higher you got up the food chain, the harder it was to distinguish who was a sleazy, connected, ruthless cartel murderer, and who was a sleazy, connected, ruthless CEO. Once a guy bosses up and gets posh, it's hard to differentiate.

But he must have some cover business, some money laundering gig to explain away all his riches, so I looked at his bookshelf. The usual things about business startup, being an entrepreneur, and *Personal Finance for Dummies* told me pretty much nothing. He didn't even have a laptop on the empty desk.

I had learned nothing by the time a side door opened and the broad, tall man himself sauntered in. He wore a suit, and wore it well, which tapped into my daddy chasing side. I had to remind myself I'd been brought here under duress and wasn't going to like anything this man told me.

"Turk Blackburn!" he barked.

I shrugged. My arms were loose now, and I could have attempted an escape out the window, but I still didn't know where Lock was, or the fate of that hapless native. "Mr. Rojas," I said respectfully. "Where's my partner, Lock Singer?"

Instead of going behind the desk to assert his authority, he leaned against a side of it. He unbuttoned his jacket, and crossing his feet enhanced the nicely made package in his crotch. I shamed myself for having noticed that. *But who the fuck wouldn't? Old habits die hard.* Hand on hip, Rojas gazed at me levelly, assessing. This was exactly the sort of authoritative, macho older man I used to melt for, and I was ashamed for even thinking of it.

"Lock Singer will be fine as long as you work with me."

"All right. What is it you need? That goon of yours wouldn't explain a thing—just whipped Lock and kept kicking that fucking Indian."

"Never mind about the fucking Indian." With a simple lift of his chin, he *willed* me to approach him. I was such an accomplished submissive, having trained myself to pick up on clues, ticks, and telltale body signals from other men, I obeyed. Just as I was taking a few steps toward him, I admonished myself. *What the fuck are you doing, Blackburn? You're not in a nightclub or even in a truck stop. This epic asshat holds your fucking fate in his hands—and you still don't know where Lock is.* I made myself stand still.

He continued, "My runner told me you were doing an errand for him."

"Stumpy? Yeah, he sort of forced us to go into the Rez for him. But we didn't take the original H, Mr. Rojas. Stumpy did. He was blackmailing us into doing the errand for him."

Rojas didn't seem to have heard me. He had a musing, faraway look in his eye. I got the impression he wasn't talking about the same thing I was. "Of course I googled your name. I like to know who's working for me. I knew about Lock Singer. Sort of an obnoxious little twerp, although banging hot."

Banging hot? That was an odd choice of words for a major trafficker like Rojas. "He's a good man," I said lamely.

"Oh, so I *heard*, from Stumpy. I heard you think Singer is an *extremely* good man."

Oh Jesus. Here we go again. Is this destined to be my lifestyle for the next forty years? I knew that gays were persecuted, but this was ridiculous. It seemed like everyone we ran into was some kind of fucking deviant, violent homophobe.

I held out my hands, palms to the floor. "Look. I'm tired of defending who I am. No, we can't fucking deny that we're lovers. I don't know why everyone is making such a big fucking deal of it. I was just helping Lock with the task Stumpy gave him. He threatened to out us to our clubs if we didn't. I guess you're going to go ahead and do that anyway, so you might as well—"

"No," snarled Rojas. With one bear's claw, he swiped at my neck. Intuitively, I reared back, but he caught my neck in his grip and yanked me to him. Smashing me against the desk until I was bent backward almost in half, he loomed over me with intent, amorous eyes. "I googled you, Turk. I admire the way you've kept yourself underground, off social media and the public eye."

"I'm an outlaw," I gasped. My hands had slapped up against the desk and he completely dominated me with his big, beefy body. He was straddling one of my thighs, his big package juicy and heavy against me. He must have been commando under the pinstripe suit, because his long dick lay heavy against my thigh like a two by four. A month ago I'd already be on my knees slurping that tool into my mouth. I'd be tearing his button-down shirt in two to get at that hairy, teddy bear chest. A muscular, potent daddy Dom in a suit? It didn't get better than that. A month ago. "Outlaws don't go on Facebook."

I was hoping he'd be proud of me, such a good little soldier keeping off the fed's radar like that. He planted his fists against the desk on either side of my hips, looking rapidly from one of my eyes to the other. "I admire that the only information out there about you is your dispensary and things related to your legitimate business."

"Well, of course." I was starting to sweat. It was air conditioned in there—Lake Havasu in May and all that—but I was becoming uncomfortable on many different levels. I hadn't eaten in a long time. I was light-headed, it had been a fucking long day, and I was literally in the clutches of this feral monster who could extinguish my life with one twist of his wrist. The unspoken threat was that if I didn't go along with whatever he wanted, he'd harm Lock. I needed to discern what the fuck he wanted. "That's how we roll in this business, Mr. Rojas. Not long ago, even medical marijuana wasn't legal, so we learned to step very lightly."

"Good," he snarled, his eyes sparkling. And it was *not* my imagination that he began to do the slow hump against my thigh. The big tool loose under the pinstripe wool rolled from side to side as he undulated his spine with dog-like rubbing, his thighs clamped down around mine. "There was one photo I saw of you. Just one. But that one was enough to convince me that I needed to meet you in person."

So it had not been my imagination. Mr. Rojas was pumping and preening to sexually impress little old *me*. I should have been flattered. But now, maybe since having met and hooked up with my sweet Lock, I was oddly apathetic. "Which picture? I didn't know there was a picture of me out there."

"Ah." Rojas seemed lost in the fantasy of the photograph as he lifted the bottom hem of my plaid shirt. He slid a hammy hand up my fluttering abdomen till he reached my nipple, which he thumbed eagerly. "What a picture it is." He stopped fingering me long enough to whip a cell from his pocket. Now, as he thumbed the phone, his rod twitched inside his trousers. He must've gotten to the correct photo. He turned the phone to face me.

I squinted. Was that fucking *me*? "Where is that? It looks like I have makeup on."

Rojas turned it back to face him. It made him smile. "Indeed you do. You're on the set of *The Hunger Games* in North Carolina."

"Oh, *that?* Caesar's Ghost. I was just tagging along with my brother Faux Pas. He's a special effects makeup artist. I needed to do a run out there to reach out to a brother club, so I tagged along to his set for one day. Just one day," I protested. There was no point in lying to the crime boss about what he could easily discover for himself.

Still grinning like a buffoon at the photo, Rojas diddled my nipple even more ferociously. I admit, his toying with me was stiffening my dick. It was plumping up just inches from his boner, pulsating in time with my heartbeat. Who doesn't like to be admired? "Yes, but this picture is the epitome of beauty. When I saw this, I knew I had to call you here." He flipped through some more photos that also seemed to please him, and when he put his phone back down on the desk, I saw he had swiped over to another nude, bare-chested young twink. I was older, more muscular, virile, and was proud of my Vandyke. I wondered why he'd singled me out. I was more of an otter—or even a gym bunny—than a twink or a pup. The photo he had of me wasn't even shirtless.

"Are you a fan of the franchise? *Hunger Games* is, uh, a great series of films." At the moment, I couldn't recall a damned thing about the fucking movie. Some futuristic sci-fi thing, maybe post-apocalyptic—weren't they all?

Now his hand roamed freely over my chest. His spatulate fingers unbuttoned the lumberjack shirt so he could feast openly on my torso. I wasn't a fuzzy teddy by a long shot, but my pecs were sprinkled with more than enough chest hair to tell the world I was no twink. His hands roamed passionately over my chest, and his long shaft trembled against my thigh. He rubbed his thumb over the silken line of hair that arrowed down my abdomen, sending a thrill rolling through my groin. "Ah, my lovely, sweet boy. Your beauty surpasses your intelligence. Did you not shoot bows in that movie?"

I frowned. "Bows? Yes, I suppose there was some bow-shooting going on." To be honest, my dong was plumping up with all that stroking. The head poked out the worn pocket of my jeans, where the denim was so threadbare only the thinnest layer of cotton kept the air from caressing it. The man was a smoking hot animal, and a month ago I would've had his salami in my fist and been spreading my thighs for it. Boss or no boss, I would've given myself up to this beefy daddy within minutes. *What the fuck?* I was used to doing it in truck stops or clubs where one couldn't always choose one's ideal partner. Carmine Rojas *was* my ideal partner, as of a couple weeks ago. Brawny, brutal, and dominant to the core.

However, things were different now.

"Ah, that's what I like. Don't The Bare Bones own an archery shop?"

I wasn't sure whether to be delighted or appalled that he was unbuckling my belt with the precision of a machinist. "Yes, The Hip Quiver. You like…archery?" What sort of twisted game was he playing? Was archery a sort of metaphor for something? It could easily be sexual, so I went with that. I tried to distract him. I put my hand over his, stopping him from opening up my belt. "Listen. I'm with Lock now. I can't just run around letting anyone feel me up."

For the first time, he frowned too. "Who said I'm 'anyone'? Were you not informed who I am?"

"Um…Carmine Rojas? I know you're the boss running the whole Colorado River operation. But you don't oversee The Bare Bones. We don't work with your side of things. We have other partners, other people we do business with. We don't need you."

Now he fisted his hand around my ponytail, exerting just

enough pressure to make me uncomfortable. My Adam's apple was bared to him. I was literally laid vulnerable to this wolf about to rip out my throat. "You listen here, little boy." I was hardly "little." I was thirty fucking two years old, a strapping stud, or so I'd been told, but I wasn't about to argue semantics with this feral bruiser. "I can make or break you, *regardless* of the name of your asinine little club. I can break your dickwad buddy Lock Singer. I can break his fucking spine in two and bury him in the desert. I could give a shit less what happens to that low-level spitter. It's in your best interests to allow me to seek my pleasure."

I gulped drily. The message was loud and clear. "Yes, sir." I slipped into a role that was in my comfort zone. "Tell me what you want."

He snapped my neck once just to show he was in control, then he smiled like a snake. "You're just a sexy Robin Hood, aren't you?"

"I am," I agreed. I was flying blind here, feeling my way around. "I like...shooting people with my arrows."

Rojas' eyes rolled up into his skull. "Ah," he moaned, humping my leg with his pulsating knob. "Robin Hood thinks he can steal from the rich."

"But I only want to give it to the poor." It was the old me who reached out and rapidly unbuttoned his shirt. Renting it in two, his broad, grey-haired chest was revealed. He stood tall with a regal bearing, proud of his body, of his manliness. Semen stained the crotch of his trousers. It was this regal, forceful machismo that I used to crave, used to seek out at truck stops. Those men were much more base, uneducated, and earthy than this daddy Dom in a tailored suit who was manipulating me to save my lover's ass. He knew which game he was playing, all right. He knew which side his bread was buttered on. He was a slick, domineering operator, and I was certain he *always* got what he wanted.

His entire hulking body shuddered, and he gripped his handful of my hair tighter. "Ah, Robin Hood," he murmured against my mouth. *Dear God, is he going to kiss me?* He had some kind of archer fetish, that was obvious. And I thought I'd heard of them all.

My brain cells were lighting up the midnight sky thinking of the quickest, most expedient way to dispatch with this guy. He was rich, he was powerful, and most of all, he held Lock's safety in his fucking hands. Maybe I could get out of this without even making him come. Some men weren't necessarily that interested in that. "Robin Hood is here to save the day," I murmured back, hoping I hit the nail on the head.

That worked. "*Ah!*" he cried orgasmically, and kissed me.

Survival instinct kicked in. I knew what I had to do, and my brain transmitted that information to my body. I have to admit straight up—I kissed him back.

I pretended it was two years ago, before I hooked up with Dayton. Things had been promiscuous back then—before I thought I needed to be monogamous with Dayton. I would have eagerly kissed this grey fox back with vigor, so that's what I did now.

I was experienced in fantasy and role play. I knew what it took to convince myself of something. I often pretended to be submissive, the bottom in a scene, when in reality both I and my partner knew otherwise. I was always in control. Being a seductive, pleasing bastard gives you the upper hand. A power bottom controls all, lets the top think he is getting what he wants. Little does he know every move has been dictated by the bottom. The power bottom can orchestrate the scene, discover what turns on the Dom using subtle ploys. You feel the push and the pull, both physical and mental. You gauge the ebb and flow of the power tide, submit when necessary, push back when begged to.

As I twined my tongue with Rojas', I evaluated the lay of the land. He slurped and practically licked my face, diving down to suck on my throat. I wondered briefly if he was going to be one of those men who keep their violence barely swept underneath the rug, just hovering under the surface waiting to burst forth at strange moments. He grunted like a stuck pig as he humped his drooling dong against my leg.

The better I was able to fool myself into believing the fantasy, the hornier I got, too. It wasn't such a giant leap to make, since daddy chasing had been such an important part of my persona. Big hairy teddies like Dayton fucking *lived* to hump me—Lock was actually not even my "type," or the type I thought I liked. I used to revel in seducing the beefy, virile brawn of a man like Rojas, and I did it now, gyrating my erection against his. He was drilling his tool right against mine, just a couple thin layers of fabric separating our penises. Who was he pretending to be? I had to take a chance at it, using what little I knew about Robin Fucking Hood.

I gave his bulging dick a big squeeze and muttered, "I'm just looking for a few good merry men."

Now I didn't know whether it was the squeeze or the folklore reference, but something sent him over the edge. "*Dios mio!*" he wheezed, stabbing his tool into my fist. "*Yo soy el rey y tú eres mi esclavo!*"

I didn't know *exactly* what this meant at the time, but I knew *rey* was *king*, so I went with the flow. Rubbing my face against his, I sighed heavily. "Oh my king, please let me give you release. Your big wand"—or whatever the hell those lordly people held in their hands while sitting on the throne—"is crying out for release." I squeezed his wang lustily now, hoping he'd just release inside the pinstripe trousers and be done with it.

Or, I should say, *half* of me wished he'd just shoot and get it over with. The other half, the half I was easily able to compartmentalize in my head, was aroused beyond belief to be wrangling with such a silver daddy. I got off on powerful men, and it didn't get much more powerful than Carmine Rojas. His hungry mouth slurping at my throat and slashing across my mouth, his hands feeling and massaging my chest, his long tool thrusting against my thigh—it was all good, and I drank it in with pride.

Suddenly he drew back, standing tall again. He gazed at me with fire in his eyes. We both panted uncontrollably, but suddenly he had retaken the reins of power, and I didn't like it.

He slapped my face. It stung as tears came to my eyes, just as though a beloved had slapped me.

He snarled with disgust, "You worthless sack of shit. I'll teach you to steal all that money and keep it for yourself."

Now I wasn't sure if he still thought I was Robin Hood or just a simple hood who had stolen some of his heroin. He backhanded me again.

"You think you can outwit the king? I'll fucking show you how the king does it."

He seemed almost enraged as he tore apart my buckle from my belt. I coiled with tension, unsure what he intended to do. After all, his minion had whipped the hell out of Lock's prick. Angrily, Rojas yanked my jeans down to my knees. I was leaning back on the desk on my palms, and my dick sprung free, bobbing.

Rojas eyeballed it greedily. "I'll fucking show *you* what happens to thieves." Gripping my penis by the base so it bulged from his fist, he whacked it with his palm several times, hard. The initial sensation was always painful, but if the beating wasn't too hard, pleasure always spread through my balls and thighs, a haze of luscious warmth. Yet there was that sense hanging over me that he might snap at any moment and take things too far, far beyond the safeword zone. "There. Take that. And that."

I leaned against my hands, threading my thumbs together behind my tailbone. I knew it made me look helpless, at the other man's powerful whim. But I was unsure how much power to let Rojas think he had. "I swear I'll never steal again!" I cried. I hedged my bet. "But being near your immense manhood is driving me insane!"

That did it. Every man lives to be worshiped, and this fucking trafficker was no exception. He was still human, in some subterranean part of his soul. Gratitude washed over his face, the anger evaporated, and he took my chin in the palm that had been striking me. "*Mi Dios, mijo,*" he said with awe. "You are the most beautiful boy I have ever kissed. Let your king lick your lance and bring you pleasure." And he dropped to his knees and sucked down my dick.

"*Ah!*" At first I was overwhelmed. Lust surged through my groin, pooling in the cockhead that he rubbed convulsively against the back of his throat. He ate me voraciously, as though he hadn't had dick in a while. He was married, but being a kingpin meant he could do whatever the fuck he wanted. The fact that he was sucking another man's dick a few rooms down from his wife's office told me that he had no regard for her.

The greed he put into the skull job told me his goal was to swallow some hot spunk, and he quickly brought me to that point, pistoning his head up and down on my pole. He slurped me up like a chocolate fountain, his tongue stroking me inexorably toward orgasm. If all went well, that would satisfy him and he'd let us the fuck go. He might even owe me one, in the perilous and delicate power play of bondage and discipline. If I could get him to actually *like* me, I could use that to our advantage.

But all didn't go well.

Things had changed a lot in my life in the past two weeks since running into Lock at The Racquet Club.

Things had changed *too much* in the past two weeks.

Evidently I couldn't follow through with this deviant act. Evidently I was too honest, too upright, too fucking good.

Two weeks ago, it would've been a no brainer. I would have flooded this salt and pepper daddy's throat with my hot jism—taken the money, if any was offered—and be done with it. Mission accomplished, right? Wrong.

I could no longer fake it. I'd always been a horrible actor, and now even my *dick* couldn't fake it. This had never happened to me before, but I started getting soft.

Horror of horrors. My dick started deflating in his mouth, like a melting piece of candy!

At first, his tongue stroked to keep me afloat. But soon even Rojas had to admit I wasn't going to come to the party, and he detached with a big sucking sound, gripping my hips, glaring up at me. My cock just flopped like a dead rubber hose. Once again, it had made my decision for me.

"You don't want me?" he shouted. "I don't turn you on? What the fuck is this?"

Believe you me, I was mortified beyond belief. My fidelity to Lock Singer was getting the upper hand. Even brainwashing myself with the knowledge that this tough motherfucker was holding my lover hostage, even that didn't cut it. My dick had a brain of its own, and it was thinking *You can't do this. Lock would get mad*. Of all the fucking times for my promiscuous prick to start asserting itself. *Fuck off, prick!* It had a job to do, to get us out of this mess, and it chose *now* to stop performing?

"I don't know what the fuck," I stammered. "This has never happened before."

"And it happens with *me?*" he roared. Staggering to his feet, his own dick tented out his trousers, and the dark area on his crotch was even bigger. He had no problems getting it up. But the thief he was trying to pleasure sure as hell did.

He pointed at the carpet. "This has *never* happened with me either. And I'll see to it that it never happens again."

I closed my eyes. I was doomed.

CHAPTER THIRTEEN
LOCK

They kept Lock in the back seat of the Caddy for the longest time, as though they didn't know what to do with him.

Wrists zip tied behind his back, with that hood over his head starting to feel way too claustrophobic, Lock was a miserable wreck.

Not only had he been dick-whipped by some sadist he'd never seen before, both him and his lover were now in the custody of the Colorado River crime boss. What little Lock had heard about Carmine Rojas didn't warm his heart. As could be expected from a Marin cartel boss, he was a heartless money-making machine. There were rumors he worked with human traffickers, too. Lock doubted that Stumpy even dealt directly with Rojas. There had to be at least one more level of authority between them. But somehow, Stumpy had succeeded in planting lies in Rojas' head. Rojas now thought *they* had stolen the heroin—not a good position to be in.

Lock had nothing better to do than to berate himself. *If Turk hadn't been giving me a skull job in that hotel room, we wouldn't be in this fix. I'm the worst thing that ever happened to him. I'm the reason he's even in this fucking mess. Why did he hook up with me, anyway? I'm bad news, nothing but human garbage.*

He'd always been convinced he was responsible for Park

Langham's death. It had been Lock's idea to fly deep behind enemy lines purposefully seeking to draw SAM fire. It had seemed like tactical genius at the time. He had evaded being hit. It was when he was returning to destroy the threat that they'd been shot down.

The guilt was an unbelievable burden on Lock. The Air Force shrink had tried to draw it out of him, but he'd never unloaded on anyone. He just took the PTSD meds, finding out how they'd been helping him when he stopped taking them. He'd come to at a rally with his hands around a brother's throat. Luckily only Tim Breakiron had seen him, counseling him to get back on the meds. But Lock had never been able to shake the conviction that he alone was responsible for Park's death.

He knew Turk wouldn't even *be* in this part of Arizona if it wasn't for him. Although the sadistic Roland seemed to be sparing Turk for some reason, guilt was just eating away at Lock. Because the real heart of the matter, Lock was beginning to suspect, the thing that had originally set these wheels spinning in motion, was his original beef with Stumpy Meadows.

Years ago, before Lock hooked up with Ruby, he'd been pretty handy with the ladies. Losing Park in Iraq had put the zap on his head, and he'd never been the same since. So he was determined to make an even bigger push for the gashes. He and Breakiron must have passed around at least thirty, maybe forty different slashes before Lock decided he wanted to settle on one gal named Hilary, at least for fender fluff purposes.

Well. The second he put Hilary on the back of his bike, out of the fucking woodwork came Stumpy Meadows. Like a whirling dervish, the guy attacked Lock with brass knuckles and a fucking ball peen hammer, the signature weapon of the Hell's Angels, which made everyone wonder. Lock had been so taken by surprise he'd wound up with a concussion before Breakiron and a couple other brothers had pulled Stumpy off of him. It was an unfair fight what with the weapons, and most of all, nobody had known Stumpy had claimed Hilary. She was his old lady only in his own mind, so the whole altercation was laid at Stumpy's feet. Stumpy hated a lot of guys—pretty much everyone on the whole planet, really—but he had a special hatred now for Lock, so Lock usually tried to avoid him.

He had only offered to track down the source of the bogus weed because he wanted to get closer to Turk. Even back then, when he was still fighting his desire for Turk, thinking he could go square and return to fucking sweetbutts, he wanted to be physically close to the beautiful, exotic biker. And, he had to admit, it was stimulating and exciting, never knowing how much closer to the flame he could get without getting burned. The thrill of risk, the possibility of exposure, that all enhanced the illicit aura of what he was doing with Turk. As a former fighter pilot and current bounty hunter, danger was his middle name.

His emotions ran much deeper than that. Lock already knew, even before Turk so expertly tongued his anus and made him shoot his wad, that he'd never be able to give up the sultry ganjier. They were pushing things ever closer to the edge, but they could've gone quite a while without being discovered. After all, they lived four hours away from each other. Lock would have to go up through Flag to get to Turk, and how many days off did he have from his business, his club? None. They'd have to have an *extremely* long distance relationship that could easily avoid detection.

Now, even if they made it out of this mess intact, Stumpy's threat still dangled over their heads. And after accusing them of being the heroin thieves, Lock doubted that Stumpy intended for them to get out alive.

Lock started a sort of prayer in his head. He used to do that while flying missions with or without Park. *I love you, Turk. Feel my spirit reaching out to you. Stay safe, buddy. We'll make it. We'll make it.*

That was when the Caddy's door was flung open, someone grabbed his bicep, and he was dragged from the car.

"Hey, *listen*, you BGs!" A BG was a baby gangster, and Lock was sick of those fucking hyenas yanking him around. "You tell me *what the fuck is going on*, or I'll—"

"Or you'll what?" goofed one BG.

"Tell your mommy on us?" snickered the other.

They were right, though. Lock wasn't in any position to protest. Instead, they led him stumbling through a room that seemed to be the kitchen from the scent of a tomato-based sauce. Lock hadn't eaten in a fuck of a long time, but that was the least of his worries. He knew the BGs wouldn't answer any questions and would just taunt him, so he held onto what little dignity he had left and allowed them to take him through many hallways and into a room. After shoving him into a chair, they left him alone.

Well, this is a fine fucking thing. I wonder what happened to that poor fucking Hopi. No, I don't wonder. Those guys are expendable. They get them hooked on drugs so they hand over their subsistence checks every month. They—we—pay them peanuts for ferrying our junk into the States. They have no fucking alternative, do they?

It was a conundrum Lock could not solve. If he could, he'd be President of the US.

He perked up when someone entered the room. A soft moan told him it was a woman, so he ventured, "Hey. What's going on, do you know?"

The door closed, and Lock's heart jolted with despair. But she was still here—he heard a rustle of skirts, and she was taking off his hood.

"This is just getting out of control," the woman said, whipping the hood off.

Lock blinked to adjust his eyes to the indoor lighting. It was dark out now, it had been the longest day of his life, but at least now he was sitting across from a forty-something woman, maybe Rojas' lawyer come to tell him to dial it back a bit, trying to eliminate any blowback on Rojas. "Oh, thank you, thank you. Do you know what the fuck is going on around here?"

"Not exactly, but I'm not going to turn a blind eye to it anymore. You're with the Assassins of Youth? You're not wearing that leather vest with the patches."

"Right, because we thought we were doing undercover work for our club. *Helping* Mr. Rojas. Turns out it was a double-cross, and Rojas thinks we're rats. God knows what he's doing to my partner, or where."

"They're down the hall." The woman squeezed her eyes shut with the patience of a Madonna. "And I can guess what they're doing. My husband picks the prettiest boys. I saw your partner walking by. He fits the bill."

"Your…husband?"

"Yes." She laughed bitterly. "Don't ask how I came to be in this position. Let's just say Carmine has a vast ability to fool people. He's very slick. I guess I was the proper 'citizen wife' he needed at the time."

Lock nodded. Papa Ewey had a citizen wife—a lawyer, in fact. She had gotten them out of many scrapes before. "So you don't think he's in danger?"

"Not as long as he plays along with Carmine's game."

"Listen. There was a Hopi guy. A bloody, bashed-in Hopi."

She shrugged. "Haven't seen anyone like that. What's your name? I want to tell you something."

"Lock Singer."

"Lock. I'm Carmen. I know, Carmen and Carmine, ha ha. I have a plan up my sleeve. I can't take this fucking bullshit anymore. Dead bodies everywhere, people being tortured in my own home, the strange comings and goings, acting like a fucking Mafioso, I just can't take it anymore. We've been married twenty-one years, but I just discovered he found a way to funnel almost all his income, laundering it through his daughter's sunglass business. In essence he's turning all his income over to her, and that's just the final straw in twenty years of betrayal. I should've been tipped off when he made me sign a prenup allowing him to list his daughter as primary beneficiary on the five million life insurance policy."

"Why'd you sign off on such a bum deal?"

Carmen sighed. "Youthful idealism. I figured since he was well off, he'd provide for me in other ways. I suppose he has, but the lion's share of the business has gone to his daughter, who loathes me for marrying her father. I was never allowed to have a child—his daughter knew it would take his attention away from her. But it's I who have been here for him through thick and thin. The second that bastard winds up in a wheelchair, she'll be out of here. I suppose that's what they're saving me for—a nursemaid. Anyway, I know you don't care about that. It's the outcome you might be interested in.

"I'm ready to make a move, Lock. I'm filing a suit under the RICO Act. Carmine has been paying himself insane royalties on this stupid sunglass patent they filed. He's set up a network of sham companies from Bermuda to Hong Kong, paying for services that weren't provided and products that don't exist."

Lock snorted. "In other words, typical badass drug kingpin shit."

"I suppose so, huh? He's got a personal slush fund he uses

to cavort with young men around the world. He had me convinced I should donate my community assets in some of his companies and waive inheritance rights in exchange for being made the beneficiary of a private Panama foundation. After I did that, he went and changed the sole beneficiary to—"

"His daughter," Lock filled in. "You can avoid that if you make yourself the owner of the policy."

Carmen nodded, her mouth a thin line. "I know that now. I know I don't have much sympathy here. Lots of people have daughters, and lots of people believe he's 'doing right' by his daughter. He's not a deadbeat dad, that's for sure. But to me, it's a bit—"

"Excessive."

"—excessive, and basically if he's by some miracle shot dead, I'd be left with nothing."

Lock nodded. "Same if you divorced him."

"Right. Of course I've pondered that for years. Besides, it goes beyond that now. Now, I want fucking *revenge*. I don't care about Christian forgiveness anymore, Lock. He's wrung all that sort of kind, charitable feeling from me. My agenda is revenge, to get this motherfucker off the street. You live in Lake Havasu?"

"Is that where we are? I thought so. I live up in Rough and Ready. I run Los Toro Hermanos Bail Bonds. That's where you can find me—I hope—when it comes time to take him down. I'm all in, that's for fucking sure."

"Good. I thought I could count on you. We're here on Armour Drive near the golf course, if anything goes south."

"If I make it through this with all my body parts still attached, my life and rep won't be worth a pile of dinosaur shit. I'd ask for a piece to take him out with, but then we'd never make it off your property alive."

"Right. And taking him out would just funnel everything to his daughter, who would continue the scheme."

"Can you fucking find out something for me? Can you fucking find out where my partner—"

The yells and shouts of a tussle at the end of the hall outside stopped Lock short. He frowned fiercely as he strained to make out what was being said.

"—I'm going to get my lawyer on this! You can't just fucking grab an innocent biker off the street and take him into custody without reading him his rights! I have a civil right to remain free and clear and bear arms, and so what if I was packing a Glock? Since when is it illegal to take up arms against your oppressors?"

"I'll give *you* a fucking oppressor!" yelled Roland, and the door to Lock's room was flung wide open.

The heap of bones and limbs that was Twinkletoes was flung into the room. Lock's wrists were still bound, but he wrenched himself to his knees next to Turk's Prospect. "Twinkletoes! What the fuck?"

The skinny Prospect was wailing, "This is oppression without representation! I demand to see my lawyer. Your mother sucks bears in the forest!"

Roland said smoothly, "Good. I always hated my mother." He then glared, but not at the Prospect. He glared at Carmen. She was standing and attempting to inch herself out of the room, to wash her hands of the whole mess.

Roland stopped just short of wrenching her by the arm. He shot at her, "What the fuck is *this*, Carmen? Aiding and abetting the enemy again? Playing Nurse Ratched? I'm telling Mr. Rojas you took off his hood. What *else* were you talking about?"

Great, just fucking great. Now poor Carmen would be in hot water as well. Meanwhile, Twinkletoes continued to writhe like a bucket of fishing worms.

"I demand the due process of law! You can only hold me for twenty-four hours without charging me! *Elif air ab dinikh!*"

From what little Arabic Lock remembered, he knew that Twinkletoes' oath had something to do with dicks and religion. Carmen darted from the room after casting a last longing look at Lock. Roland slammed and locked the door, and Lock was able to ask Twinkletoes, "What the fuck? Last time I saw you, we left you at the Motel 6."

Hands bound at the small of his back too, Twinkletoes struggled to sit upright. He was a frail guy, with some sort of wasting disease. It took a giant bully of the lowest sort to throw him around. Twinkletoes panted, "Well, you remember how I put a tracker on Turk's bike. I noticed it was down in Poston, which baffled me, so I started down there in your cage. On my way, I passed two Caddies with blacked-out windows. On a hunch, I followed them here. Saw you guys with hoods, like some fucking journalists in Iraq, like some drug dealers in a National Geographic drug documentary. Un-fucking-fortunately, they saw me in the street, too."

Lock sighed deeply. "Well, that's just fucking great. Now they've got all three of us. They've really got the drop on us."

"Nothing's gone our way, that's for sure," lamented the Prospect. "Let's just hope Turk can convince Rojas to let us go. Or whatever."

Lock's empty stomach practically flipped, thinking of what a good job Turk could do convincing Rojas. He was glad he hadn't seen Rojas, so he couldn't graphically imagine Turk on his knees servicing the guy who was sure to be a giant, muscular bull. Or—was this worse?—the douchetard on his knees pleasuring Turk. He didn't know which was fucking worse, so he made small talk with Twinkletoes.

"I've got to thank you for trying, Twinkletoes. You're a loyal Prospect to your club."

"I try. It's not hard to be loyal to someone as exemplary as Turk. He's just a stand-up guy in every way. I can't think of one bad thing to say about him. He doesn't even snore. Seriously, his one bad quality might be that sometimes he's *too nice*." Twinkletoes looked away when he said, "I'm glad you hooked up with him. He deserves someone better than that Dayton Navarro asshole."

Lock was pleasantly shocked to hear Twinkletoes was aware of Turk's homosexuality. "Oh yeah? You knew about him and Dayton?"

The Prospect looked back at Lock. "Who doesn't? We don't go around discussing it openly, but it's sort of a not very closely guarded secret that Turk prefers the company of men. Doesn't bother me. He's a chick magnet, so it leaves more slash for me. The sloppy seconds."

Lock was about to ask Twinkletoes what would happen if Turk came out to their club, but again several pairs of boots were coming down the hallway outside. Body parts bumped and tussled, and when the door was kicked open, that damned Hopi was flung into the room.

Or, the shell of the Hopi. All the fight had gone out of Kwahu Johnson now. He was a barely breathing pile of bloody bones, and it was lucky this room wasn't carpeted, much less furnished. Lock thought about that LIBRARY MUSEUM ARTS & CRAFTS sign that was the highlight of Kwahu's interior decorating scheme. This guy had never stood a chance. Protesting the Redskins name was probably the highlight of his patriotic life—a life that now looked on the cusp of being over, for all practical purposes.

Roland loomed largely in the doorway now, handling Turk

with a bit more care. Even so, Turk was shoved into the room, and he fell to his knees next to Lock. Turk's hands were free, and he took Lock's face between his palms, turning his head every which way, inspecting him for signs of damage.

"What the fuck, Twinkletoes?" he asked his Prospect. "Don't tell me how you got here."

"I won't," the Prospect said sullenly.

Roland stepped in imperiously. He never seemed to sully his perfectly dry cleaned suit. "Mr. Rojas isn't too thrilled with this pretty boy here. He wants me to show you what happens to people who don't completely thrill him."

With three large steps, Roland came toward Kwahu. Suddenly what looked like an axe flashed in his hand. The old adage "it happened so fast" was definitely the case as a vicious cast came over Roland's face, literally making him resemble a demon, and the next thing Lock knew, most of Kwahu's foot was separated from the leg.

The majority of the blood splattered poor Twinkletoes, who recoiled in disgust up against the wall. It splashed his arm so heavily it dripped like glossy paint. Turk, too, automatically recoiled from the gore, halfway climbing up into Lock's lap. Lock only wished his arms were free to shield his lover from the gruesome sight. He knew Turk had seen worse in his time, but Lock's guilt at having gotten Turk into this mess in the first place took precedence. *Turk would not have that blood splashed on his leg if it weren't for me. He wouldn't have to look at a severed foot if not for me.*

"Fuck!" Lock shouted. "You're a disgusting, sadistic pig, do you fucking know that?"

Standing tall, Roland stood like a jolly giant holding the bloody axe. He even nodded with satisfaction at his handiwork, although he had to kick Kwahu to make sure he was still alive.

He was, although he only gave a few feeble groans. *If I had my piece, I'd shoot this poor bastard to put him out of his misery. After I shot this torture dungeon master.*

"Okay," Roland said brightly. He nodded at some shadowy figures in the doorway, and a BG came forward holding a sealed FedEx box. Roland waved the bloody axe around as he spoke, as though it were a lecturer's laser pointer. "Give that to the pretty boy. We've got to put these hoods back on you because we don't want you knowing where we are, naturally. But Mr. Rojas has decided to give you one more chance to prove yourselves worthy of his trust."

"Who cares?" spat Lock.

"Listen to him," Turk whispered, probably a wise move. Raining sarcasm and resentment on the cruel right hand man wouldn't help their plight.

Roland continued suavely, "We've brought your bikes back to a spot in Lake Havasu. There you'll get the coordinates of where we want this FedEx box delivered in person."

Turk cut Lock off at the pass by responding first. "Who are we looking for?"

"Guy by the name of Heriberto Orozco."

Lock asked, "By any chance does he work for the Marin cartel family?"

"Don't know. Doesn't matter. Do you want this chance to gain your freedom or not?"

Turk snapped, "We'll take it."

Roland nodded at a BG, who picked up Lock's hood from the floor and yanked it down over his head. *Well, at least we're free. For now.*

As they were hustled down to the side door, they passed an authoritative man yelling into his cell. Lock assumed it was Rojas, and he was shouting,

"Just take the fucking shipment up to La Paz on the next Rez and bury them! I'll set those fucking Cocopahs straight later."

It was pretty strange to be taking *any* shipment to La Paz on the Colorado River Reservation, because Lock knew that to be a ghost town. He hated Rojas so much he didn't care what or who they were burying.

Lock didn't realize until the Caddy was underway again that they'd only placed hoods over his and Turk's head. Twinkletoes was still back at the mansion, being held as a hostage until they completed their stupid fucking mission.

CHAPTER FOURTEEN

TURK

I was filled with admiration for the clean lines and sparse furnishings of Lock's midcentury modern house.

I had always liked that sort of architecture. Cropper Illuminati had rented an Eichler house in Pure and Easy before hooking up with Madison's mother. Back then, we had loathed the hollow plywood walls over which sound traveled, walls that didn't go all the way to the ceiling, like feeble partitions in a rat's maze. You were fucked into jackhammering if the hot water pipes underneath the cement slab broke, and birds were constantly committing hara-kiri against the large expanses of glass. The electric stovetop didn't work for shit, took forever just to boil water, but on the up side, the spotted floor tiles looked as though someone had already puked on them, so rarely needed cleaning, at least according to three bachelors.

We had loathed the style back then, but Lock's house was different. For one, his walls went all the way to the ceiling. He had invested in period-appropriate remodels, like a top of the line electric stove, cabinets that weren't made of particle board, and Jetsons-like quartz countertops. He even had retro furnishings, like an atomic wall clock, a TV in a turquoise housing, and a chenille bedspread that I glimpsed when Lock first gave me a tour of the house. I soaked in all the personal touches that showed me unseen sides of Lock, like the framed photo on his mantel of him and the Little League team he apparently used to coach, sponsored by Los Toro Hermanos Bail Bonds. It went against the grain of his tough, impervious image. The assistant coach evidently was the Indian guy I'd seen going into his office near the highway.

Best, a kidney-shaped pool was heated to perfection and beckoned to us after our grueling day. After we chowed down on some hamburger patties Lock tossed into a frying pan, we stripped and soothed ourselves in the calming pool waters. The house backed up against the open space of a high desert mesa, and I presumed the neighbors on either side were either asleep or cool.

We hadn't talked at all about our ordeal. The elephant in the room was the giant question, "What did Carmine Rojas do to you in his private office?" Lock was sensitive enough not to bring it up, although I knew he was dying to know. It was enough that we were taking an evening off to soothe ourselves, to recharge, to sleep while Twinkletoes sat in that room with the dying Indian. He'd come to save us and was being held hostage instead. But we wouldn't be worth a damn on our next run if we didn't have some sleep and food.

I had finally been allowed to call my club once they set us loose where they'd parked our bikes. I talked to Lytton, but only briefed him on the most basic of details. I had to admit that Rojas was holding Twinkletoes. That was club business, and they had every right to know.

"But all we have to do is deliver this package tomorrow, and they'll set him free."

Lytton harrumphed. "Sounds like a house of cards that just keeps falling, one after the other, man. I always knew those Assassins were bad news, but this is fucking crazy. They can't just hold our Prospect while some low-level scumbag is blackmailing you." I noticed how Lytton didn't ask *why* they were blackmailing us, what they had on us. "We're fucking riding out there first thing in the morning to set those assholes straight. I've heard nothing but bad things about that Stumpy dirtbag. I heard he bailed on his own brother while they were doing a jewelry store heist. Left him holding the bag while he got away. I've heard about the way Stumpy uses those poor bastards on the Rez. At least we pay our men an honest wage and we do *not* get them hooked on the stuff. I even heard Stumpy was booted out of the Hell's Angels for being too brutal. Too brutal for the Angels."

"Don't come down. They'll let Twinkletoes go when we report this mission as completed."

"It sounds like another fucking setup to me," said Lytton, but he backed off.

"Tell me about your first experience with another guy," Lock said now.

We'd done a bunch of laps, the better to exercise our arms that had been bound so long. We'd washed off all the dried blood, sweat, and piss with chlorinated water, and we were finally somewhat refreshed. I still didn't want to get out of the pool, so I flung my arms over the edge of the concrete and panted with the exertion of my swim. The second Lock made me think of Evo Tognozzi from high school, the second my prick began to swell underwater.

I smiled slyly, exhausted. "I was sixteen the first time I sucked another boy in a high school locker room."

"*Holy shit*," Lock whispered, coming closer. His hard-on touched my hip under the water, and I knew we didn't have to worry about major shrinkage. "Are you fucking kidding me?"

"Serious as a heart attack. Isn't that every closeted boy's wet dream?"

"Fuck *yeah*. Tell me about it."

That's when I started telling Lock about Tognozzi. Lock cupped my ass in his palm and squeezed my hard-on as I told him the locker room story. The hazing that had been intended to torment and embarrass me had turned into a giant teenaged hormonal fuckfest. I had never been a good speaker, but the story just flowed, encouraged by Lock's squeezes and nibbles to my shoulder. "When the first boy called out 'bukkake!' and came forward with his erection in his fist, it broke open a floodgate. Suddenly about six boys stood around me shining their poles."

"What did the main asshole do—Baumgardner? You think he was closeted?"

"Oh, no fucking doubt. All these hazing rituals that involve tormenting some guy's genitals? It's their way of taking out their sexual frustrations. Baumgardner had a towel around his waist, but it was obvious his willie was pretty hard, too. When the boys started whacking off on me, Baumgardner became unhinged. 'What the fuck? Is everyone around here a fag?' He fisted my dick at the base and began striking me even harder with the ruler, almost like in a frenzy. He really looked like he was crying at that point. 'Fag! Fag!' he kept yelling.

"'Oh, God, I'm coming!' yelled the original boy. And he splashed me with a big, hot load. It pooled in my abdomen, ran down my sides, it was such a heavy load. That was when Baumgardner really went crazy."

Lock gripped my hip, now placing his hard-on in my ass crack, between my thighs. I could feel his thick tool pulsing near my anus. Warm water lapped at my balls, setting them to tingling. "I'll bet. Did the other guys start jizzing on you too?"

"Well, get this. The guy I had the crush on, Tognozzi, I

guess he'd been hanging around toward the back. Baumgardner was in a frenzy of sadism by this time, and he snarled, 'I'll fucking get *you*, you damned homo. Let's see how much you like munching man meat.' And he whipped off his towel, just like in some gladiator flick."

"Was he hard? Were you right? Let's go up on that patch of lawn."

"Course he was hard." We hauled ourselves over the edge of the pool and half walked, half crawled to a small lawn where Joshua trees cast long shadows from the outdoor lighting. Lock had spread out a couple of towels here, and I fell on my ass, my prick wet and shiny. Lock immediately positioned himself between my outspread thighs, the taut cap of his penis pointing right at my asshole. He nuzzled and lapped at my nipples as he squeezed my dick. I'd been servicing other men all week long, and hadn't had a single chance to come myself.

"What was he going to do, do you think?" Lock seemed to be taking my story with a grain of salt. I couldn't prove any of it, of course, but it was so firmly ingrained in my memory banks, every detail had been saved, down to the sour smell of Baumgardner's crotch. He hadn't showered yet, and I actually did *not* want to suck his dick. "Did he shove it in your mouth?"

"Well, no," I purred, squirming under the hard, flat planes of Lock's torso. "He never got around to it, because Tognozzi suddenly busted to the front of the line. After being silent as the grave all fucking day, he suddenly couldn't resist coming forward with a giant erection in his hand."

"Tell me more," Lock murmured.

I hissed and jumped, not expecting the handful of lube he pressed between my ass cheeks. I soon exhaled and relaxed, though, remembering to trust in him. He must've thrown the motion lotion down when he placed the towels there. *How thoughtful.* He massaged the slimy stuff around my hole, occasionally slipping a finger in to the first knuckle, tantalizing me, prepping me. My voice was mellower now, almost trance-like. "Well, he shoved that moron Baumgardner aside and straddled me as I sat in the chair. I'll never fucking forget the sight of his gorgeous face looking down at me, superior, haughty like. Lock, you wouldn't believe what a hot sight it was, this erection just inches from my hungry mouth."

"Oh, I'd fucking believe it," he mumbled, now sliding two fingers inside me.

My hands woven together at the back of my head, I swiveled my hips into Lock's finger-fucking, the better to grind his fingers deeper inside me. I gasped when his fingertips brushed against that sweet spot. Now my hips bounced like a ping pong paddle, my cock the ball that danced frantically. "He growled at me, all superior and dominant. 'All right, you cocksucker. You were ogling me in the fucking shower. You want my meat in your mouth. Say it.'"

"Did you?" Lock was humping the towel now as he finger-banged me. "Say it, I mean."

"I did. I said it real low, hoping not everyone in the entire room heard me. 'I want to suck your dick.' But by now a couple of other boys had jerked off on me, and my chest was just a swimming mass of cum. Every time a boy would release on me, he'd fade out and another one would take his place. But Tognozzi was bold. He had everything in control, even though he was a new transfer student. He just grabbed his own beef and rubbed it against my lips. I'll never forget the sweet taste of his pre-come, and I stuck out my tongue to taste it. It was the first jizz I'd ever tasted, other than my own, and he kept encouraging me. 'Go ahead, you know you want it. Suck me.'"

Lock's fingers slipped out of me, replaced by the sizzling

heat of his cockhead. My severe physical exhaustion almost added to the erotic bliss of him nudging that fat dickhead into my hole. His panting against my throat came shallow and rapid, misting my skin. "So did you? Oh, God, tell me you did. Tell me how you swallowed that football player's sword."

I rotated my hips lasciviously, like a stripper at the pole, encouraging his dick to sink deeper and deeper inside me. I hadn't been used in a while—it had been two months since my last fuck session with Dayton—and I really had to relax into it. I was grateful he wasn't plundering my ass like a lot of eager bicurious men would have, but taking it slow, although it meant holding his breath in between pants, his hips shuddering with his effort at control. "What do you think, Mr. Singer? The second I opened my jaw to take him in, he grabbed the back of my head and jammed it in so far it hit my gag reflex. I opened up wide and tried to deep-throat him like a fucking noob, trying to take every inch of that big tool. He groaned and fucked my mouth, and I was practically choking and puking—while turned on in every cell of my being."

Lock groaned too, and jabbed his dick another two inches inside me. I wrapped one naked thigh around the back of his haunches, wide open for him. His cock flexed and expanded inside my ass, and a subterranean tremor ran up his arms as he held his torso off me. Now he was hunched over me, his thighs lifting my hips off the towel, pulsating deep inside me. "Don't stop," he whispered. "I'm gonna come just like that hunky football player."

"And I'm gonna love it just as much. He kept snarling macho, domineering things at me while I slurped away at his dick. 'You love that, don't you? This isn't the first time you've swallowed a dick, I can tell."

"Was it?" Lock choked back a grunt. "Your first dick? Are

you sure? You're so fucking good, it can't have been your first."

I knew he was chiding me, so I slid a hand from under my head to caress his. It was heaven spearing my fingers through those thick spiky locks while gyrating my pelvis against him. "That's what he said. 'That's right, suck it down like you've done before. Do the same thing to me you've done to all those other dicks.'" My erection was smashed between our pubic bones, Lock massaging it with his every stroke. He now fucked me aggressively, his fingers digging into my ass as he held me to his crotch, every thrust against my gland sending me higher into a vortex of ecstasy. Tiny spurts of pre-come dribbled from my dick and I rotated my hips for maximum pleasure. "The last thing he managed to say was, 'You just love eating a whole load of prick juice,' and he blew in my mouth."

The moment I said that, Lock shot his wad. Holding his breath, his hips trembled as his prick twitched inside of me. I couldn't really feel the hot load he deposited up against my core, but gooseflesh rose on his shoulders and the juicy globes of his ass.

He was just a grunting, mindless hunched ball of ecstasy, and I jiggled my pubic mound against him, squeezing his spurting dick tight with my inner muscles. "That's it…come inside me, you blond god, my Master…I want to take all of you, all of it. Just keep coming. Cumon…you can do it…" Like a trainer encouraging a puppy to swim, I encouraged Lock to keep his spurting cock deep inside me, to draw out his orgasm.

Finally the jets petered out, and Lock breathed freely, gulping drily, huffing and puffing. Touching his nose to mine, he tried to kiss me, but he was panting too heavily. "God, Turk. You're a fucking beautiful stallion. You really let me in. That was the deepest, most intense fuck I've ever had."

I gave him a peck on the lips, but my mouth was dry, too.

"You sure love to ball," I panted, quoting an old Marvin Gaye song. Every Bare Boner worth his salt knew all those old R&B songs. One brother, Gollywow, sang backup in an R&B group, so we were all aficionados.

"Agh." Unceremoniously, Lock rolled off me and onto his back on the other towel. His hand was flung over his abdomen like a piece of tissue paper. "Finish telling me about the locker room. What did the Greek statue do after he blew in your mouth?"

Now I'd lost the taste for the story, and really, the rest of it wasn't nearly as spectacular. "Well, everyone was kind of embarrassed by then. Nobody wanted to look at anyone. I still had a big old honking hard-on, but even Baumgardner didn't want to spank me with the ruler anymore. Everyone couldn't wait to get the hell out of there. Even the kid who was still choking the sheriff and dripping on my chest did a moonwalk out of there. I almost thought I'd be stuck tied to the fucking chair helplessly for the coach to find me all dripping with semen."

"You could've sucked off the coach, to get him to untie you."

I glanced at Lock. He was grinning crookedly at me with an exhausted smile. "I didn't start being a daddy chaser until later. Well, did anything like that happen to *you* in high school? What kind of high school did you go to?" I realized I knew nothing about Lock's childhood, where he was from. Did he grow up in Lake Havasu?

"I went to Brentwood School," said Lock distantly, as though talking about someone else.

I felt he expected me to know what that implied. "And?"

"And that place was so white they thought Malcolm X's name was Malcolm the Tenth. That's what."

"So? White boys suck cock."

"Not these boys. I would've been tarred and feathered about as bad as we're going to be if Stumpy outs us to our clubs. Well, my club, anyway. I get the feeling your club already knows, right?"

"I'm fairly sure." I raised myself on an elbow and lightly ran my fingers through Lock's chest hair. "Bareback, eh? You trust me that much?"

His eyes were relaxed, open. Trusting, I might've even called them. "I believe you've only been with Dayton for the past two years. And I didn't get anything from him. Yet."

"No, you're cool. Dayton's clean. So you didn't touch another boy in high school?"

"No. I was in denial, especially to myself, I think, until I was in the Air Force."

I was intrigued. My stiffie already rubbed deliciously against the towel, and without thinking, my hand moved to lightly stroke myself. "You did it with another jock?"

Lock's face took on a shy cast. "Yeah. Me and Park did it every way from Sunday for almost two years. And don't give me any shit about the Mile High Club."

"Oh," I said casually, "lots of people give you shit about that?"

He smiled wryly. "Not a one, because I haven't told even one person."

"Where is he now?"

"Dead."

Oh, Jesus. I didn't fucking know what to say. I dropped my cock. Again, something came out of my mouth before I had a chance to censor it. It must've been my exhaustion talking. "If it's any consolation, I lost my Fender too."

"The white power jail guy?"

"Right. New blood came in that had it out for Fender. They got him with a shiv they'd smuggled in. I saw the murderer running away from the scene of the crime, but I couldn't prove anything. I just held my man and sobbed and screamed like a fucking baby. I was never the same again."

Lock looked distantly at the stars above. "Then you know how it feels. Only I didn't get to hold any body. I gathered up several body parts, but I couldn't sit there holding them and sobbing." He came down to earth a bit when he asked me, "Is that when you got the teardrop tat?"

"Exactly. I walked around like a zombie for another few months, and then my time was up. No one dared touch me in the meantime."

"I get that. I was a zombie for a long fucking time after that crash in the desert." His eyes finally flickered to my face. "I really only got over it when I met you."

My heart nearly stopped. *Met me?* "You mean, met me like two weeks ago met me?"

He nodded once. "Two weeks ago."

"You were a zombie until then?"

"I didn't really come alive until I met you. I was just walking around, going through the motions. I hooked up with Ruby because I never wanted to be with another man. That, and my club wouldn't tolerate it, of course. I even thought I'd marry her. I guess I was kind of half-hearted about it, because I didn't get upset when she walked out. I kept thinking 'I'll get upset tomorrow,' only tomorrow never came. *You* came instead."

Uncomfortable with intimate talk, I turned it into a joke. "Well, I haven't really *come*, if you look at it."

Lock's face became dead serious. "Listen, I know you haven't been satisfied in a hella long time. All that'll change tomorrow once we spring Twinkletoes from that peckerhead's house. We'll come here, relax, grill a decent dinner instead of some prefab hamburgers. Wish I could tell you I'd have some of my friends over, but I can't. I wouldn't. You know. But I want you to know this isn't all one-sided. I want to satisfy you too, Turk." He closed his hand over mine.

"But we should get some Zs," I said, giving him an out. "We won't be worth a damn to Twinkletoes if we don't get any rest."

Lock withdrew his hand and struggled to a sitting position. "Yeah. I wonder what's in that damned FedEx box."

"Yeah. And what it means for ol' Heriberto Orozco."

I helped Lock to his feet. He said, "Box feels heavy enough to be a piece."

"Yeah, but why would they be sending a piece to anyone? You don't need to wrap a piece up in a sealed box."

"Got to be drugs then."

We started walking back to the house. I said, "Same thing. Why bother wrapping up drugs?" We had to take our scoots to Yuma the next day, a good two hour ride. "You know that area of Yuma it's addressed to? What's it like?"

Lock said, "As expected from the Spanish name of our contact, it's a pretty bad barrio. Heriberto Orozco is probably a dope boy in a trap, so it could be coin to pay him. Either way, I don't give a shit. Don't want to be there when he opens it."

"Me either. It's not our beef."

"I know my club does business with Rojas, but I wouldn't mind seeing him taken down. You wouldn't believe the backstabbing shit his wife was telling me about him. She plans on filing a RICO case against him but I don't want to wait that long. Want to see that guy gone *now*."

Lock went to get a glass of water, and I went to piss. By the time we joined each other underneath his cool, clean sheets, I was pretty much out like a light.

Even then, it was the best sleep of my entire fucking life. Occasionally between bouts of REM sleep, I'd be aware he was holding me, his skin against mine, patches of his velvety goodness licking at my body like a steady flame. I fairly buzzed with the energy he imparted to me. We literally had good chemistry.

I drifted for what felt like hours, sometimes dipping into a dream where Lock was the cocksucker. Lock's shaggy hair tickled the insides of my thighs as he mouthed my erect dick. His dream tongue was spongey and ticklish as he sucked me into a heavenly, seedless orgasm. But when roadrunners started their clicking and rattling outside Lock's open window, I groggily woke. In the dim light before sunrise, Lock lay on his back like an angel, his arms flung out above his head, the owl tattoo a blur on his pec.

I knew it had only been a dream. But it gave me something to hope for.

CHAPTER FIFTEEN
LOCK

They'd jumped out of bed at the buttcrack of dawn. There was no lolling about, fondling each other.

In a way, Lock was relieved. He knew he'd vaguely promised Turk some sexual relief and now he was regretting his words. Nerves, that's all it was. He was glad he couldn't talk to Turk as they ripped it up going south down the highway.

It was a huge step to take. There had been that unwritten line in the sand with Park that Lock was never forced to go there, to take the aggressive position in pleasuring his lover. Frankly, he didn't know what Park did to satisfy himself. It wasn't Lock's business and he didn't care. He was simply never, ever going to put a shred of effort into giving another man sexual pleasure. He didn't roll that way. It would mean he was definitively, irrevocably gay, and Lock would never admit to that. Not even to his own self. He was really just nailing Park for lack of any tolerable women around.

Now that he admitted he was in it with Turk for the long haul, though, he had to rethink that stance. Riding free past the mines of the barren Dome Rock Mountains gave him a bit of leeway to actually think about it. The idea that Carmine Rojas had touched his lover really tweaked him. Although Roland had been rougher with Turk when he tossed him back into that little room with Lock, he knew something had gone down between the kingpin and his lover. It had to have, or they wouldn't have been given this last chance to redeem themselves.

That explained all the strange stuff Roland had been saying to Turk, calling him a "pretty boy" whom Rojas was "interested in," and saying that Rojas wasn't "completely thrilled" with him. Had Turk sucked Rojas' cock? Done an inadequate job? That had to be it, because if Rojas had sucked Turk off, there was no way for Turk to fail to thrill. Lock concluded that Turk had been unable to follow through with the cocksucking, had literally choked or even bitten the sadistic monster. It was just one of those things Lock knew he had to erase from his memory banks, but he was still left with a bitter, smoldering rage against the crime boss.

The idea of patching over into The Bare Bones had even crossed Lock's mind. Staying with The Assassins of Youth was just a lousy, pissed-off concept. He loathed Stumpy Meadows and would be stuck seeing him at least once a month in chapel, not to mention rallies and club fish fries or business. But patching over would only bring a slew of fresh problems with it. Mainly, having daily access to the wonderland that was Turk Blackburn's body would be irresistible. They were bound to get busted by Turk's club sooner or later. No matter how tolerant those brothers were, two homosexuals were worse than one, and eventually they'd have to leave anyway—in good standing, or otherwise. Besides, Lock didn't want to leave the bail bonds business he'd worked so hard to build from the ground up.

Lock thought about Stumpy's use of meth and heroin. He had heard that ongoing heavy drug use was a patch-pulling offense. Maybe that's why Stumpy had been booted from the Hell's Angels. He could bring this up to Papa Ewey. It still didn't address the fact that the Assassins were dealing with

Carmine Rojas, a thug who had held them hostage and abused Lock's boyfriend under duress. Lock didn't do business with people he had no respect for.

There had to be a mental and spiritual prize in running with his club. Just the money and camaraderie wasn't good enough. Lock had to be rewarded on more esoteric levels, which was why he'd coached Little League and been a Big Brother for years. His club had always fulfilled his primitive need for freedom, equality, democracy. Every brother had a vote. Decisions were clear-cut, sharply defined, easy to follow. Now, knowing the sleazy hand of Carmine Rojas was on a lot of, if not most, of his club's business, Lock no longer felt part of a righteous brotherhood. He was only a minion, a cog in a corrupt, sordid empire that was just putting simple people to death while making buttloads of coin for the unscrupulous powers that be.

Lock and Turk were deviant, bent men, he knew that. But they soared head and shoulders above the reprobates at the top of the cartel heap. They were idealistic, pure, and romantic bent zealots. Lock might as well hand over all of his rockers right now to Papa Ewey and walk away with a shred of pride from the club that had meant the whole world to him. Before Turk Blackburn had assaulted him, broken his nose, and forced him to love him.

Oh, holy Jesus on a stick. A cop was suddenly behind Lock, his cherry blaring. He must've been hiding behind that billboard like a typical fucking pig. They were going about ten miles over the speed limit, but they really should've been doing more, the sooner to spring Twinkletoes from that house of horrors.

Waving at Turk to continue on—Turk had the FedEx box in his saddlebag—Lock decided to take the fall, accept the Fast Riding Award from the cop. He worked closely with the courts and could even make the ticket go away back in Mohave County. He could even play the "fellow law enforcement official" card.

"Sorry, Officer," Lock said smoothly after cutting his engine and removing his helmet respectfully. The portly county sheriff was maybe only in his forties but wrinkly from squinting at sun all the time. "I'm a bail bondsman from Lake Havasu, on the trail of a child molester."

"Is that so?" Sheriff D. Greenspan didn't seem all that intrigued by what Lock thought was a pretty damned intriguing. He scratched his belly over the tan, button-down shirt that stretched it like a condom. He held out his hand for Lock's driver's license. Lock handed him that, plus his Los Toro Hermanos business card. "You look more like a biker we've got an ATL on."

"I don't know why there would be an Attempt to Locate out on me. I'm the guy catching the criminals. Wasn't I speeding?" Lock really hoped he'd been speeding. Who the hell would put an ATL out on him? Maybe Stumpy, for some weird reason. Maybe he'd heard they'd made it out of Rojas' house alive and he didn't like that. But would he have involved the cops? Doubtful. Highly doubtful. Outlaws never reached out to cops. It just wasn't done.

"Oh, yeah, sure, and speeding," Greenspan said distantly, waddling back to his vehicle to run the license.

Lock could do nothing but wait. He couldn't even get off his ride without freaking out the overly dogmatic pig. And sitting there, the image of that fucked Hopi and his cut-off foot kept flashing in his mind's eye. *I have to seriously do something to get retribution on that fucker Rojas. Look at his sad, sorry wife. He treats her like he beats her. I guess she'll get hers eventually. But think of all the body parts he's chopping off in the meantime.* It was like colonial Africa over in that golf course mansion what with all the hacked-off limbs. Maybe Lock could do something to hurry Carmen's plan along.

"All right, looks like your record's clean. Kind of important for a registered bounty hunter, isn't it?"

Lock forced a smile. "Sure is."

Greenspan looked at him over the top of his mirrored shades. "Look. I don't want to give a fellow officer of the law a ticket. It really rubs me the wrong way having to do that."

Lock nodded. "And I'm not that ATL subject…right?"

"Right. Must be another biker they're attempting to locate. But you *were* going eighty-two. Listen. If you get off that bike and follow me over there, I might just let you pay off that ticket. Things might go real nice for you."

"Pay off" the ticket? This cop was looking for some sort of bribe. Lock calculated quickly. He hadn't had a chance to get to an ATM for a couple of days, but he had been buying gas and gas station junk food, so he had like twenty dollars in his wallet. D. Greenspan had waved at the cop car. He must want Lock to go on the lee side of the car so people driving by wouldn't see him handing him money.

"All right," Lock said slowly, dismounting just as slowly. "I'm not sure how much money I've got on me, though. You'll have to let me check my wallet."

"Right," agreed Greenspan. "After I frisk you, of course. Wouldn't want you going for your piece."

"My piece is in my waistband. A forty cal Glock." Lock meandered to the desert side of the car with his hands held away from his sides. "Wallet's attached to that chain."

Officer Greenspan shoved Lock's shoulder, got him to lean against the car's hood on his palms in the attitude of someone being frisked. "Good to know. You've got some nice toys here.

I use this brand and model of Taser myself."

"It's a good one," Lock said conversationally, although the sheriff was taking an excessively long time feeling his calf. He hadn't even removed his Glock first. "Works at fifteen feet."

Greenspan took forever squeezing Lock's thigh. His fingers pressed uncomfortably close to Lock's testicles. Lock knew the guy would be obligated to pat his crotch, but it was when the cop said, "I *really* like your tools," that a feeling of dread knifed through Lock's entrails. So it wasn't totally unexpected when Greenspan slid his palm around the fly of Lock's jeans and squeezed a big handful of his prick.

Oh. That sort of payoff. How could I have been so fucking stupid not to realize that? Maybe he'll take money. "Listen," Lock said feebly, "I'm not into that sort of payment plan, Officer. You saw that guy riding with me. He's my partner. We're…" Lock couldn't even think of the word, that's how often it came up in real life. Whatever it was, it meant "two people committed to have sex only with each other."

Officer Greenspan squeezed his tool almost lovingly. "That's all right. I don't care. Most bikers around these parts don't hesitate to get on their knees to get out of a ticket. No one wants that on their record."

Seriously? Most bikers do that? The bikers Lock knew would rather suck bloody glass from a rubber hose than blow a cop. Who the fuck lived around here? "Well, I'm not one of them, Officer. I guess I'll just take the ticket. It won't affect my bondsman's license. It's not a felony." Lock attempted to turn around, but Greenspan's hand between his shoulder blades told him to stay put. The officer's free hand now threateningly clinked a pair of handcuffs.

"But it *is* a felony to commit a crime while possessing a deadly weapon."

Fuck. The guy was going to be a total douche about it. "Seriously? You know that I'm licensed to carry this piece."

Greenspan was taking one of Lock's arms off the roof of the car in preparation for cuffing. "Won't be licensed for long if you don't get on your fucking knees like a good submissive and lap up my dick."

Fuck and double fuck. Lock's brain was lightning fast gauging how he could elbow the hefty guy in the gut and pull his piece on him. He could reach his piece faster, get to it first. He'd hold it on the guy while he made his getaway. *But he's got my license number.* Greenspan could make life hard on him. Greenspan would issue the ticket anyway, and then some. There'd be a serious ATL out on him if he pulled his piece and escaped. Then there really *would* be a felony. *Triple fuck.* He would've issued the perverted policeman a beatdown even if he *wasn't* attached to Turk Blackburn. He just didn't go in for being bossed around by anyone, cop or no. But he had to calm down and evaluate to what extent he wanted to tweak the emotional officer.

A hugely lucky thing happened just then.

"Who's this?" Lock said, glad a fellow biker was pulling onto the shoulder. Greenspan seemed to perk up, too, and backed off. Lock exhaled with relief. The new arrival wasn't an outlaw, didn't fly any colors, and only wore a few patches on his cut that were associated with a regular riding club. So he couldn't have been pulling over to help out Lock's ass.

"Ormond," said the cop warmly. He even shook the biker's hand after the guy removed his riding club helmet, complete with face guard. No self-respecting one percenter wore that style of lid, unless the guy was riding undercover. Still, Lock would've seen him around if he belonged to a brother club. Ormond wasn't even a nomad. The final nail in his coffin was

A DANGEROUS REALITY

that he was *friendly* to a cop. That just about tore it. Not only was he in a regular riding club, it was a *very lame* one.

Lock took advantage of this interruption to sneak sideways back to his ride. Ormond was incredibly handsome in a model-perfect, Turk Blackburn way. He was beefier than Turk, with that natural, sultry eyeliner that had marked his lover Park. He wore his white wifebeater like a proud flag, showing off his carved torso. Just the sort of guy to distract Officer Greenspan, and Lock straddled his saddle again. *Thank you, Ormond.* Lock waited to be given the all clear to leave. He didn't want to risk pissing off the touchy pig again. Ormond seemed to be putting Greenspan in a good mood.

In fact, the sheriff's mood was so elevated, Ormond even got off his bike and went around the rear of the cop car. Lock grinned. *This is getting interesting.* When the riding club member's head vanished at the feet of the cop who leaned back against a car window, Lock became so intrigued he even dismounted and tiptoed closer.

He wanted to know who the fuck had just saved his ass, and why. Who was this guy not affiliated with any MC who had interrupted what was certain to end unpleasantly? Ormond had Greenspan so gaga the guy appeared to have forgotten all about Lock, when he'd literally had him in the palm of his hands seconds ago. Maybe it was an insult to Lock's twisted sense of pride that this new rider was able to distract the pig so easily. But it was like a highway pileup—he had to slow down and look.

Clusterfuck! The beautiful biker was on his leather-clad knees. He'd already whipped the beefy cop's dick out and was slathering his artistic tongue all up and down its length. It wasn't even an impressive or attractive dick, but the biker was acting like it was cotton candy lube the way he licked it up. The fleshy cop's jaw was slack with attention and he licked his lip while rubbing his hand all over the biker's spiky hairdo. He was uttering shit Lock couldn't hear over the whooshing of highway traffic, but Lock got the general picture. Officer Greenspan was loving every second of the excellent blowjob.

Lock guffawed in disbelief when Ormond took the little tool in his mouth and hoovered away enthusiastically. *This must be the cocksucking biker Greenspan mentioned. And he's not even trying to get out of a ticket. Is he doing* me *a favor?* I think I want to stick around and talk to this guy.

So Lock waited with folded arms as Ormond worked like a hooker to satisfy the portly cop. Lock was fascinated with the danger of the scene. This was something Turk might've done a couple years back—if Turk was into blowing cops, that was, which Lock doubted. But the sheer danger of the act, right beside a busy highway, with an officer of the law to boot—that was up Turk's alley. The exhibitionistic thrill of almost being caught was a turn-on for Lock, too. He mulled over the possibility of doing something like this with Turk, then decided against it. There was a lot more than a speeding ticket at stake if they were seen by someone they knew. Someone who could Instagram a picture of them in about ten seconds.

Sorry to be so late, he texted Turk. *Cop's got a scene you won't believe when I tell you in person. Behind you about twenty minutes.*

Meantime, Lock was getting a good chuckle out of Ormond's enthusiastic talents. So many questions and so little time. Greenspan had to hold his belly out of the way in order to get an eyeful of the gorgeous motorcyclist polishing his knob. Lock was surprised the guy didn't climax sooner what with that pretty face wringing it dry. But Greenspan jumped a little when his radio crackled with a 215, a carjacking not far away. The officer finished up fast then, swiveling his hips like a belly dancer to plunge his dinky tool between those shapely lips. Ormond sure appeared to enjoy giving that guy a pipe job, and Lock was hugely relieved when the cop waved him away in his rush to jump into the driver's seat. He was so rushed he barely tucked his shirt back into his pants.

Alone finally in the cop car's dust, Ormond looked at Lock like the cat who ate the canary. Standing upright now, he sported a giant erection nestled between his chaps that told Lock he'd actually been into the pipe job. Lazily, he wiped his mouth with the back of his hand and approached Lock.

"See? I knew he'd let you go. Not everyone is into his style of payment like I am." Ormond had a heavy Latin accent. He was too tall to be from south of the border, so Lock decided he was a Spaniard, from Spain. "Sorry you had to see that."

Lock grinned. "All right, now. You want to tell me what the fuck that was all about? Because I don't think we've met before, and you're not affiliated with any MC that I can tell. For that matter, you can't possibly know that *I* am affiliated with an MC because I'm undercover right now and not flying my colors. So what goes on, brother?"

Ormond laughed, suddenly shy. Pulling a cigarette from his cut pocket, he leaned back against his bike casually as though this happened every day, giving blowjobs to cops. "All the Quartzsite cops know me. I've just got a thing for men in uniforms. It's constantly screwing me up, this kink. When will I ever learn? These men are just using me. But I'm a sucker for it every time."

Lock nodded. He got it. He used to think it was mostly Park's uniform that had made him fall in love. There was something about a hot stud wearing badges and patches—maybe part of his attraction to Turk. "It's something about authority figures. You like being bossed around. Nothing wrong with that." *Especially if your kink gets me off the hook with that cop.*

But Ormond shook his head. "That's the thing. I *don't* like being bossed. I am not a submissive, not a weakling. To me, getting on my knees is a way of, how do you say it, *control*. When I know the big man is putty in my hands, I know I control him, I know I can get him to do anything for me." A blush seemed to rise in his beautiful dusky skin, and he looked at the ground. "But I know a big, bad biker like you doesn't want to hear this disgusting stuff."

That's when it suddenly came pouring out of Lock. He'd been keeping it secret so long when he really wanted to shout it to the world. Ormond was an aficionado of the two things closest to Lock's heart—bikes, and other men. This stranger had just helped him out of an enormous scrape. Lock didn't plan to pour out his heart. At the very least, the guy was a stranger from Quartzsite, so he'd stay a stranger. Lock didn't need to ever face him again. "No, it's cool. You're a power bottom. That's understandable. So is my…" And he said the word. "…boyfriend."

Ormond's eyebrows shot up. He dropped his cigarette to the dirt and stood up straighter. "Boyfriend?" he asked skeptically.

Lock repeated, "Boyfriend. That guy you might've seen me riding with. He's with a different club, one out of Pure and Easy. I'm with The Assassins of Youth out of—"

"Bullhead City, I know," Ormond said in his thick Latin accent. "You know that asshole Stumpy Meadows? He's constantly harassing me and my friends. What a homophobe."

"Yes, unfortunately, I know him. He's the reason we're stuck on this run down to Yuma, which is where I'd best head right now."

"But wait. You are a…gay biker? I presume Stumpy does

not know?"

Lock guffawed. "That's why we're on this idiotic run. Stumpy got a visual of us doing it in a Motel 6 a couple of days ago and we've been in debt to him ever since."

Ormond pointed at the ground. "That is why I do not join a fucking MC! You think I would not like to? I would *love* to have a fine brotherhood of men like that—they do not even have to be homosexual! What do I care? I have the human need for companionship and brotherhood that would be fulfilled with a club. My bike is an extension of my very soul. The Harley is not a sewing machine like those rice rockets! Riders don't have the same connection we do, and only other Harley riders feel that, no?"

"I'm with you, brother." Lock's heart sped up when Ormond said he would like to join a club. *Why the hell not? Why haven't I thought of this before? Because I barely have time to think.* "I've been trying to think on what Turk and I are going to wind up doing. You say you have other gay brothers—friend who also ride?"

"Oh, yes! There are maybe ten of us who get together in the Quartzsite area." Again, Ormond shaded a little with embarrassment. "But not all of them like to toy with men wearing badges. They each have their own kinks. But none can join an MC because we cannot be ourselves in a club like that!"

So many ideas clamored to find a footing in Lock's brain. He knew only another ride down the highway would blow the dust from his soul and allow those ideas to organize themselves. He was loaded with questions for Ormond, but he had to get going or Turk would think he pussed out. "You know what, I'd like to meet up again and toss some ideas around. You're definitely giving me some ideas, but I've got to run." He shook the guy's hand. "I'm Lock Singer, but don't go around repeating that in mixed company. What do you do in Quartzsite?"

"Ormond Tangier at your service. Well, not in *that* way, I do not mean! I work in the special effects makeup business. I run my own studio, but I have to fly to LA quite often."

Quickly, Lock whipped a bail bonds business card from his wallet and wrote on the back. "Here. I'm attempting to locate this loser. He molested several young boys and jumped bail. Let me know if you see his Lexus anywhere, you and your men. You ride this corridor often. Keep an eye out."

"Most definitely," said Ormond, who Lock was starting to suspect was Italian. The makeup business, that explained how picture-perfect the guy was. His spiky hair was tipped with silver-gold frosting, his five o'clock shadow just the right stubbly length. "And here is my card if you ever wish to…to talk with others like you."

"Sure thing," said Lock, saluting the man with his own card.

A thrilling, dangerous tingle tickled at Lock's innards as he plummeted toward the Chocolate Mountains. *Was it possible…*He almost didn't dare to think it might be.

He needed to feel the nonstop, throbbing vibration of his bike beneath him. He fell into a trance when he rode, as though a hundred Buddhist monks chanted in his head. The roar of his tailpipes expressed his frustration and rage, and most of all his impotence at finding himself the helpless victim of Stumpy Meadows and, now, Carmine Rojas.

He needed a way out of this fucked predicament. Meeting Ormond Tangier just might've given him that out.

CHAPTER SIXTEEN
TURK

"Let's park our rides a few doors down from Orozco's trap house," said Lock.

We were paused at a stop sign in a hood that was just wall-to-wall graffiti and roach coaches, with a spitter or a spotter on every corner. It was hard to tell the difference because they were all liberally covered in colorful ink sleeves, defiantly sagging their pants to the point where they couldn't run away even if a pig was chasing them. Low riders on their way to a sideshow bounced their Impalas or other cheaper muscle cars. We had just stopped at a roach coach for shrimp tacos and ceviche. If all went well, by sunset we'd be back at Lock's house with Twinkletoes safe and sound, barbecuing something even better.

But things hadn't been going very well, had they?

"Good idea," I said. "That way if things go south we can make a quick getaway. Let's park them facing the highway."

In a hood like that, we even had to take our lids with us instead of leaving them on the seat or hanging from the handlebars. I carried the express mail box. We were glad it was still only noon. Any later, and a place like that would explode into a regular tornado of dangerous activities, and we didn't need any strangers getting in our way. We hoped to fuck

Heriberto Orozco would be there in person so we wouldn't have to wait around.

"What was the scene the cop had going? You texted me," I reminded Lock.

The scene seemed to amuse him. "I'll tell you the details later. Let's just say I've got an idea for forming a new club."

Seriously? Ideas of that nature had been knocking at the back of my brain, but I hadn't been able to find a way to make any of them work. Mainly, the thought of leaving The Bare Bones just put the fear of God into me. And why would a cop handing Lock a speeding coupon be giving him ideas for a new club?

We were passing through Orozco's chain link fence. His half-dead grass looked like a lumpy dog park lawn and was littered with Sol and Tecate cans. As we went up the front path, some guy peeked around the corner of the house. *Great.* Already Orozco was warned that two sinister *gabachos* were heading his way. There was a big likelihood we'd get rolled just by being in the yard.

I knocked, because what else could I do? Eventually a woman answered. I hated how criminals sometimes got their women to do their dirty work for them. For all Orozco knew, we were there to mow him down in cold blood.

Lock spoke, as he knew Spanish better than I did. "*Sólo estamos aquí para dar un paquete a Orozco.*" *We're just here to give Orozco a package.*

I displayed the package. Her eyes were large and terrified like a deer's, as though someone behind her held a gun to her, which pissed me off. So I shouted, "Listen, Orozco. All we need to do is hand you this package from Carmine Rojas. We don't care what your job or problem is. This is *our* job, and Carmine told us to do it, *comprende?* If we don't hand you this box, we'll be in deep *mierde.* Do you get my drift, *ese?*"

I shoved the box at the woman, and she cringed back as though it was a box of *mierde*. Waving her hands as though sprinkling fairy dust, she cried, "No, no, no!"

I rolled my eyes. "Look, Orozco, we're just trying to do our job. You have to take this fucking box, or we won't be able to tell Rojas we did our job."

Lock added, *"Tiene a nuestro amigo de rehén."* He's holding our friend hostage.

I wasn't sure if this was cool, showing our hand like that, but amazingly, it seemed to work. Maybe Orozco was familiar with Rojas' tactics, and actually felt for us. Whatever the case, he removed the woman, who fled gratefully.

He actually seemed like a timid guy, not a tough gangster with gold teeth, not a hit man or *sicario*. He wore one of those simple countryman's shirts, Dickies pants, and a fade haircut. There was just something about him, like a lack of ink or accessories, that didn't scream out "cholo." Lock and I shared glances. *This* guy was so important to Rojas he needed to send two guys down practically to the border to hand him a box?

"Look, just take it," I told Orozco wearily. "Once you take it, we can call Rojas and he'll release our man."

Orozco looked warily at us. "He has your man?"

"Sí," I said. "And our man is weak and feeble and not used to being held hostage. Just take the fucking thing. I'm sure it's just marijuana or other *drogas*."

Orozco finally took it. We saluted him crisply, and sauntered off down his path. As the door slammed behind us, Lock said, "Let's wait until we get back to our scoots to text Rojas."

I was already thumbing my phone. "No fucking way. We did what we were asked to do. I don't care if it's a fucking IED or poison—that's none of our concern. Rojas can verify with Orozco that we did it." I was texting Rojas, probably to one of his many burner phones. *The job is done. We're leaving Orozco's right now.*

But a piercing wail coming from inside the shabby house almost prevented me from hitting the *SEND* button. We both froze, staring at each other wide-eyed. Was it a man or woman shrieking? Lock was the first to make a move back to the house, and I had to hold a hand to his shoulder to stay him.

"Let God do the accounting," I urged. "This is none of our beef. Our job is done."

Lock took my hand from his person and threw it away. "I can't stand to hear a woman cry."

Sighing heavily, I followed Lock back to the house. It was evident it was both a man *and* a woman wailing to the heavens above, crying out all sorts of Ave Marias.

"Look," I seethed at Lock as he made for the door, "that's *my* Prospect back in that room with the dead Indian. I don't care what these fucking beaners do. Let's not jeopardize it all just to help some asswipes we don't even know."

But Lock was inside the house already.

I had no fucking choice. What was I going to do, burn rubber out of there and leave my lover consoling some strangers? As angry as it made me, I had to follow.

And nearly puked up my ceviche.

I had to hold onto the doorjamb to stop myself from keeling right over. The Sonoran woman was holding a mass of bloody human tissue and Ziploc bags, which explained why I hadn't smelled anything. Both her and Orozco were on their knees sobbing their hearts out, the female Orozco smearing her chin and neck with the bloody flesh. I was too dizzy to figure out which body part it was, but Lock filled me in.

"It's a dick," he said with awe.

I remembered his experience with his lover's body parts, so

I tried to take control and breathe. "That's not just a dick. Look at this other stuff. Looks like a fucking nose and maybe a hand."

I couldn't believe I had couriered *fucking body parts* for a hundred and fifty miles.

Then, as Orozco screeched profanities about his *hermano* Mateo to the gods the meaning of the whole thing sunk in to my brain.

This was one of those situations where the runner's relatives were being held in Sonora as assurance that they wouldn't turn rat or vanish or go into witness protection.

In this case, it seemed to be Orozco's brother, or his brother-in-law, and judging from the wide variety and extent of body parts, Mateo was probably not on this earth any longer.

"*Fuck*," said Lock. "But what can we do about it?"

I wanted to say, "I *told* you not to come back in here!" but something stopped me. Suddenly, I *wanted* to know the deal behind Mateo's demise. Lock, Twinkletoes, and myself had already suffered enough at the hands of Carmine Rojas and his pathetic minion, Stumpy Meadows. Maybe we could do something to hurry along Rojas' wife's RICO case.

I grabbed Heriberto's arm and yanked him toward the kitchen. As could be expected, it took several long minutes for him to compose himself, crossing himself and exclaiming to his mother in heaven. I kneeled by the woman and manfully tried to pry the body parts from her clutch. Eventually I gave up and went looking for a box to bury them in. The frozen lasagna box I found was more respectful than the bloody, smelly FedEx box.

Heriberto told us a sad tale. My businessman's brain quickly saw the advantage to offering him a deal. Some Boners in our Phoenix charter could find a safe place for the Orozcos, after making sure our man Twinkletoes was safe, of course. Heriberto had nothing left to lose—no more relatives were being held in the Sonora trap house. In return, Heriberto would give us the location and keys to a tractor trailer belonging to Rojas. Rojas had had Mateo killed when Heriberto had reported that both the Cocopah and the Fort Yuma Indian Reservations had refused to accept the load and he would have to drive it hellaway up to the Colorado River Rez.

Heriberto didn't want to. He was fed up with the whole thing. He could give us bills of lading, manifests, and driver's logs that confirmed Rojas' shell company as the transporter. Mrs. Rojas could use this information in her RICO case. Our club lawyer Slushy—and Twinkletoes himself—were experts at getting to the bottom of legal mazes like that. And we'd have a free shitload of A-1 heroin.

I was washing my hands at the kitchen sink after putting the penis into the lasagna box.

Lock said, "That H can go a long way toward our startup MC."

I had no idea what he was talking about. Heriberto and his wife were on their knees praying when I wanted to hurry them along packing necessities to get the fuck out of there. I had to text or call Twinkletoes and probably Lytton as well, because I wasn't risking a snowball in hell until I knew all was safe with my crew. "Oh, fucking thank *god*." I nearly sobbed with relief. Twinkletoes had just texted *I'm out of that house of horrors. Taking Lock's cage to get a Big Mac or three.*

I was toweling off my hands when I finally looked at Lock. I kept forgetting how banging hot he was. He was sweating with nerves and the exertion of the day's activities, but it made him look vital and macho. "Our new club. I'll be President or you'll be President, I don't really care. But I know the name of the

A DANGEROUS REALITY

new club. The Bent Zealots. Because that's what we are."

And that's how we began formulating the founding of a new motorcycle club.

CHAPTER SEVENTEEN
LOCK

"All right. *Now*," said Lock. "I'm going to give you what you deserve."

Just as Lock had been hoping and dreading for weeks, Turk Blackburn trembled under his palms as he pressed him back into the wall of the loading dock.

"You don't have to do this," murmured Turk, but his eyes were heavily lidded with pleasure. He practically purred with sheer joy as Lock palmed his pulsating erection through his 501s, Lock's body plastered to his. "I know it's not your thing. You don't need to prove anything to me, Lock. Besides, we've got a job to do."

Lock smiled as he took a bite out of Turk's lower lip. "Judging from what I know of you, this won't take long."

Turk smiled lasciviously when he said, "*Vete a la mierda!* Fuck you!*"

"Oh, don't you wish." Lock set to eagerly undoing Turk's belt buckle.

He knew they should be getting a move on. When they had noisily ridden their bikes inside the trucking dock in Quartzsite, a few teamsters had looked at them with curiosity. But it was a Saturday, and there wasn't a lot of activity going on, and the Freightliner Orozco had promised was already backed up to the bay doors waiting for them to take their bikes up the ramp. A hundred kilos of H wouldn't exactly fit in their saddlebags, and the manifest said there were some pallets of frozen Brussels sprouts in there as well. So the plan was to drive to a warehouse Lock's club rented in Lake Havasu—driving *around* the Rez, since they didn't want to piss off the natives with the unwanted cargo—unload most of the H, then dump the truck at a high-visibility truck stop with all of the incriminating paperwork inside and just enough A-1 to bolster a RICO case against Rojas. One of Lock's many eyes and ears up and down the corridor would accidentally discover the abandoned truck.

Lock was satisfied with the plan, so right now he had another man's dick in his fist.

He'd never jacked another man. Of course he'd done it to himself a hundred thousand times, and he knew enough to spit into his palm as a way to heighten the lubricious pleasure. Judging from the way Turk twitched, hissed, and fluttered his eyelids, Lock knew he was already close to the edge.

He saw the power in it, making someone else come. It was an ego boost to know you literally held the other man's crisis in your hands. Before, in all of his encounters with the exotic stallion, Lock's power had been in Turk's hunger for him. Turk's lust for Lock's prick was where Lock held sway over him. Now, although the tables were turned in their physical roles, Lock still felt that he ruled supreme, because every tiny movement of his fist around the hot meat made Turk jump and suck in air. If he stopped now, Turk would probably collapse or sob from need.

And that was some power.

And caving in more to the acceptance that he was at least bisexual at his core, Lock could see where he might be doing this again. And again. So he'd better practice it.

He speared his free hand through Turk's hair, loosened it from the man bun at the nape, feasted on the hot gooseflesh of his throat. He had to leave enough space between them to jack the dick efficiently, he discovered, and that was frustrating to him, too. He wanted to rub his erection against Turk, to smear their hard chests together, to dry hump his lover so hard that he creamed inside his jeans, but he had to maintain some distance.

Lock found that, in a weird way, it was sexier to jack a man off than to give a blowjob. Looking in Turk's eyes, capturing Turk's glance with his own, being able to lick Turk's luscious lips and talk face to face was dirtier, more erotic than even fucking him.

"I can't wait to start The Bent Zealots with you, love," he whispered. "A bunch of deviant, twisted faggots roaming the highways raising just as much hell as the other MCs." They hadn't discussed exactly *where* this club would be founded—they hadn't exactly had any time to get into details.

"No twinks in our club," Turk gasped. One hand grasped a fistful of Lock's hair. The other tantalizingly squeezed and fingered Lock's pec. "Just bulls, bears, and wolves—real players."

"Right. We have to be able to take all the fag-baiting that's bound to come our way. We have to fight the powers that be."

"People might not know, Lock. It's not like we're wearing colored hankies in our pockets."

Lock had to chuckle, remembering his own experience with colored handkerchiefs. "Oh, everyone will know, all right, once Stumpy shouts it to the four corners of the earth. And he will, even though we kept our part of the bargain. And then some."

"And then some." Turk said something that shocked the crap out of Lock. "Unless we take him down."

Lock nearly paused his corkscrewing of the delicious dick.

He remembered himself, remembered his duty, and renewed his attentions. The cock was shiny, hot, slippery as greased metal in his palm. He tried to sound casual. "You mean, have him booted for being a fucking drug addict?"

"No," gasped Turk, gyrating his hips in time to Lock's pumping. Turk nearly scalped Lock, he gripped his hair so tightly. "Take him out. And I don't mean to the Olive Garden. Oh, Great Caesar's Ghost, Lock! Don't stop! Don't fucking sto—"

It was too late for Lock to stop anyway, because Turk's dick was spurting hot come. Lock pulled back a few inches to enjoy the sight and was hit in the chin with the force of the jet. The lanky biker was shooting an amazing load that had been held back way too long, and now the dam was breached. *Hijo de puta!* Lock reveled in the flood of delicious jism that now dripped from his wrist, and he coaxed every last drop with more nasty talk.

"Good, babe. Come in my hand. Come all over me. You know I want to lick it from my fingers. I want to watch you eat your own come from my hand, to lick it from my mouth."

That did seem to squeeze a few more spurts from the aroused dick. Apparently talking about ending Stumpy Meadows was a massive turn-on for this elegant-looking biker. It reminded Lock of the myth that had earned Turk his bones, the story about him, Ford Illuminati, and Ford's dead pops down in that desert near Nogales. How many men had Turk actually buried?

But some asshat rolling up a bay door nearby shocked Lock into a sense of reality. They had a job to do. Suddenly all was hustle and bustle, and Lock barely had time to wipe his hand on the tail of his wifebeater before the teamster came waddling around their side of the Freightliner's trailer.

Lock slapped Turk on the shoulder as though they'd just been swapping some Twinkies and Doritos. They nodded and lifted their hands in greeting at the grizzled driver. Of course neither one of them had a trucker's license, so they needed to keep a low profile for a while. Thinking about safety on the road reminded Lock of Turk's parents. They stood by their bikes waiting for the trucker to waddle away, so Lock asked lightly,

"How *did* your folks pass away, then? You said it wasn't a drunk driver."

A tense shadow passed over Turk's face, and he looked away. He seemed to have to force the words from his mouth. They came out as separate little hard rocks of anger. "An old, senile guy who should've had his license revoked a long time before. No one wants to take away licenses from seniors, so it's not a popular sentiment, or anything to lobby for in Congress. But it happens a fuck of a lot more than you'd know. I agree drunk and high people are incapacitated, of course. But people who don't know the difference between the gas and the brake are just as big of a hazard."

Jiminy Christmas. Lock stumbled around for words to say. "I heard of a senior who drove happily down the middle of a farmer's market, I think in Southern California. He took out about ten people before his car finally stopped, probably by a brick wall. He was all dazed. He thought he was going for a Sunday drive."

Turk's jaw was set. He finally looked at Lock. "Exactly. I really dread getting old, Lock. I dread not knowing if I'm going for a Sunday drive or am plowing through a packed concert hall. I *really* hope I die before I get old."

"Don't fucking say that," Lock said lamely.

Turk forced some more words out. "If he would've been a

young drunk guy, preferably a biker, he would've done life for manslaughter, for wiping out both my parents. But this senile fuck? No one wants to throw the book at a mild-mannered eighty-five year old who was too confused to know what he'd done."

Lock was appalled. He'd really never thought about it before. "Nothing happened to him? *Something* needed to happen."

"*Nothing* happened. I was ten and my entire life was over, but the courts argued 'why should we ruin the oldster's life too?'"

"It's a tough call to make," Lock said lamely. "No jury would convict him."

The very planes of Turk's face seemed to have become angular. His eyes flashed with the sick, wobbly kind of rage Lock had seen often in men overseas. "It's why I'm very interested in retribution now."

Lock nodded. "I get it."

The trucker had finally vanished, so it was time to roll up the trailer doors, inspect their cargo, and move their bikes in. Turk, having dealt with many big rigs in his profession as a budtender, opened up the doors of the Freightliner. Together they extended the ramp in preparation for loading their bikes. First, they wanted to inspect the cargo. Turk would get his Phoenix crew to put the squeeze on Orozco if there wasn't as much H as he'd told them to expect.

Sure enough, what could possibly be a hundred kilos of shrink-wrapped mustard-yellow heroin was in the far back, under pallets of individual ketchup destined for restaurants. Turk, as an experienced marijuana taste tester, poked a hole in one package with his switchblade and took a bit on his tongue. He nodded. "A-1," he confirmed, wiping his blade on his pants leg. "Let's shake it."

Lock had to grab Turk by his sleeve. "Wait. What about the Brussels sprouts?"

Turk smiled. "Who cares about any fucking sprouts? Maybe Orozco confused sprouts with ketchup. Or maybe we misunderstood."

"Pretty hard to confuse *coles de Bruselas* with *salsa de tomate*. What the fuck are these coolers? They look like the kind hunters use to put deer in. These must be the sprouts."

"Maybe more H," said Turk, practically rubbing his hands together.

There were about ten of those big game coolers stacked along one wall of the trailer, ten on the other wall. Lock ambled to the closest one he could easily open. "I used to go ocean fishing as a kid off Long Beach for mahi mahi. We'd put them in coolers like this on the party boat. Man, that was some good eating."

Turk said from behind him, "I wonder if the Mexicans are bringing in fish? They still have some good *tiburon* and other great *pescado* down there in the Sea of Cortez off Guaymas. Some of those can be pretty expensive. I know a guy who sells giant fish to fancy restau—"

"*Holy mother of God!*"

Banging the hinged lid of the cooler back against the cooler behind it, Lock instinctively staggered back from the putrid contents of the box. He hadn't stayed long enough for a thorough exam, but just the unseeing eyeball of that Mexican staring back at him was enough to give him the 411. The mouth was set in a grimace like a Halloween fright mask, his entire body wasn't in one piece, and there appeared to have been at least one other head and torso jammed in behind him. Someone had just made a nominal effort at keeping the bodies from rotting by throwing a few of those ice blocks in there, but apparently they didn't want to waste valuable room.

Lock stood in the middle of the trailer dry heaving, hands on knees. He did not do well with body parts, not since he'd picked up the pieces of Park in the desert.

"What? What?" said Turk, going forward to the cooler. Lock waited, gagging, for the horrified reaction, but none ever came. Turk just quietly went to a couple of other coolers and opened them. Still, no reaction.

Maybe he's got PTSD. Maybe he'll have a delayed reaction. Turk's lack of horror gave Lock the gumption to go forward again and at least stand by Turk's shoulder, gazing into another cooler.

More men. Boys, really. All of them seemed to be teenagers, shot execution style in the head, then chopped up as efficiently as possible to fit into the coolers.

"*Why?*" Turk mused quietly, fingers tapping on his chin as though studying a math problem.

Turk's reaction horrified Lock even further, if such a thing were possible. "*What the fuck, Turk? Why?* I'll tell you why. Because the Marin cartel are a bunch of bloodsucking, ruthless motherfuckers who only give a shit about coin. No *wonder* the Indians didn't want to accept this truck! This fucking explains why Rojas wanted Orozco to drive this truck to La Paz which is a fucking ghost town—they were gonna *bury* these bodies there. Rojas was planning on burying the bodies on their land, where even top level federal agents don't dare tread. No wonder the Indians and Orozco wanted no part of it, and I don't either, man. That's it. We're out of here. Let's just take enough H to fit in our saddlebags and go. I can still have my guy find the truck here with all the paperwork, so we can still nail Rojas. Come on, man. This is bad juju. I'll shoulder the financial load for starting the new club. Let's just cut our losses."

Turk still appeared to be thinking. He was practically stroking his beard like a mad scientist. "Wait, Lock. This could be just what we need."

Lock's heart was pounding out of his chest, but he had stopped breathing. Was Turk even darker, more twisted than he'd ever imagined? Turk had just been talking about how much he loved revenge. He had every reason to loathe Rojas and Stumpy and hell, even *him*, his own lover, for getting him into this fucking mess in the first place. Had Lock inadvertently been drawn to someone who was even darker and more bent than him?

"Wait *what*, Turk? The plan is pretty fucking self-evident. We take off, man. How many dead beaners are we surrounded by? Fifteen?"

"Twenty," Turk answered with an alacrity that was starting to make Lock panic. But Turk finally broke free of his thinking mode and slammed the lid on the cooler. He spun about to face Lock, who hadn't seen an excitement like that in Turk's face for a while.

Turk held up a forefinger. "We've got a delivery to make, my friend. I'll just make sure not to speed."

Oh, clusterfuck. What the fuck have I gotten into now?

At the same time, Lock knew he would go along with whatever Turk wanted. He always had. He always would.

CHAPTER EIGHTEEN
TURK

It was the most deliciously evil plan of my entire vengeful life.

I may seem like a mild-mannered guy who runs a weed dispensary—most of the time. You sort of have to be mellow in this business. Mellowness is in the job description of marijuana workers, something that sets us apart from the frenetic, hyped-up unpredictability of, say, meth dealers.

I also have a sort of composed, still face. I don't do many different facial expressions. People think of me as this supremely calm, level-headed dude.

But fuck with me, my crew, my loved ones, and vengeance sinks its tentacles into my soul.

Rojas had messed with me in a perverted way. It wasn't so much the aborted blowjob—that had been a normal enough thing, up until recently—but holding Lock and Twinkletoes over my head as hostages, that really tweaked me. Twinkletoes had texted that poor Kwahu Johnson had died sometime during that night while I'd slept securely and peacefully in Lock's arms. The guy probably hadn't even pinched any product from Rojas to begin with.

This whole sequence of shitty events had been put in motion thanks to that old redneck, homophobe, and Hell's Angel reject, Stumpy Meadows. I knew we were going to face a shit ton more Stumpies in our careers as The Bent Zealots MC. Having done time, I knew how valuable it was to make your bones early in this world. For instance, lots of people seemed to think that *I* had something to do with Cropper Illuminati's death in that desert. I was there, sure. I take no credit for burying him, but I'm not going to dissuade folks who want to think that.

If we wanted to start our new club off on the right foot, we were going to have to make a big statement. Go large—register our brand, as it were. I was going to have to take a page from Ford Illuminati's book if I wanted to guarantee the fate of our newborn club.

But I had a bit of a problem convincing Lock.

I was the one who knew how to handle an eighteen-wheeler, so after we secured our bikes in the trailer, I took the wheel. I think at first Lock was just going along with me like a zombie, and we were almost to Parker before doubts really started getting ahold of him.

"Are we fucking being followed?" He was as jumpy as a virgin at a prison rodeo.

I think you're conditioned to dislike or fear things during your formative years. I had to put myself in Lock's shoes. Putting the pieces of his lover back together in that Iraqi desert had given him a fear of body parts. And probably death in general, although who didn't dislike that? For my part, the guy who inadvertently murdered not one but both of my parents had gotten off scot free. So my particular fetish was for seeking vengeance. Not letting people get away with murder.

"Don't panic, Thor," I said. I just liked calling him Thor because he was a blond god. "You're jumping at ghosts. This'll be a simple op. Then we'll be sitting in the catbird's seat. Hell, we can even keep those ketchup packages. Too bad there weren't really any Brussels sprouts. Don't worry about blowback, buddy."

It seemed that Lock glared at me, but I was busy keeping my eyes on the road. "Well, of *course* there's going to be blowback. Who the hell do you think Stumpy's going to blame for this? Us, that's who. I'd like to leave my club in good standing, not go out with a blowtorch to my back pack."

"How's anyone going to know it was us? They'll assume it was Orozco, the last driver of this vehicle. No one in the Assassins will know where he is by then."

Lock harrumphed. "Easy for *you* to say. You'll just ride back to Pure and Easy and go back to your weed job and your beloved club. Stumpy's going to put two and two together because why would Orozco—"

"Whoa, whoa. Hold your horses, Thor. In the first fucking place, 'go back to my club'? Before we found these stiffs, we were talking about starting our own club."

"In general terms! No one's said a damned thing about who is going to quit whose job yet, in case you haven't noticed. Pure and Easy is way too far from Lake Havasu for us to commute."

I was starting to feel uneasy. "Besides, the P&E territory is already staked by The Bare Bones. We'd have to carve out a whole new territory that isn't already claimed by either the Boners *or* the Assassholes. You sure this Ormond guy is equipped to deal with levelling up like this? Or does he just want to ride the byways giving skull jobs to pigs?" Lock had told me the incredible story about the fairy who had saved his ass by distracting the pig who was about to ticket him. The guy had no motive for such an act of charity, as far as I could tell, other than he really liked eating pork. I was eager to reach out to Ormond Tangier, though, if he had a bunch of other bent bikers in the palm of his hand. We could use the muscle. You couldn't set up a new club with only two guys. We needed a crew.

"He's up for it," Lock groused. "I can get a read on a guy a mile away. He's tough, he's been through the wringer. He's got the grit. Sounds like him and his crew have the Quartzsite area sewn up, but it'd mean bumping Stumpy out of his own backyard."

"No, it doesn't." I had no intention of pushing into Stumpy's backyard. I had other fucking plans for Stumpy. "You leave your club in good standing, we can come to some agreement about carving out territories."

"Sounds like you're planning to come out this way."

"That *was* the plan." It really was. I had known for months, years probably, that eventually I'd have to strike out on my own if I wanted to live even a halfway truthful life. I'd always known I'd meet someone I wanted to actually live with, maybe even enact one of those cornball gay wedding ceremonies with. Who the hell knew? Never say never.

I had even come to the realization that I'd have to leave my precious Pure and Easy area in order to stretch my wings. My range extended so far and wide from the P&E location that I knew everyone who was anyone in central Arizona. I'd have to start over fresh somewhere far enough that nobody knew my name. A new locale, a new base, a new rep. I liked what little I'd seen of Rough and Ready, Lock's suburbia haven east of Lake Havasu City. The downtown had bars, sporting goods stores, a bookstore, even a movie theater. All the essentials for life as we know it. If we could bring down Carmine Rojas…big plans, I know. But Ford Illuminati had taught me to always keep your eye on the prize.

"I like your house," I told Lock, "and I don't own one. No reason to. Got my own wing at Ford's house, but I'm sure his old lady wouldn't mind seeing my sorry mossy face go."

This seemed to soothe Lock, as it was intended to. What we were doing was monumental, and of course we'd get tweaked. Forming a new club wasn't something to be taken lightly. "Your face isn't too mossy. You just need to get out of your cage, hit the open road, blow the dust from your soul."

"Ain't that the truth, brother." Lock hadn't asked me to move in with him. I was just being presumptuous. Then again, he hadn't said no, had he? "Is this the turnoff for Stumpy's?"

"Yeah. We're approaching it from a different direction, and I know just the spot to stop."

As I took the turn, I asked, "You're on board with this?"

"I'd go to the wall for you, you know that, Turk. We both made the decision to go rogue and there's no turning back."

"That's what I'm trying to impart to you, Thor. The only target we're going to have on our back is the rainbow colored one. And that's probably a bigger cross to bear than the rep of being the ones who dumped the bodies of twenty Mexican teenagers on Stumpy Meadows' ranch."

"Wait a second," Lock said cautiously. "I thought you said people would assume that Orozco—"

He quieted down when I gave him that silent, sidelong stare. Lock had to know that I fully planned on taking the rap for our actions. It would make our bones on the streets. It would rocket us up the food chain, boss us up in one giant swoop.

I said, "You know Stumpy's already told your club that you're gay. Us playing his errand boy hasn't changed any of that."

"Yes…" Lock said uncertainly. "I haven't talked to any of my crew in days."

"Well, I'm sure it's crossed your mind that Stumpy Meadows isn't exactly a man of his word."

"Yes…"

"And what's a man worth in a club if his word's no good?"

"Not much," Lock said with real anger. He lit a cigarette with the finality of a man going to the scaffolding. The smoke seethed from between his teeth with viciousness as he, no doubt, thought of Stumpy Meadows and the agony he'd piled on us. Lock leaned back in his seat, one tanned arm running along the open window. His nose that I'd broken was nearly healed now, its crookedness giving him a thuggish, gangster look that really suited him.

We drove in silence until Lock pointed with his cigarette. "There. See that barn? That's Stumpy's. He stores alfalfa or hay or whatever in there. If we do a real sloppy job and just fling the coolers everywhere, it'll be a matter of minutes before someone stumbles on them."

Twinkletoes had just done an investigation on the possible IDs of the teenagers. Within minutes, he'd reported back about forty students missing from the city of Magdalena in Sonora last month. They'd been protesting cuts to their state-financed school. About ten shallow graves had been found in the hills by farmers calling themselves "community police" who had taken over when the *federales* failed to do jack shit to cover up their own handiwork. The outcry became bigger with each grave found, so no doubt the cops had handed the remaining bodies to the cartel to dispose of.

So we had the bodies of student protestors whose biggest crime was to want better education. Nothing chapped my hide more than that sort of unjust, unpunished shit. Having finally told Lock the story of my parents' death had lifted an enormous burden off me. Only Ford, Lytton, and maybe their old ladies knew the details of the pathetic, senile old man who had gone for a Sunday drive on my parents' hood. Everyone else in my club probably assumed it'd been a drunk driver, too. But having brought it into the open sort of tore the bandage off the wound, and now I furiously flung bodies around with abandon. Everyone else with dead parents at least had their retribution. I had never had mine.

I'd backed the truck up to the barn. Luckily there was nobody there at the moment—although I doubt I really cared, at that point, if anyone saw me. I just yanked the coolers down the ramp as though pulling sleighs loaded with seal meat. Fury overtook me, like those mothers who lift school buses that have run over their children. Lock backed out of my way as I hauled the coolers full of dead students across the hay-strewn dirt, opened them, and rolled the coolers on their sides to dump the contents.

It was extremely gross work. I'd been inside a slaughterhouse once when I was about sixteen. Cropper Illuminati had thought he might purchase one, as another of his diverse business interests. But after slipping around in the blood and guts and eyeballs of the processing room for about ten minutes, we were all off like a prom dress in May. If it was too disgusting for Cropper Illuminati, then it was as disgusting as a dog eating her puppies, and we were history.

I had put on some gloves I'd found in the cab and tied a bandanna around my face, and I probably looked just as brutal as those *sicarios* who had originally shot the helpless kids through the foreheads.

"Let me help," said Lock, as I barreled back up the ramp for another cooler.

I practically shoved him out of my way. "I can do it. I'm halfway done."

"I don't want you doing everything alone. We're in this

together, for better or worse."

I was bent over in the dark, dragging another cooler from the stack. "Doesn't matter. Doesn't matter who does it. What matters is it gets done. Then let's get some distance in our rearview before you call your CI and give him directions where to accidentally find this site. While you're out there, can you grab some of that paperwork from the console? Let's stick it in a—*oh*."

I was halfway down the ramp with the latest container of gore when I happened to glance aside at Lock. Only, there were four legs, not two. Straightening up, I saw that one of the BGs belonging to Rojas had his forearm wrapped around Lock's throat, a pistol to his head. Lock gripped the forearm, but there was nothing he could do. Where the fuck had the baby gangster come from?

Lock had been getting me in all sorts of hot water lately. Now, at last, I'd inadvertently done the same to him.

It was a no-brainer. I didn't even have to think. I dropped the cooler, whipped my Glock from my waistband, and squarely shot the BG in the face.

CHAPTER NINETEEN
LOCK

It all happened so fast.

One minute, Lock was mindlessly watching Turk haul cooler after cooler down the trailer's ramp. Turk was in a haze of rage, surrounded by a cloud so angry it almost had a face, like some kind of genie escaped from a bottle. Lock had seen this sort of angry activity before, in Iraq. Anger was good when it drove men in times of war. And they were definitely in the middle of a blood feud. The lines were blurred, where one faction began and the other ended. But the wheels were in motion, and Lock couldn't stop them.

He felt like he should help Turk. But suddenly he was paralyzed with some strange kind of PTSD-driven flashback. He knew he hadn't taken his meds for a couple of days, but this was fucking ridiculous. *I can deal with fucking body parts.* But seeing as Turk seemed to have it all under control, Lock just stood by lamely. Until that gangbanger snuck up behind him and stuck the barrel of a pistol to his head.

What the fuck. The hyena must've been waiting behind the barn or something, because he came out of nowhere. The guy seemed all prepared for a giant speech, but Turk, quick as a dart, whipped his piece from the small of his back and nailed the guy right in the forehead.

It must've been the forehead, because when the hyena dragged Lock backward with him and they hit the ground together, Lock's cheek landed against his face, slimy and metallic with blood. The BG's arm was still in a death grip around Lock's neck, but the guy was dead as a dodo, and Lock instantly recoiled. He scrabbled backward like a crab to get away from the splattered guy with the gold teeth.

"*Great Caesar's Ghost!*" Turk bellowed his signature line, but his voice seemed to come from another planet, like a theater next door that's playing a louder movie. Glock still in hand, Turk ran for Lock.

That's when that bald-headed sadist Roland stepped from behind the Freightliner. They had thwarted his plans, but now he had a profound speech already bursting from his eloquent throat.

Lock and Turk froze like players in a Christmas pageant. Maybe they wanted to hear what Roland had to say. Maybe they were taken by surprise. But since when had a BG acted alone? Of course he had backup. He was just a puppet on a string. And Roland was the puppet master.

"You think you were pretty slick operators," Roland boomed out. "Jacking this fucking truck and dumping these bodies. But looking in your rearview mirror is Stealth 101, brothers. The fame of your homosexual activities has already run far and wide. You think you can get the drop on someone as powerful as Carmine Rojas? Well, you'd better think again. Not only are we going to ruin you, we're going to frame you for the murders of these beaner kids, and you're going to be doing fifty to life in the ghetto penthouse at—"

Looking back later, maybe Lock had imagined that grand speech from Roland. Because the next thing he knew, Roland was flying back, jerking like a backup dancer in a Miley Cyrus video.

And once again, the barrel of Turk's Glock was smoking.

Turk should've been panting, at least from the exertion of the body-filled coolers. Shooting someone was no big deal, Lock knew that. All you had to do was raise your arm and squeeze the trigger. You could hardly get buff and muscular from doing that. But Turk was still as a deep pool, his eyes dark and mystical as he looked down at his handiwork. Standing straight like that, the cloudless Arizona sun at his back, made him look like a superhero in a graphic novel. His untucked plaid shirt flowed manfully from his broad shoulders, his pecs straining against the tightness of the wifebeater under it. His skull and crossbones belt buckle glinted in the sun, and his engineer boots were spread with virility. The veins in Turk's forearm practically throbbed with power.

Lock felt ashamed. Turk had literally saved his life twice in a row within the space of minutes. And Lock hadn't even drawn his weapon. Doing so now, he shouted, "Fuck! Where the fuck did they come from? I don't see any fucking vehicle!"

"Are there any more? You go that way, I'll go this way."

They each darted around separate sides of the building. Lock first came to the ATV—he thought he remembered seeing Stumpy riding around on that thing. Roland, in his arrogance and supreme self-assurance, had only taken one BG with him to do a man's work. And Turk was just pissed off enough to take them both out, almost within the same minute. Lock had to hand it to Turk. He didn't wait to hear Roland's threat, his punchline. Lock believed Roland that their fame was already ringing in the streets. They were doomed on at least that front, so they might as well finish their job and get the fuck out of there.

Turk skidded around his side of the barn, saw the ATV, and

dashed back toward the Freightliner. Lock followed suit, wholeheartedly helping now, grabbing a cooler handle in tandem with Turk.

Turk said, "I can't believe there aren't more of them, or they don't have any backup."

"I know. Seems weird. And how did Roland even know we were here? Did they nab Orozco? I watched as your Phoenix brothers took him away in that cage."

"Right! Diz Evans and Don Loos are righteous, dependable men. I don't fucking know! Maybe that BG has been following us this whole time, although you'd think I would've noticed that."

By this time, so many bodies were piled in clumps inside the alfalfa barn, they had to carry the final cooler down the row of feed bales and dump it in the dark. Lock was glad not to have to look at much, but the absolute worst was the middle part of a torso spilling what seemed like miles of intestines like sausage links. They had to find a truck stop pronto, to wash up.

"That's it," said Turk. "Let me just fasten up the back of the trailer and we're out of here. Why don't you jump in the passenger seat and text your CI buddy to get out here? Tell him to wait an hour. By then we should be safely at your Havasu warehouse."

"All right. But listen, Turk…What Roland just said about how our, ah, fame has already spread far and wide."

Turk nodded curtly. "I know. Means Stumpy didn't even keep *that* half of the bargain."

"Right. But also, it means that, well, that our fame has spread."

Turk grinned crookedly. "You didn't think we could keep that under wraps for long, did you?"

He had a point. Their goal was to confess anyway. Turk's

club might be tolerant, but that confession would just hasten Lock's departure from the Assassins of Youth anyway. It was just all so new. Things had been happening at a lightning pace lately. Lock hadn't even begun to process it all.

He nodded and smiled. "Yeah." He really wanted to wrap his arms around Turk, slap him on the back, anything, but the idea of the layer of gore that must coat their skin stopped him. Whipping off the bandanna that had covered the lower half of his face, an idea occurred to him. He had to slightly rotate Roland's body by moving the hip with his boot, and he stuck the brown kerchief in Roland's back right pocket.

"Wish I remembered what brown meant," said Lock.

Turk was prompt with his answer. "Scat."

Lock frowned. The word vaguely had a hunting meaning, as far as he knew. "What's that?"

"It tells the world that he likes eating shit."

Lock was too tweaked to laugh—although he would definitely do a lot of that in the future, looking back—and he hopped into the passenger seat to text his buddy who lived in Parker.

He heard Turk closing up the back of the trailer. After several long moments, it occurred to him that Turk wasn't coming around the driver's side. Leaning over the console to see in the driver's side rearview mirror, Lock caught a sight that made the blood run cold in his veins.

Stumpy Meadows stood behind Turk, the barrel of his Magnum glued to the back of Turk's head.

He must've made Turk give up his weapon, because Turk's surrendering hands were empty. Stumpy had probably been hiding near the ATV the whole time while Turk offed his business partners. "That's right," yelled Stumpy. "Come on out, you butt-fucking asshole, because I've got your boyfriend. I'm gonna bury him just like you done tried to frame me for all these fucking Mexican students."

So they *were* the missing students. Lock's brain was on fire. There were any number of tactical things he could've done—sneak out the door, go around the front, go around the back, try to take out Stumpy from a sniper's position—but all of them ended up in the same scenario. Turk dead.

"Tell him," growled Stumpy.

Turk shouted, "It's okay, Lock. Just come on out. Don't do anything stupid. It's not worth it."

Stumpy yelled, "Listen to your gay boyfriend. For once he makes sense. We're coming around the front of the truck, so you just ease on out that door, nice and slowly. Throw your Glock on the ground in front of you so's I can see it." Stumpy knew Lock always packed the Glock. "And that knife, too, that Italian flick blade. Throw that out, then step on down."

Lock did as ordered. What fucking option did he have? He did quickly scan the cab of the truck for anything he could use as a weapon. Just a pen and a plastic fork, so for shits and giggles he stuck those in his back pocket, where Stumpy would probably find them when he was searched, anyway.

Lock faced Turk when he stepped out of the truck. It was strange to the nth degree, facing both his lover and his immediate demise. He prayed they'd both go out at the same time. His overly controlling father, who had wanted him to be a lawyer, had also forced church upon him and his siblings. Until Lock had rebelled at age fifteen, they'd attended a Presbyterian church in Bel Air. The Presbyterians had never talked much, if at all, about an afterlife.

But Lock knew. He'd seen too much to deny it was a fact. When he'd sprawled in that Iraqi desert, for all intents and purposes dead to the mortal world, he had soared high above the wreckage of his plane. His spirit did a reverse zoom so fast that his tiny body was like an action figure, and soon he was in space. Not black, dead space, but a space alive with many planets, asteroid clouds, and prisms of the most brilliant intensity. Best of all there were *people*, or at least the personalities of people, since he couldn't *see* them.

Two people in particular he had spoken with at length. He got the impression one was a man, one a woman. They were so highly advanced, so evolved in their concepts, they would shame Albert Einstein. He nearly sobbed with grief when they told him he had to go back—the old corny adage that it "wasn't his time to go yet." He woke up in that desert with a mouth full of sand and blood, and he had to spit it out in order to sob his frustration. *He couldn't recall a thing the angels had told him.*

But he'd always known the wisdom would come back to him the second he departed this earth again. That looked to be imminent now as Stumpy frisked him with one hand, keeping the Magnum trained on Turk.

Stumpy muttered in a haphazard fashion as he checked Lock's pockets, tossing away the pen and the fork. Lock could tell he was flying on meth, probably the rave drug MDMA. He was sweating bullets, and his pungent, acrid scent raked Lock's nostrils. "Hands up, goombah. You gay boys think you can outsmart us. Well, I'm glad you shot that bald-headed spade. He was always acting like he was the kingpin of the whole operation when he didn't do none of the work. He just drove around with his fucking chauffeur acting all hoity-toity, like he was the big dog of the tan yard. Who the fuck needed him? And that nethead Orozco squealed like a pig when we squeezed him. He sure gave you guys up in a flash."

So they had gotten to Orozco? Lock wondered what had happened to Turk's two men. Stumpy waved his piece now, indicating the two men should walk over to a wall of alfalfa bales like men going to their execution. Which they probably were. Stumpy continued to ramble.

"Come on, you panty waists." He viciously shoved Turk in the ass with the gun barrel. Lock and Turk exchanged glances, but it was impossible to read Turk's mind. What sort of plan could Turk have in mind, anyway? They were helpless douchebags, all because they'd allowed Stumpy to get the jump on them, and he had a bigger piece. War was like that. It was always all about who had the most, and best, armament.

"Before I give you a back door parole, I'm going to let the entire world know who was responsible for this whole fucking student mess. That's right. Flyboy, you go stand over on that pile of limbs there. Don't give me any smoke. You, pretty boy, you go over there and"—Stumpy started chuckling to himself with the wit of what he was about to suggest—"pick up that head by the hair and hold it up, you know, like it's some kind of trophy. Flyboy, you put your foot on that pile like it's a giant pile of doves you just shot."

The men ambled slowly, not eager to do Stumpy's bidding. They were so slow, in fact, that Stumpy put a boot in the small of Turk's back and shoved violently. Turk went sprawling to his hands and knees.

"Ha ha!" crowed Stumpy. "I like you that way, you three-legged beaver. Maybe I'll even fuck you that way so the whole world can see what a sissy you are."

Lock couldn't hold his tongue any longer. The longer he talked, the more it enabled Turk to get to his feet with a bit of dignity. "They're only going to see what a sissy *you* are, you dumb fucking asshole. Only a guy who was really a closeted gay would want to butt fuck another. Why would that even occur to you if it wasn't in the back of your mind the whole time, like it was in Rojas' mind?"

"Oh, yeah?" Stumpy said wittily. "Well, I can tell by his teardrop ink that he's been in the big house. No one gets out of there without someone putting it in his toaster."

Brushing himself off as though he wasn't already covered with other people's innards, Turk sneered. "Don't tell me you haven't been a prison wolf yourself. I can see by the Alice Baker on your arm."

Stumpy had always been particularly proud of his Aryan Brotherhood shamrock on his bicep—why he always went sleeveless under his cut. "Yeah, so what? I did Buck Rogers time in Tent City. Doesn't mean I ever had to visit the chocolate speedway."

"Tent City's the worst," Turk snarled. "It's one wall-to-wall keister stab."

"Whatever!" yelled Stumpy, waving his piece around. "I fucking advise you to do what I say or I'm going to blow your head clean off."

Lock said, "What difference does it make whether we do what you tell us to? You're going to bury us either way."

It looked as though that thought hadn't occurred to Stumpy. "Just do it, before I change my mind! Flyboy! Put your foot on that pile. Pretty boy, pick up that fucking head."

Stumpy had to transfer his Magnum into his left hand in order to take his smartphone from its cradle and thumb around for the camera feature. Again, Lock and Turk exchanged looks. This time, Lock imagined he could tell what Turk was thinking. *If we could just distract him for a fraction of a second. We could jump him and disarm him. Then only one of us'll get killed in the rumble. That means a fifty-fifty chance. I'm not taking those odds. Let's just go along and see what he wants. Oh, you think he's actually going to let us go after we dumped these fucking bodies on his property? He was booted from the*

Angels for being too brutal, *man. No, we're going to have to get the jump on him. It's our only chance.*

These thoughts were jumbled together in Lock's mind, and he knew that Turk was thinking at least a few of them.

"Okay," yelled Stumpy, "hold that head up higher. Turn it so I can see the eyeballs bulging."

Turk shouted, "Clockwise or counter-clockwise?"

"Clock—counter—just make it face me! There, heh-heh. Good one. Flyboy, don't look so serious. Look more proud, like, proud of your work."

Lock only rolled his eyes. "You know what, back there under the barn there are some even gorier bodies. Remember, Turk? That's where we put that guy whose intestines are spilling out of his chest."

"Like sausages," Turk agreed. "We could drape some of the sausages across our shoulders."

"Right. Does that thing have a flash, Stumpy?"

Stumpy turned the phone around so the lens faced him. He shrugged. "Dunno. Never thought much about it." Frowning, he looked back at his hostages. "Who cares if there are better bodies back there? We can hack some of these ones up and get some innards that way."

"With what tool?" Lock pointed out. "You took away my blade. You're the one with all the weapons."

"True," agreed Stumpy, almost cheerfully. "Okay. Let's go back and see these sausages. Hands up!" He waved his iron to indicate they should proceed into the darkened barn.

With his eyes and a slight lift of his chin, Lock told Turk to walk first. They filed between two walls of alfalfa bales. Lock knew Stumpy was already favoring his right dominant hand to take the photos. It would've been smarter to use the dominant hand for the pistol, but then Stumpy had always been a few trucks short of a convoy.

The pitchfork was where Lock remembered it had been, leaning against one of the walls. Apparently Stumpy didn't see it as a weapon, because he seemed completely taken aback when Lock ducked down low to grab the pitchfork's handle about midway. He spun around like a stick fighter, twirling the pitchfork in a scything manner that kneecapped Stumpy. The last thing Lock saw was the O of Stumpy's snaggletoothed mouth as he flew up and back like a plastic action figure.

"*Get the gun!*" Lock shouted at his partner. He could already tell as Stumpy soared in midair that he still gripped the pistol, although the phone had gone flying. Standing tall now, he jogged toward where he believed Stumpy would meet the ground. Like a medieval jouster, Lock lunged at Stumpy with all his might, with the pitchfork prongs set to meet Stumpy's midsection.

Lock's aim was true. The prongs pierced Stumpy's stomach as though slicing through a steak. A satisfying resistance to his furious pressure reverberated up the pitchfork's handle and through Lock's arms. Leaping, he toppled Stumpy, his weight adding force to the stabbing. When Lock stood on it like a pogo stick and bounced up and down, he thought he even felt the fork's tines bash through some ribs to exit the other side. Stumpy was pinned good and proper, the two pieces he'd taken from the men still stuck in the back of his pants. But he was far from dead, and his flailing arm squeezed off a shot from the gun.

A flash. Turk must've been heading for them to disarm Stumpy. Turk was blown back out of Lock's line of vision. Lock made a frenzied, wild kick at the arm that held the gun. He missed, and Stumpy got off another shot. The second kick connected, and the gun went pinwheeling up and somewhere into the wall of bales. Lock returned his force to putting weight on the pitchfork while stomping the hell out of his rival with his steel-toed boot. Lock thought he felt a thigh bone crunch under his frenzied stomps. The guy screeched and flailed like an insect specimen, but he was held fast, true and well. "Turk!" shouted Lock. "Are you okay? Where the fuck are you?"

Lock looked around crazily as well he could without releasing the pressure that kept Stumpy pinned. It would take for-fucking-ever for the idiot to die this way, and by that time, the CI that Lock had texted would be there to witness the carnage with instructions to call the cops.

"I'm here," Turk said, somewhere behind him. "I'm okay."

He didn't sound okay. Turk staggered forward like a slow zombie, holding his hand to his pectoral, where a crimson bloom told where he'd been hit. Lock spat, "Fuck! Did you see where the gun went?"

"Yeah," said Turk, weakly, possibly in shock from his injury. He tossed his head. It was difficult to hear him over the squeals and curses of the stuck pig at their feet. Turk bashed the homophobe in the shin with his own boot, and the guy quieted down. "It's up there smack on top of that stack of bales. Go get it, I'll take care of this."

Turk took over pitchfork duties while Lock clambered up the wall of alfalfa to feel around for the piece. Meanwhile, Stumpy was hollering,

"You fucking fairies! You're already doomed! Nothing you can do to me is going to compare to the world of hurt you're gonna feel when the club gets ahold of you. I already told Papa Ewey and your best butt-fucking friend Breakiron about your gay boy activities. I told him how you were screwing this Boner up the butt with a beer bottle while licking his dick and—"

The gun grip was still hot from Stumpy's sweaty hand.

A DANGEROUS REALITY

When Lock squeezed the trigger it felt like butter. Very little report or recoil, just a cotton headed almost slow-mo sensation of seeing the bullet piercing Stumpy's stupid brain and finally, at last, putting that insect to rest. He stopped quivering and fighting and his jaw went slack, but Turk gave a few extra shoves on the pitchfork just for good measure.

Lock didn't even need to wipe off prints from the gun, as he wore gloves. He just dropped it next to Stumpy. It was Stumpy's, after all. Lock volunteered for the unpleasant task of sliding his hand beneath Stumpy's back and retrieving their pieces. Lock found the phone where it had been flung and pocketed it. They looked at each other and nodded crisply at a job well done.

Lock was worried about Turk driving the truck after being shot. A quick exam revealed luckily only a flesh wound, and Lock was able to bandage it up with another clean bandanna from his saddlebag.

Everything was foggy, dreamlike as they drove the straight line to Lake Havasu City. It all came rushing back to Lock what this feeling was like after a major fire fight or engagement. The rush of adrenaline must numb out the brain, which made sense from a biological angle. It wasn't survival of the fittest to have a bunch of screaming, emotional thoughts plaguing you when you were fighting for your life. It made sense for God or whoever to put man's brain on autopilot when doing what had to be done. The fuzzy sensation lingered long after the battle was over.

They were halfway to Lock's warehouse before anyone spoke.

Turk said, "Are you sure you're ready for what's next? Because what's next is going to make what happened back there look like child's play."

Lock speared his fingers through his hair and sighed a giant sigh. "Yeah, well. The wheels are in motion. And I'm glad I'm going there with you, babe. I trust you. You've got my back, you know? We worked pretty well as a team back there." It was as close to a romantic, sappy speech as Lock was ever going to give.

Turk wasn't one for flowery words, either. "'If we could read our enemies' secret histories, we'd find sorrow and suffering enough to disarm all hostility.'"

What was Turk saying? That they should feel *sorry* for ol' Stumpy Meadows, mass murderer? "I'm sure Stumpy had secret suffering, too. But it's the *way* he chose to take it out on other—"

"I'm not saying that," Turk said slyly. "What I'm getting at is, you and I started out as enemies. But I saw the sorrow and pain in your face. I knew you were carrying a huge weight of loss and loneliness, just like I was. So I dropped all hostilities."

Oh. Lock squirmed uncomfortably in the passenger seat. Turk had just seen clear through him. "We share the same burden," Lock admitted.

Turk's sideways smile was genuine as he shifted gears. "It's a lot easier when you bear the weight together."

That was true. And the more Lock breathed in deeply, he felt the calming spirit of Turk's companionship soaking into his blood.

EPILOGUE

TURK

S ome days you just really don't want to get out of bed.
Some days you just don't want to face at all.

Which isn't to say I didn't *want* to face the music. The unknown terrifies most people, but my entire life has been about the unknown.

It doesn't get any more unexpected, sketchy, or random than the life of an MC patch holder. We're all about being trained to expect the unexpected, especially when it rains on you from the damned sky.

Some weeks it's just horror upon horror, like before The Bare Bones went on lockdown after hitting back at the Presención cartel. For weeks it had been one random act of violence after another, whether it was in apple orchards, Crate and Barrel, or in the case of poor Kneecap, while waiting in line for Judas Priest tickets. Yes, that poor hapless guy, who already walked with a cane, was hit once again with a baseball bat in the knees, causing havoc to ensue, and Kneecap to lose his place in line. That guy just couldn't buy a break.

Then the randomness became skull-crushing boredom during the lockdown. I alone was given my freedom, and in the meantime things had seemed to normalize in the world of Pure and Easy. Apparently Ford and Lytton had reached out to kingpin Abel Presención and had reached a kind of détente. We could come out of lockdown and resume our normal activities without fear of blowback from the cartel.

As Veep I should've been in on the details, but by the time I got back to P&E, I frankly didn't care so much. I spent half the night sitting up in Ford's living room with him and Lytton giving them a blow by blow on what had happened along the Colorado River. Of course I was completely honest about the whole Stumpy Meadows thing and how we had basically ruined the empire of Carmine Rojas, with assistance from his wife, of course. The Illuminati brothers laughed with glee, seeing a whole new business chasm opening before their very eyes, but I told them I had plans for that giant kingpin void. *Me.*

They were mournful to lose me, but they accepted it. I had lived with and loved Ford Illuminati as more than a brother for over twenty years now. In the world of an MC brotherhood you endure way more together than any normal, white bread family. So when I say "we had been through hell and high water together," I mean it. There is never a dull moment in an MC— unless you're in lockdown, start to grow moss, and begin fighting over the latest issue of *People* magazine, that is. But the life is so action-packed, you learn to thrive on the adrenaline boost. You develop a fight-or-flight instinct that gives you lightning reflexes.

My new life would be an even more tangled, dark, and dangerous jungle than the one I'd just left. I'd be kicking and scratching just to get by in the beginning. But fuck it, I was going to *miss* my brothers. I know, we'd be brother clubs, and we'd be invited to the monthly fish fries and all, but it'd hardly be the same. We had lived, and some of us had died, by the sword for so long now. My brain had been firing on the same set of neurons for so long, I was going to have to retrain it, to re-establish new patterns. I'd been following in the deep wagon wheel ruts of The Bare Bones for almost my entire life. This was the most terrifying new venture I had yet to undertake.

"Our one and only item for the meeting," said Ford. He took a deep breath, exhaled, and looked pointedly at me. "Well, I'll leave it up to our brother Turk to explain. It's his story, so he deserves to tell it."

I'd been practicing this speech in my head for months, years probably. Just when it came time to speak, facing a sea of my brethren's faces at the chapel table like that, I stumbled. I literally choked like a fucking sap looking into the craggy, experienced face of Duji, and the craggy, pockmarked face of Tuzigoot. These were our elders, our uncles who had raised me and Ford, had guided us through the hormonal and violent maze of adolescence. There was always a father figure there for us, even if Cropper was out of town on business, or fucking some whore in the next room. I was abandoning all of this to start out fresh in a club where *I* would be the father figure to a bunch of bumbling, clueless Prospects, bikers who had never been in an MC before.

"I'm gay," I blurted, just like Ellen in that infamous sitcom. I might as well have had a mic, too, for how fucking loud it sounded to my ears, reverberating against the fake wood paneled walls of the chapel. I had expected to make a preamble that would lead eloquently up to this point, but the statement had been festering for so long inside me, like boiling lava under the crusty surface, that it came out in one eruption like that.

To their credit, nobody looked too shocked. Tuzigoot and Faux Pas even smiled and looked at each other—had they had a *bet* going on?—while the others nodded sagely. No one said anything, though, so I blustered on.

"Some of you may have guessed, but I wasn't ready to come

out. That needs to be each man's prerogative, and I'm glad Ford left that up to me, to do in my own time. Well, uh, that time has come, brothers. Some shit went down in Lake Havasu City—all up and down the Colorado River, actually—that can't be undone, and I have to bow out of The Bare Bones."

Now there was murmuring and a bunch of "what the fuck"s. Ford and Lytton were obviously the only two who had prescience of this announcement, because they remained straight-faced. It was Faux Pas, my uncle if ever there was one, who outright demanded,

"Why the fuck, Theodore? No one here is demanding that you hand over your cut and step down! That is the last thing we would do!"

"Yeah!" added Duji. "We don't care what the fuck you do in your spare time. Just, you know, don't go draping The Citadel with rainbow banners or watching *Showgirls.*"

"Hey," said Gollywow. "That was a good movie. But I second what you're saying, Duji. Just don't start reading Gore Vidal or walking around stark naked."

"Hey," I protested feebly, "at least I don't walk around with a penis pump hanging from my dick." I referred to our ex-sergeant-at-arms, Riker, a coarse guy who had been there the day in the desert when Cropper had met his demise.

Knoxie said, "Or a urethral dilator sticking out of your cut pocket."

Everyone cringed and laughed, and the tension was broken. Brother after brother started protesting that I didn't have to leave. It became evident that I'd need to explain farther.

"I met a guy," I started, but the *ooos* and *ahhs* overwhelmed me.

"Let me guess," shouted Speed, "Dayton Navarro. I knew it! I saw you two walking from behind the toilet trailer once all adjusting your cuts and wiping off your mouths. Didn't look like any drug *I* ever heard of."

"No, not Dayton. Someone new, someone I want to start a whole new club with."

Everyone hushed up at that. Tuzigoot, so famous for his craggy face he was named after an ancient Aztec god found carved into a pyramid, went absolutely stone-faced. Now I had to race on, to keep the momentum going.

"I know it's a big undertaking. I'm not going to step on anyone's toes because the club'll be based in Lake Havasu City."

"Backyard of the Assassins of Youth," Wild Man said with wonder. The Assassins weren't our enemies, but they we weren't on back-slapping terms with them either.

"Yeah, well, some things have changed. Papa Ewey has agreed to let us have Lake Havasu and its backyard, and we've pretty much got Parker and Quartzsite locked up. Papa Ewey doesn't have anyone living down there anymore since Stumpy Meadows met his maker a few days ago, in case you hadn't heard."

Every last man jack looked at each other with fresh surprise. Of course they'd heard how the hated Stumpy Meadows had been discovered sprawled upon the corpses of a dozen missing Mexican students, stabbed with a pitchfork through his vitals. The trucking papers—and the body of Rojas' head of security—strewn nearby and held down with body parts as paperweights had proven Rojas' involvement with the Marin cartel in Sonora. Feds had arrested Rojas at his palatial estate, since his wife Carmen had already opened up RICO negotiations with them. A fresh turf war was afoot with the remaining Rojas henchmen scrambling to make or break alliances with various factions of the extensive operations. It wouldn't be a pleasant place to step into, but it was our only choice.

"And my new partner"—I wasn't comfortable yet using the word "lover" out loud—"is based in Lake Havasu City. We've already got a few guys who want to patch into the new club. Of course there are a zillion details to iron out. Anyway, that's not your concern. What concerns you is that I'm stepping down as Vice President of The Bare Bones effective immediately."

As I stood, most of the men looked to Ford and Lytton for confirmation. Ford nodded. "Lytton, although a fucking bang-up sergeant-at-arms with all of his scientific know-how, is the logical guy to step in as Vice Prez. This has all happened so fast we're going to leave the sergeant-at-arms position open for now, so right now you need to vote on one thing. Will we allow brother Turk Blackburn to leave The Bare Bones, Red Rocks Original, in good standing? I say yea."

"Yea," Lytton echoed immediately.

As they went round the table, everyone had no other option than to say yea also. When the moment came for me to remove my cut, hot tears boiled in my eye sockets. I had worn that cut so fucking long, I'd actually had to start over from scratch with a new one when I had a growth spurt while in jail and shot up like a foot in one year. The rockers were all original, filthy beyond belief, but that was how we rolled. It was quite literally a part of me, conforming to my size and shape, reeking of me, no doubt, depending on what sort of diet I ate, who I was banging, and how much beer I drank.

Carefully folding the cut, I placed it on the table. "Our world is different from the regular citizen," I told everyone. They all nodded sagely. "The straight world is like a smoke world full of deception and lies. Those businessmen and lovers stab each other in the back while smiling in each other's faces. Here, that would never fly. We tell it like it is. We're true blooded brothers, bonded in the rules of the road. We can depend on each other to act a certain way, and this reliability creates a network of solid bonds.

"I plan on relying on these bonds of ours in the upcoming years, brothers. You know my new club will be filled mostly with gay bikers. You can vote later on whether or not you want to do business with us. But we want to do business with *you*. I'm pretty sure we've got at least the safe passage through the Colorado River Rez sewn up in our back pocket, and we're reaching out to Papa Ewey on rights to the other Rezes. Let's just say he owes us one, and the tribes are more liable to look fondly upon me and Lock Singer than upon Papa Ewey and Stumpy Meadows. Papa Ewey is willing to give up some of his power base to retain control in the Bullhead City and Laughlin area."

Duji nodded. "Lock Singer. Good man. He runs a bail bonds company in Lake Havasu, right? I had him search for some fucktard who took a powder once. He found him in half a day."

Ford pointed at Duji. "That's the one. I've had a couple of sit-downs with him myself. He's straightforward, easy to read, doesn't have any hidden agendas. Can't say the same for Papa Ewey. You all remember what went down during last year's Laughlin Run."

I'd been afraid Ford would bring that up. That same bumbling Prospect of ours, Mergatroyd, had inadvertently hit on one of Papa Ewey's favorite sweetbutts. I was there—she was actually seeming very *into it* with Mergatroyd—when Papa Ewey came roaring in and chased Mergatroyd up a tree. I kid you not. We were all sort of halfway laughing, but halfway tweaked about how we were going to save our Prospect. He'd been caught doing something legitimately bad in the MC world, but the Assassholes started throwing beer bottles and lighted flares at Mergatroyd. It was all settled amicably—*after* Ford had been forced to call on Laughlin firemen to put out the fire under the tree. You know how much bikers love to call on the law. It was the only way to put the fire out, and get our Prospect down in shame. And Papa Ewey had laughed.

"Speaking of Prospects," I said. Ford had allowed me to bring this up, too. "I'm taking Twinkletoes with me."

A fresh round of chagrin rolled over the room. I continued speaking louder through the protests. "I know Twinkletoes is a favorite. That's why I'm taking him." I laughed, trying to lighten the mood. Twinkletoes wasn't there because he was still a Prospect.

Gollywow yelled, "I always knew he was a bit light in the loafers."

I rolled my eyes, but I knew I had to make myself immune to immature remarks like that. I'd be hearing plenty of them. "He's not gay. But with his name, he gets plenty of this shit anyway, so he's already got a head start on the loads of crap we're going to be putting up with coming down the pipeline. His technical expertise was invaluable during this op, and he's a good loyal man."

"But that's why we want him!" cried Faux Pas. "He was helping me with computer modeling for some zombies and werewolf attack victims."

Wild Man moaned, "He was helping me break into the Baal's Minions cash vault."

I said, "Well, you're stuck with Tobiah as far as computer expertise goes. He's excellent in his own right." Tobiah was Lytton's office manager up at the Leaves of Grass pot farm on Mormon Mountain, not a brother. But of course he did a lot of technical surveillance work for the club.

"What're you going to do about The Joint System?" Speed

asked, mentioning my dispensary on Bargain Boulevard.

I looked at Lytton. He'd created, founded, and nurtured Leaves of Grass, our main supplier of primo, dank bud, and it was his turn to speak. "August will get bumped up to manager. He's good enough to be a ganjier." August raised two fingers to an imaginary cap on his head in recognition of the promotion. "I'm going to let Crybaby come down off his mountain and help August in the store. I'm just going to have to find a new cultivator up at the ranch."

Speed asked me, "But what're you going to do in Lake Havasu? Open another dispensary?"

"That's the goal," I said, "since they only have a really shitty one that only delivers to the seniors, not a storefront open to cardholders. As you know, A Joint System is a full service, one stop shopping op. Hell, I've already got the majority of my suppliers sitting right in this room."

"Plus the Ochoas," Lytton added, mentioning my other supplier near Show Low. It wouldn't do to only feature weed from one plantation.

"In the meantime, I got a gig with the Lake Havasu newspaper as their pot critic." I really had. Lock had just happened to mention me to a friend of his who worked at the paper, and a new job description was born.

I expected the scoffing that came with that revelation. "What?" sputtered Bobo Segrist. "There's such a thing as *pot critic*? What's the fucking world coming to?"

I held out a calming hand. "Sure. You don't go to a restaurant and just order a red wine, like they do on TV. You want to see the list, hear their offerings, make a choice. It's my job to write about my opinions. Not that I won't have enough to do, setting up a new charter and all. In fact, I'm going to borrow Slushy for a couple of weeks. Drawing up new bylaws and all that."

"*What?*" whined Kneecap. "Slushy was helping me arrange a plea bargain with the DA on that public indecency charge."

"Typical," sneered Knoxie, never a big fan of the guy who looked like Ronald McDonald and had fucked his old lady.

Duji chimed in. "Slushy is helping me set up a shell corporation for my club income." He held up idealistic hands. "We're going to call it the Blendin Corporation. Get it? Blend in. We blend into the background."

"You hope," said Ford.

"What is the new club going to be called?" asked Faux Pas.

"The Bent Zealots," I said proudly. "We're zealots about our gayness, and the rest of the world thinks we're bent."

Faux Pas, a special effects man for the movies, nodded with pursed lips. "I like it. It conjures up a lot of images. You can have a hooded Middle Eastern fellow with a sword on the logo."

"Something like that," I agreed, "only maybe not too Arabic, if you know what I mean."

"Why not? The Shriners have been known as the Ancient Arabic Order of the Nobles of the Mystic Shrine for over a hundred years just because one of the founders took a trip to Egypt and thought some images looked cool. They've got a scimitar and a head of a sphinx for their logo. Something like that could be very cool."

I actually agreed. "Put a fez on our rocker," I halfway joked.

Gollywow said, "Ride around in those tiny cars in parades."

"Right," I said. "Tiny Harleys."

"Actually," said Tuzigoot, "I wanted to bring something to the table about a rumor I heard about The Cutlasses, a new direction they're taking."

The table went silent, and everyone looked at me wide-eyed.

Then I remembered.

I had retired my cut. I was no longer a member of The Bare Bones MC. I couldn't listen in on whatever Tuzigoot had to say about The Cutlasses.

I cleared my throat. "Well," I said feebly. "You guys know how much I love you, each and every last one of you. You've been my family, and that's never going to stop."

"No, no," everyone agreed.

"You've been here for me, and I hope that continues."

To my left, Lytton stood. "We wish you all the best, brother Turk."

We hugged and slapped each other on the back heartily, sort of gripping each other's backs with our fingers in desperation. It was one of those horrible, emotional moments everyone dreads, because you never know when you're going to burst into fucking tears.

And I had to go through it with every brother in the room. I slapped back after back, embraced brother after brother, each one smelling a bit different. Each man had a distinct scent all his own, scents the amalgamation of who they were, what they ate, the air they breathed, the cuts they'd been wearing for years, even decades.

I did start crying, and eventually had to casually wipe a tear from one eye with the back of my hand as I left the chapel, head held high.

So that was how I walked out of my club and into a new life. Nobody wanted me to go. I could've hung around there—forever, as a matter of fact, even without a cut or any colors.

But I had to leave eventually. I had forced myself to do thousands of things in my life that were outside my comfort zone. Kiss my first girl. Kiss my first boy. Ride alone cross country. Watch as my stepfather was murdered in cold blood by my best friend. Dump the body parts of twenty students in an alfalfa barn. Cross the border into Nogales, make a hit, and return.

But never had anything seemed as unreal, life-changing, or momentous as walking out the fucking hangar doors of The Citadel with only Twinkletoes at my side.

LOCK

"I want to add a bylaw," said Hobie Cleminshaw. That high-voiced, enormous man looked like someone's roly poly and possibly creepy clown uncle, but Lock had seen him head-butt a Baal's Minions patch holder into the middle of next week. One had to be tough to be a gay biker, presenting a powerful image and letting everyone know one was in control. Otherwise all hell broke loose. "I want to add that members must be of sound mind when attending church. In other words"—and he looked pointedly at Rover Florkowski, a craggy guy who had been sadly a pizza face as a teenager—"sober."

Rover got the picture, all right, and he wanted to add a bylaw of his own. "Oh, yeah? Well I'd like to add that during church there's no talking unless the President gives you the floor."

"The President's not here," said Dipstick Hunziger. He was probably called that because he was six foot five and about as thin as that tool. Or, he could be a pretty big dipstick with his rapier wit.

Lock, as Veep, took control of the messy meeting by banging a hammer on the long conference table they'd had brought into The Happy Hour Bar and Grill. He didn't have a gavel yet, and like most things, he'd had to improvise with some of the carpenters' tools. "I'd like a free give and take, especially since we're a startup. I don't want anyone feeling stifled by our roles as President or what have you."

"Yes," said Hobie, "but it's going to be absolute anarchy if everyone talks at once! Especially if they talk too fast for me to write. I don't know shorthand."

"Yeah," said Dipstick, a chef. "We also don't eat jello molds with little marshmallows anymore, Hobie."

Hobie pointed at Dipstick with his pen. "That doesn't mean they aren't delicious."

Lock rolled his eyes. He wouldn't have picked Hobie if he wasn't so badass with his martial arts skills and if he wasn't such an organized secretary. With his ladylike voice and penchant for drama and calling everyone "girl," Hobie pretty much epitomized the stereotype of the effeminate bear. They argued amongst themselves just like any club, just like the Assassins of Youth had. But Lock wanted them to beware of coming across as infighting in public.

"All right, guys. So far we've agreed on about four things. We're running this club on a parliamentary basis. Cuts must be worn at all times. Prospects must own their own Harley and be sponsored by a member. And we must be constantly stocked with three-ply toilet paper."

"Here, here," said Dipstick.

Rover made a face. "I've got hemorrhoids."

Hobie pointed at Thymus. "And no hip-hop on the jukebox."

Dr. Thymus Moog—who was actually a medical doctor, cardiology, Lock thought, as well as the son of the inventor of the Moog synthesizer—pointed back at the roly-poly secretary. "Hey. If you can have that obnoxious show music that makes it sound like a Hugh Jackman special in here, then I can play hip-hop."

For the twentieth time, Lock banged his hammer. He was already wearing a pattern into the top of the conference table with that thing. "Men, men. We can figure out all the details later, like about the fucking toilet paper, Doritos versus Fritos, and whether or not we're allowed to put 'hippie shit' on the front of our cuts. That can all be figured out later, once we're up to full strength. Right now it's just the five of us, six with Ormond Tangier, eight when Turk and Twinkletoes get here."

The doctor chuckled. "Twinkletoes."

Lock glowered at the small, impish guy. He increased the volume and authority of his tone. "Listen, we've got to get it together and take this fucking seriously. Do as you say or walk the line. Respect your colors. No stealing from other members. Don't fuck around with a brother's old man. You're representing your club in all business transactions. We have to present a united front. We have to be *more* united, *more* together, *more* solid than any other MC out there. Dipstick, you left the Baal's Minions to join us. You and I are the only ones with actual MC experience. I'm nominating you as the treasurer." Dipstick nodded with satisfaction. "And I want the rest of you men to look to us for guidance if you're not sure how to proceed with anything. I don't want a club full of whiners running to me every time some scumbag on the street calls you a fairy, but if there are credible threats, bring them to me, Dipstick, or Turk."

"Or Twinkletoes," pointed out Hobie. "He's got MC experience."

"But he's just a Prospect," said Thymus.

Lock said firmly, "Twinkletoes is patching in with a full rocker as soon as we get the patches back from the place that's making them. He deserves to be a fully patched member. I don't want anyone feeling pity for him or razzing him 'cause he's got multiple sclerosis. He's put in his time."

The doctor said, "Secondary progressive MS, from what I was told. His symptoms have begun a steady march."

"Right. That." Lock spread his hands on the table, palms down. "But other than that, I don't want to be weighed down with every minor scrape you guys are bound to get into. I picked you, or Ormond did, because you're tough, resilient, intelligent, and you all know how to handle yourselves. You're all familiar with firearms and aren't afraid to use them in a predicament. Rover, you were in Kingman the same time Turk was."

"Weapons charge," said the craggy biker. "It was a bum beef."

"I'm sure it was," Lock said unconvincingly. "My point is, we've all agreed to dedicate our lives to an outlaw life, to outlaw justice. Turk and I didn't found this club in the blood of dead students for nothing."

Lock had given the club the 411 on the whole Stumpy Meadows story. He had to. If he didn't he was withholding vital information. There might eventually be blowback from that chain of events, and it was the basis of their entire foundation. Papa Ewey had conceded a large part of his own backyard to The Bent Zealots because he agreed that Stumpy Meadows was a "loose cannon," a drug addict who never should have been allowed to stay in The Assassins. Papa Ewey had known a lot of that, yet he'd allowed Stumpy to continue operating in the Colorado River Rez. As much as Papa Ewey loathed homos, he conceded that Lock and Turk had been put through the wringer. He would let Lock leave in semi-good standing as long as he agreed to have his Assassins back pack removed. Papa Ewey would personally check on that in about a month.

In addition to this, Carmine Rojas and nearly his entire empire had been dismantled. Carmen Rojas had gone into witness protection and was naming names right and left. A heat wave was sweeping throughout all of southwestern Arizona, taking out one runner and spitter after another and everyone on the totem pole in between. There was a giant void to fill, but it was anyone's guess who the Marins in Sonora would appoint to fill Carmine's shoes. In the meantime, laying low was the best policy. Regrouping, rebanding.

"I also selected each of you based upon what you can bring to this club's table. Dipstick, you bring all your Minions connections. Rover, you've been working with Tony Tormenta, El Tisico, and Los Marlines Risitas down in Nogales. The doctor here obviously has great medical skill but also has connections in Mexico and Canada for any type of prescription drug known to man."

"Really?" said Hobie. "I've been unable to get my hands on any Dinitrophenol, a diet pill."

"Banned for good reason," said Thymus, "but I can hook you up with some pills that actually work."

"Hook me up, too," said Rover.

"Why?" whined Hobie. "You're perfectly fit and trim."

"I know." Rover grinned. "I just want some speed."

Lock sighed. It would take a while to whip this club into shape. And they were going to have to get whipped fast. Rumors were starting to leak out onto the street about what had gone down at Stumpy's alfalfa barn. There were still some Carmine Rojas loyalists who would like to get payback on whoever had taken down their boss. Nobody seemed to care much about Roland or Stumpy.

Thymus started rising from his seat. "I've got to get into surgery."

Lock said, "Okay. One last thing. We need Prospects. If anyone sees anyone they think is likely, let me know."

"I know a few tough baby gangsters," said Rover.

Lock pointed his hammer at Rover. "No drug addicts. OK, meeting adjourned."

When Thymus hit the swinging front door of the ancient Happy Hour lounge, that's when Lock saw Turk. The guys had all briefly met Turk before Turk had returned to Pure and Easy. Turk had approved of them—with reservations about the sheer craziness of Rover Florkowski—and had gone off to deal with his club.

It had been a long-ass week of fumbling sexts and even more bumbling phonesex, and now here Turk was, in the flesh. He banged into the still-smoky, run-down bar like the long-legged stallion he was. He was wearing a black cut that was completely empty, devoid of any rockers or patches, a blank slate. Twinkletoes followed him, greeting Rover, with whom he seemed to have formed a particular attachment. There was another guy, too, that Lock didn't bother even looking at. Suddenly men were pouring beer and playing pool, and Turk zeroed in on Lock.

It was thrilling and alien to be in public like that, completely open and free about the fact that another man was heading for him with sex on the brain. Turk was so single-minded in his quest that he practically slammed into Lock, smashing him against the long, polished bar.

They kissed like two starving men on a desert island. Turk stroked Lock's tongue with long, adoring licks while grinding his pelvis against Lock's. Other clubs allowed sex in their clubhouses so Lock knew theirs shouldn't be any different. Carpenters were still working on finishing a dilapidated room in back that would be their chapel, and there would obviously be no sex in there. For now, they couldn't enforce rules that wouldn't be enforced in any hetero club, so Turk ground his eager erection against Lock's. The flutter of expectant sensuality tightened Lock's abdomen. This was going to be good.

"Hey, listen. If you don't mind, I've had enough of this sort of thing in Gladiator School. I had to stroll down Bosco Boulevard more times than I care to remember. Take it to the back, where you don't alarm small children and barnyard animals."

Turk pulled away with a look of mild amusement. An average-looking, mild-mannered guy in a suit with a bad combover was next to them at the bar shuffling through a briefcase of papers. "Lock, this is Slushy. Our lawyer."

Slushy said, "I'll be your lawyer until you can find someone local. I'll help you sort through this whole mess you've created." He hitched a thumb at Turk and said to Lock, "I always thought Turk was the level-headed one. Now he finally comes out, as if it was any big surprise to anyone, and says he wants to start a gay motorcycle club. Yeah. That'll go over big at the next Sturgis Rally."

"Who goes to Sturgis anymore, Slushy?" Turk had an affectionate, teasing tone. "That rally is so in the rearview. You need to get with the times."

"I never claimed to be hip, boys. God, do I miss 1997. I just want to read my *New York Times* and do my yoga."

Lock managed to say, "The Laughlin run is still where it's at," before Turk whisked him off to a back room.

"All right, hurry it up, boys," said Slushy. "I've got some heirloom tomatoes to plant back home."

Lock's heart was full to bursting as Turk yanked him into the dark back hallway. There were several rooms off the hall that led to the bathrooms. No one had gotten around to remodeling anything yet. The only room that was halfway cleaned up was the "rumpus room," a place where the homeless Rover had been crashing. There was a stack of Marshall amps from the days when you could smoke inside a bar, a ragged Allman Brothers poster, and a single cot that no one wanted to touch.

Turk shoved Lock back against the Marshall stack and took a big, lusty bite from his jawbone. "I'm going to be fucking a rich boy."

Lock was so alive with desire and pleasure, he practically purred. "Why you calling me a rich boy? I'm just a bail bondsman."

"You're from Bel Air," Turk growled against his throat. Turk had figured out what Bel Air meant, apparently.

Grabbing a handful of Turk's man bun, Lock rubbed his nose against Turk's. "My dad is a rich lawyer, yeah. Haven't talked to him in ten years. Listen. I love you, Turk. I really do."

As Lock had feared, they both went stone still. Turk even seemed to stop breathing.

He hadn't wanted to make a big deal out of saying it. It was just the fucking L word. Brothers said they loved each other all the fucking time. But the way Turk was practically holding his breath while his pupils bore holes through Lock's skull, yeah. It was a big deal.

Lock needed to lighten the oppressive, serious air that clouded the room. "Cumon," he said casually, trying to chuckle. "Let me suck you. It's my turn to suck you. I don't want this being all one-sided and—"

"There are only two reasons for ever doing anything," intoned Turk. Now he gripped a handful of Lock's hair. *Oh, clusterfuck. He's going all literary on me.* "Love and fear."

"Well, I love you." Fear actually *was* beginning to get a grip on Lock. "No big deal about that."

"I think both things are at work here. For you *and* for me. The more I fear you, Lock, the more I love you."

Lock exhaled with relief. *He loves me too.* He took Turk's chin in his fingers. "So you won't mind if I get down on my knees and show you how much I fear you?"

TURK

I really just started out wanting to give Lock shit about having a rich, privileged upbringing.

I had no idea it would shame him into saying to me what had been on the tip of my brain for so long now. *I love you, Turk.*

We needed this. We needed to cement our relationship, because it was so bohemian and unusual, in a traditional foundation of convention. If I needed to fucking marry Lock I would. Gay marriage had just been legalized in Arizona. I never thought it'd be something I'd be remotely interested in. But I was. Other men could have old ladies, legal wives or not. There was no precedent for gay bikers. I wanted it legal.

But the idea terrified me. That's how I knew it was legitimate, real, and that it came from my heart. If it was just some passing fancy, it wouldn't put the fear of turning fifty into me. If we were going to start this new highly dangerous venture, expose ourselves to all sorts of ridicule and jeopardy, take any and all blowback entirely upon our own shoulders, we were going to have to do so from a rock solid position of knowing fully who we were, what we stood for.

"I think both things are at work here. For you *and* for me. The more I fear you, Lock, the more I love you."

Once it was out of my mouth and I couldn't take it back, I silenced Lock with a kiss. His dick was so stiff it poked me in the hip, and when I lunged my pelvis into him, the underside of my erection massaged his with a sensual thrill. My mouth watered to plunge that prick down my thirsty throat, to feel the bursting, velvety glans rub and gag me at the back of my soft palate.

But Lock squirmed free of my kiss to say, "So you won't mind if I get down on my knees and show you how much I fear you?"

What the fuck did *that* mean? I was so used to being the submissive to Lock's Dom, I was about to get down on *my* knees and show the blond god how much I worshiped him.

He torpedoed me with that question. We had just declared our love for each other, and suddenly *he* wanted to get down on *his* knees? I managed to stutter, "You don't need to do that, Lock. I know who you are, and I accept you for it. You don't have to do anything that's outside of your wheelhouse. You don't—"

I gasped when Lock suddenly plunged to his knees and plastered his mouth to my cock.

He mouthed it from outside the jean fabric, as I'd done so many times to him. I considered myself the cock and ball sadist par excellence, and I was highly skilled at keeping a man hanging on that precipice that usually existed for only a split second before orgasm burst the dam. I could go back and forth, seeing and then sawing, for half an hour or so, bringing a man to the brink, then reeling him back in.

Lock—poor, sweet, inexperienced Lock—just went for it. Slanting his face at an angle, he gummed my entire prick and gnawed like a wolf. The sudden shock of Lock dropping to his knees, the subservient way he mouthed my throbbing dick, how he gripped my meat with his mouth and blew a steaming hot lungful of air that warmed my whole pelvis—I was on the verge of coming within seconds.

I had to do something.

"God, Lock!" I launched myself up and over him. Catching a toehold between two of the amps, I managed to hold myself up on my palms like a gymnast. This position only swiveled my hips even more firmly against Lock's sweet face, and he munched away at my crotch like Robinson Crusoe. Somewhere out in the bar, someone had started a medley of show tunes on the jukebox, and I was glad that strange doctor had departed. He was a good, steely man to have on your side, for sure, but he definitely had a dark side. And he hated anything that was stereotypically gay.

I was glad the music blurred out my moans and groans as Lock opened my belt buckle and dipped his face against my naked groin. He slathered his tongue to my pubic bone where I was glad I'd shaved a nice trim Brazilian. He plastered the flat of his tongue to my mound like it was a freezing cold metal pole, his tongue stuck there so he could grunt and gum me like some toothless senior.

"*Aghhhh.*" My groan vibrated down into the pit of my stomach, wavering through my meat that was pounding so lustily I swore I could feel my heartbeat in it. My newly-pierced nipple was so taut that the cotton wifebeater rubbing against it felt like sandpaper. I wanted to rip off both my shirts, my cut, my jeans, and just fuck Lock missionary style against the Marshall stack with his head banging up against Duane Allman's boots, but he had me completely in his control. He was topping me from the bottom!

And there was nothing I could do about it.

I *tried* to take control. Fisting a handful of his scruffy blond hair, I yanked his skull away from my crotch so I could take my cock out of my jeans. It hit the cool, clean air with a shock to my system, pulsating there in midair, hanging in front of Lock's face. His panting breaths were humid against the moistness of my crotch where he'd been mouthing me. I let him get a good eyeful of what I'd been told was my horse cock. I gripped it in my other hand, rubbing the shiny, straining glans against his wet lips.

"You want to eat this dick," I told him. "Your only desire is to pleasure me. You want to suck this fat dong more than anything else you've ever seen in your life. Your only goal is my satisfaction."

Lock opened his mouth, although I wouldn't let him taste my prick. "I want it, Turk. I want to taste my first cock."

That did it—"my first cock." A penis virgin is irresistible to me—ten times more so because it was Lock Singer. I actually went weak in the knees hearing that, and had to cover up my weakness by plunging my meat down his throat.

Our power exchange was unbelievable. I pinned him to the amplifier with the firmness of my hips, barely moving as he suckled me eagerly. His tongue moved all around my cock like a tornado, coming at me from every which way. I never knew from which direction, and at what strength, his mouth would hit me next. I was the center of a hungry, blissful vortex that was the core of my universe.

And yeah, I came almost immediately.

It was more flattering to Lock than embarrassing for me, I told myself later. Jizz surged through my cock and erupted, utterly without any willpower or control on my part. Ecstasy gripped my entire pelvis as I emptied myself into Lock's hot throat. Admirably, he kept swallowing, his swirling tongue driving me to heights of euphoria I'd never imagined existed.

Eventually I had to disengage. Pleasure was turning to pain, as happened often in the world of domination and submission. I no longer gripped his hair. I caressed the crown of his skull almost lightly, hissing like a teapot taken off the burner. Fisting my own sore cock now, I held it away from him.

"Great Caesar's Ghost," I whispered.

Holding me by the hips, Lock rubbed the side of his face against my pubic mound. I soothed him as though he were a crying kid.

"That was fantastic," I said. "And don't worry, I won't call you my slave just because you're on your knees."

"Good. You'd better not. Fucking slave."

I could actually feel him smiling, his mouth steamy against the root of my cock.

Someone knocked lightly at the door. Languidly, as though in a drugged dream, I released my hold on Lock's head and turned to face the door.

"What?"

"Boss?" It sounded like that rough-and-tumble guy, Rover. I made a mental note that he would make a good sergeant-at-arms. He seemed to have a lot of cartel experience.

"What?" both Lock and I said at the same time.

I looked down at him and laughed. "We'd better figure out who's boss."

Lock stood, leaning against the stack of amps for support. "What's up, Rover?"

"Korg seems like she's hungry. She just brought in a dead rat from the back alley."

Rats? I recoiled inwardly, my cock shriveling just as fast as my brain upon hearing about rodents. I stuffed it back in my jeans as I shouted, "We'll be right there."

Korg was our new Bernese Mountain Dog puppy. Now that

there were three men living in Lock's midcentury modern home, there was certain to always be someone around. We were also training her to become immune to the antics and hubbub of our new clubhouse, a converted old timer's bar in the downtown area of Rough and Ready. She wasn't quite potty trained yet, so we had a crate near the old bar to secure her in if we had to go out on errands. She had only made about two mistakes inside the clubhouse so far. She was getting the picture. Already, Lock had taught her to sit, lie down, and shake paws. She was adorable—something for us all to love, something we could all agree on. Twinkletoes had feelers out to get a sidecar, to train Korg to tolerate the rumble of scoot pipes.

We named her Korg because she was a cave dog, in at the ground level formation of a new breed of club. And we'd gotten matching tattoos—I know, sounds corny, but gays aren't immune to any of that sappy romantic crap either. Our inner forearms sported cave paintings, stylized deer attacking moose like those prehistoric drawings in France. We were Cro Magnons, creating a new language, a new world from scratch.

As we adjusted ourselves, I became more self-conscious, remembering I'd told Lock that I loved him. It seemed like every five minutes I was stumbling on a new feeling, a new emotion, a new adventure. It was exhausting and invigorating at the same time.

I said, "I was thinking of making pasta for dinner tonight. Slushy gave us a jar of sun dried tomatoes from his garden."

"You know how to make spaghetti sauce? All I'm good at is grilling. Everything's grilled. Grilled pancakes, grilled eggs."

"Grilled yogurt. Yeah, I always cooked for The Bare Bones. Learned from the Illuminati brothers. Speaking of Italians, where's Ormond?"

Lock grinned adorably. "He's out planning a Sons of Italy

crab feed."

I pretended to roll my eyes, but deep down, I was impressed. The Bare Bones didn't have square, outsider functions like that. We schmoozed with potential mayors and members of town council, but it was more along the lines of giving them free weed to prevent new zoning laws from ruining one of our businesses. We didn't belong to any outside organizations, and we certainly didn't have any cardiologists among our patch holders. Faux Pas was about as upper echelon as it got, with his Hollywood connections. Duji was an electrician, and Tuzigoot some kind of laborer who worked on highways. Not that there was anything wrong with that.

"Maybe we can go fishing this weekend," said Lock as we exited the grimy bedroom.

I was going to say "We'll be way too busy for that," but I stopped myself. Sure, we had a buttload of work to do. But every week for the next twenty-eight years would be like that. We'd better make time now to do silly, fun things like fish, or we never would. Even as a tiny kid, I saw that happen to my parents. My dad was an anthropology professor at the Flagstaff university, my mother a lonely housekeeper. I think she had been an anthropologist of some sort before having us kids, and had given it up.

"Sure. Where's your boat parked?"

"Moored. It's at Lake Havasu Marina. It's no big deal. It's just a twenty-two foot shallow draft. I haven't taken it out in months."

I remembered fishing a few times with my dad and brother. It was a primal, innocent thing to do, reminding me of the serene years before everything had become highly fucked up. It was something I wanted to revisit, to remind myself there *were* still innocent, harmless things in this world. Activities that didn't end in disaster or death.

I fed little Korg some of her dried kibble with water and her vitamins. Slushy stood near the head of the long table shuffling papers around. Catching my eye, he gestured me over. I automatically stood next to him, being accustomed to that position at The Bare Bones' table. Immediately, I remembered my proper, new position at the head, so I moved aside a few steps. A wooden gavel was suddenly there at my place.

Slushy glanced at it. "I brought you a real gavel. Ford found Cropper's old one, so that one's Ford's. Use it in good health, hot stuff."

I banged it experimentally, lightly. Not seriously at all. A meeting hadn't been called. "What you got there?"

Slushy pulled out a chair and sat, and so did I. "Listen. I got a private note from Carmen Rojas' lawyer. Apparently she set this up before she went into the program. She had a precognition, shall we say. She socked away some money that she specially wants to go to the families of a couple of dudes you may be familiar with. One"—he shuffled more papers—"is a Heriberto Orozco. I know you don't think he's got any family left after the cartel got him and his wife while your Phoenix guys Diz and Don were in the gas station bathroom. And after they cut off the limbs of the rest of them down in Mexico. But I was able to track down a few people still living in Magdalena. That is, *if* they believe us long enough to accept the money. Carmen also wants to repay some Hopis down out of Poston, the Colorado River Indian Rez. You guys are the conduit. You need to funnel the funds."

"Kwahu Johnson," I said, awed and inspired by Carmen Rojas' foresight and generosity.

Lock was now taking his seat at the Veep's chair. "What about Kwahu Johnson?"

"Slushy's telling me that Carmen Rojas arranged for his family to receive some bank."

Happiness spread over Lock's handsome face. "You're fucking kidding me. Yeah, I guess that'd stand to reason. Poor guy died in her guest bedroom."

Slushy said, "I'll tell you guys. I worked for a couple years for the Ochoa cartel, as you know, Turk, having picked me up in the middle of the desert after I'd been savagely rolled in the back of a van by them."

I added, "After they told you, you were retiring in Nuevo Léon to manage a Cinnabon."

Slushy said pertly, "Yes! I'm flattered you remember that, Theodore." To Lock he said, "If it weren't for these guys here, my body would've become part of that gas you put in your tank. The moral of the story is, never trust a thing the bad guys tell you. There's a reason they're the bad guys. You have to be even badder than them, to keep a step ahead of them at all times. Imagine the worst thing they could possibly do, then double it. I always say 'keep your lovers close—and your enemies in bed. Hey, Spot!"

Slushy yelled at Rover, who was playing pool with Twinkletoes. Rover looked around, wondering why he was being called another dog's name.

"Rover," Lock whispered confidentially to the lawyer.

"Whatever," said Slushy. "Is he your sergeant-at-arms?"

"No," I said, "but I was thinking of making him one."

"Tell him to gather everyone around the table. I've got a few things I need to go over."

Rover did, although he wasn't thrilled at being called Spot, and cast Slushy dirty looks. Slushy looked like the kind of dodgy lawyer who would have an office in a strip mall—in fact, his office in Pure and Easy was attached to our indoor archery range—with his plaid suit, his Prius, and his bright orange tie, but he was just educated and sleazy enough to double-cross the other guy. Who cared if he got his law degree from the University of American Samoa? It was a four hour drive from Pure and Easy. I'd pay to fly Slushy in if it meant keeping him as our new club's lawyer.

Because he wasn't a patched member, Slushy stood, although there were plenty of free chairs. There weren't many of us yet. Twinkletoes joined us, although he hadn't officially been given his full colors yet.

Slushy brandished Hobie's scribbled notes. "These are good bylaws for a start. There are a shitload more I want you to incorporate, whether or not you like it." He tossed Hobie's notes on the table and slammed another document from his briefcase on top of them. "These are tried and true bylaws culled from all the organizations I've ever worked for. They work just as well for a cartel as a hot dog stand, a tuxedo rental, or a motorcycle club. You have to protect yourselves, get organized, and fucking *adhere* to these rules. No morons coming dribbling in half an hour late for chapel, crying because they had to work overtime at their tire store. No Prospects falling asleep when they're supposed to be keeping an eye on your scoots. No blitzed guys picking fights with other clubs and then sobbing when they come after you. No fighting amongst each other. The only punches may be given by the sergeant-at-arms. No explosives will be thrown into the fire."

Slushy looked around at the table full of blank faces. "What, you don't have a fireplace? Okay, then, strike that rule. What I'm trying to say is, this is a *business*, men, not fucking Animal House. Which is why I'm here to present to you my idea for a money laundering business." Slushy held his hands out like a frame for his face. "Picture it. Laser tag. Think of all the kids who come to Lake Havasu on spring break. They're all hung over, bored, wanting some way to burn off all that pointless energy. Laser tag! Boom, there it is! We just need control stations and phaser packs…"

As I listened to Slushy, it all started to come together. *We were a fucking club.* We might be a bunch of oddballs and outcasts from different walks of life. But the one thread that held us all together was the most important, the lifeline—our MC. We were here at ground zero, the formation of a new club, and we already had our backyard carved out for us. We had turf. Now we just had to get out there and claim it.

"So when the sugar rush from all those Adios Motherfuckers and Zombie Punches kicks in, the college set will have a place to—" Slushy glared at Twinkletoes when his cell chimed. "And another thing. Before church, all phones will be put in a receptacle."

"I know," said Lock. "This isn't our permanent chapel. The carpenters are still working back there."

"*Motherfuck!*" cried Twinkletoes, excited by his new text. He was so jazzed he could barely speak, and he flailed an arm in Lock's direction. "Ronald—Ronald—"

Lock frowned. "Ronald Reagan?"

We had forgotten all about that pedo. In the rush of activities, I had just assumed Lock had chalked ol' Ronnie up to "the one who got away." I knew it rankled him and ruined his perfect record of catching slimeballs, but hell, there was a lot of shit going on back then.

Twinkletoes cried, "*Yes!* Ronald Reagan is on the move again! The tracker I put on his Lexus hasn't moved in a couple of weeks and suddenly it's—"

Lock was already on his feet, racing for the bar where he kept his duty belt with stun gun, handcuffs, and so on. "Where is he?"

Twinkletoes was on his feet, too. "*He's fucking here!*" he squeaked in a funny, high voice. "He's driving right by the London Bridge Resort!"

Slushy yelled above the general hubbub. "Guys, guys. Whatever virtual presidential game you're playing, I need to get a vote on this laser tag idea."

Lock was already buckling on his belt, checking all his gadgets. "The Gipper is on the move! Turk, you've got to come with me."

"Sure thing," I said, springing for my Glock.

"I want to come, too!" whined Twinkletoes. "I put all this work in."

Lock agreed. "Come on!"

"Who the fuck is Ronald Reagan?" Rover asked. "I want to come, too."

Slushy threw up his hands. "Oy! Why do I even bother with these guys? Why the fuck didn't I just move to Nebraska and open a Cinnabon there?"

The three of us stumbled out the door of the Happy Hour bar and into the bright light of an Arizona afternoon. We might be a young club, but if we could combine our experience in the right way, we could be stronger than most. The Bent Zealots were a sanctuary for our identities, but we needed to make ourselves known in the world, to make our mark.

There was a whole world out there, ours for the taking.

Quicksilver Books

Did you like this book? Let everyone know by posting a review. You will be awesome, and Layla will be grateful!

ABOUT THE AUTHOR

Layla Wolfe lives in coastal California with a leather jacket, one bad-ass pink camo compound bow, and a vicarious outlaw lifestyle.

Layla Wolfe is the pen name of multi-published erotic romance author Karen Mercury.

Visit her at:
www.laylawolfe.com
www.facebook.com/layla.wolfe

MORE BOOKS FROM LAYLA WOLFE

The Bare Bones
Book #1 in The Bare Bones MC series

If you ain't living on the edge, you're taking up too much room.

The rose-colored illusion of Madison Shellmound's girlish crush on biker Ford Illuminati is stomped into smithereens by his crude father Cropper, Bare Bones motorcycle club President. Fearing Ford will kill Cropper if he finds out, Madison flees, becoming an upstanding cardiology nurse.

Madison and Ford have an ill-fated, star-crossed love that will last their lifetimes. Ford is a lifer in a different sort of enterprise, the gritty full-throttle club of guns, blood, and allegiance to his brothers. Twelve years and several tours of SEAL duty later, Ford is thrust back into Madison's arms on the worst day of his life. Madison's prospect brother Speed has screwed up big-time and owes the club his life. She offers herself to Cropper as a sacrificial lamb to save Speed.

But how long until the fiery, full-on outlaw Ford discovers that the woman he loves was treated like a degraded slave by his own father? Well, meet the new boss. He's not the same as the old boss.

Publisher's Note: This is not your mother's contemporary romance. Readers will encounter molestation, drugging, consensual bondage and discipline, violence, and a HEA. It's a full-length novel of 65,000 words. Recommended 18+ due to mature content.

Stay Vertical
Book #2 in The Bare Bones MC series

Publisher's Note: This is Book #2 in the Bare Bones MC series. This book is a stand-alone and can be read out of order. However, it is advised to read THE BARE BONES first to get a complete picture of the club's background, storylines, and setting. This is not your mother's contemporary romance. Daring readers will encounter sexual assault, violence against women, general violence among men, consensual BDSM, and a HEA. It is not for the faint of heart. It's a full length novel of 65,000 words with no cliffhanger. Recommended 18+ due to mature content.

One two three four five six seven. All good sinners go to heaven. Peace Corps volunteer June Shellmound returns to Arizona to care for her dying mother. At the clubhouse of The Bare Bones motorcycle club, June is swept into the drama when half-breed Lytton Driving Hawk barges in and demands recognition as president Ford Illuminati's half-brother.

Hot enough to melt steel, Lytton has forged a life apart from the reservation as a brilliant chemist, living the high times at his pot farm in the mountains. Lytton is no fortunate son, though, and the mortal secrets Ford's been hiding about their father drive the last nail into their brotherly coffin.

Lytton turns his back on the Bare Bones and sweet bleeding heart June. Blinded by vengeance, Lytton becomes ruled by his own demons, raising hell alongside Ford's mortal enemies, The Cutlasses. Alliances are torn apart within the club, loyalties are divided, and everyone's true spirits are tested. When the dust clears, Lytton and June find themselves running for their lives just to…**STAY VERTICAL**

Bad to the Bones
Book #3 in The Bare Bones MC series

Publisher's Note: This is Book #3 in the Bare Bones MC series. This book is a stand-alone and can be read out of order. This is not your mother's contemporary romance. Daring readers will encounter sexual assault, dubious consent, general violence among men, and a HEA. It is not for the faint of heart. It's a full length novel of 73,000 words with no cliffhanger. Recommended 18+ due to mature content.

Knoxie Hammett has been The Bare Bones' tattoo artist for years. He's just drifted through life, living it large and performing in their Triple Exposure films, recovering from a divorce he never wanted. Suddenly Knoxie has a reason to live and to want to prospect for The Bare Bones outlaw motorcycle club.

He'll need their help to rescue the lovely Bellamy Jager from the jaws of the cutthroat, warped cult leader who has been holding her hostage all her adult life. To the neglected, abused Bellamy, living in the desert canyons off stolen food and time, the sanctity of the ashram looked like a safe zone. But her haven turned to hell and she was drugged and abused, ignorant of any other way of life.

Knoxie will need every one of his Bare Bones brothers and every ounce of bravery he can muster. To save Bellamy and her white slave sister from the twisted swami, he'll need to pull off the most daring job of his life to prove to the club and the world that he's...**BAD TO THE BONES.** Don't ride faster than your guardian angel can fly.

MORE BOOKS FROM KAREN MERCURY

Redemption Song
(Midnight, New Orleans Style 4)

[Siren Menage Everlasting: Erotic Paranormal Menage a Trois Romance, M/M/F, light consensual BDSM, sex toys, HEA]

When five college friends reunite, one night changes their lives forever. Halloween in New Orleans. Remy Lafitte has paid a charlatan to enact a Voodoo ceremony in the cemetery. The ritual reanimates Niko Valdes, a French Quarter tutor who was damned to Everlost for murdering his sister's attacker. Mild-mannered stockbroker Heidi Purdue stumbles upon Niko and Remy in a compromising position. They are interrupted by a demon on horseback who beheads the charlatan before giving the trio a pentalpha puzzle to solve. Curvy Heidi knows that heartthrob Remy would never fall for her, but she falls for the undead tutor. Remy, jealous of the other two's closeness, agrees to an equitable menage, opening up to a male lover. The centuries-long battle against primordial evil leads them to a temple, where they find Solomon's ring. They go past the portal of Hellmouth to redeem themselves, but the real puzzle is how to fulfill the prophecy that they are intertwined inexorably – now and forever.

A Siren Erotic Romance

Questions? Comments?
Email suggestions to
laylawolfeauthor@gmail.com

Made in the USA
Las Vegas, NV
05 September 2024